The Flaneur

By

R D McGregor

Gangway Publishing

R D McGregor

Cover design by: Julie Laing

The Flaneur

For Julie and David

R D McGregor

'…my manhood is cast
Down in the flood of remembrance…'
D.H. Lawrence

The Flaneur

CONTENTS

The Flaneur

R D McGregor

The Flaneur

Foreword

The following tale might be seen as Part Two of *Bad Things*, a novel published by R D McGregor. If the reader has read this novel the s/he will recognise some characters mentioned and some incidents referred to. If the reader has not read *Bad Things,* consider said characters and said incidents to be from a fictitious and non-existent novel created by the narrator.

Robert O'Neil

Gangway Publishing

R D McGregor

RAIN

Prologue: The Bastard Author

Who are these people you have read about, with their strange names and unlikely histories? Who are these strangers who have fallen at the doorstep of your imagination and you have, hesitant at first, let enter. It's a daring thing in any day and age to be so welcoming. They've made themselves at home in your mind. Perhaps you have thought of them in quieter moments, allowed them freedom to roam amongst your own memories, your thoughts and dreams. They might have given you cause to ruminate on your own situation. You have, no doubt, considered their plight, not at first as rooted in reality, but their situations have grown on you, have convinced you that they are indeed true; and as such you have accepted them and become involved in their shenanigans. You have opened your mind to the possibility of others not like you, quite unlike anyone you have ever known. The impossible has become not only feasible, but demanded, and you've accepted its existence.

They are you – brought to the here and now by your truth and your bearings. You are the character who is never mentioned but haunts every line. In a room, the young man making a ship in a bottle, the crowd at a march, the reporter turned detective: you sit at the same table as all of them, share their food and sup their wine. You hear their lies, witness their deceptions, their violence and thuggery. But do not think for one moment that you are getting out of any of this without a guilty verdict upon your head. For you have been culpable, an active partner in crime. You have spoken about it with others, and although they have not said, they see you as an accomplice. Did you think that your listeners thought all this was just a fiction? They were watching you, every twitch and expression, falling and rising with your voice, the laughter and the thrills when you described certain parts of the story. They believe you to be those people. You have not only retold the story of these characters; you have made a confession.

In fact, if they read the story for themselves, it would be something far different from the tale you just told them. And if that is the case – and it most certainly is – then *you* have created the story and those that inhabit it. Don't think you can wash your hands of it all or wake tomorrow and forget it all; it will walk beside you to the grave. And what will haunt you forever is a question: how could you have created such a monstrous thing populated by characters so lacking a moral compass? You will try and suppress those thoughts and tell yourself to snap out of it. That, of course, will not happen. You can't snap out of your own life as though it is a daydream without the walls of your existence tumbling down. Anyhow, you couldn't live with yourself, for it would be a betrayal of those characters: they have become your friends, your confidantes.

Perhaps you have thought of creating your own? Whether like them or otherwise, they won't be too different in the end, because they are filtered through you and have only what you allow them, and what you share with others. Perhaps some incidents will be similar: a turn of the head, for instance. A blow to that head? Romance. That kiss? The meetings made and missed. The short skip across the road. What can you get away with? You might have wanted to do such a thing for a long time. You might have harboured secret thoughts of yourself as an author. How difficult can it be? You will tell yourself *not too difficult*. It is then you will start to criticise everything that *you* didn't bring to the narrative. You will criticise the story itself and its creator. How easy to make these people run around in your imagination. In fact, this was not the work of that author. No. This was you. You gave them the flesh and the blood. You instilled in them humanity. Your humanity. What were they before you arrived? Nothing. It is a wonder your name is not on the cover. The bastard author has tricked his readers; he has stolen the people you made real. He didn't have the talent to make them live. You did that.

Not only will you criticise, but you will also be angry, insulted, as though you have been used. What a scoundrel to treat his readers in such a fashion. This whole exercise has been a con; the author a flim-flam man, a plagiarist who does not deserve the copyright of a work that you helped create. How in the name of holy hell does he sleep at night? And his damn tricks. The shifts in time and the inconsistencies in style. All part of the grand plan to obfuscate the true purpose of his book: a cheap swindle to make a quick buck. Oh yes, he must have laughed as you were led by the nose along country roads, into dark public houses, dirty flats, bedrooms of floozies and flibbertigibbets, as I too was led willingly through the impossibility of time. But he is not as clever as he thought. You realised that early on when he derided the central character's God complex without levelling that charge at himself. Go back; read over that section. It's somewhere in chapter 9. He has the absolute audacity to suppose he can read the character Gladbody in the way Gladbody thinks he can read the character Calvert. This is a perfect example of projection and a man frigging his imagination. What arrogance to think that he knows anyone better than they do? I would go further: what arrogance to believe you know yourself well enough to pontificate to others?

What self-delusional fools authors are. They think they are in control, but it is we who decide whether to buy or borrow a book. It is we who decide to open that book. That's just the start of it. It is our interpretation as reader that makes meaning of the action. And at any point we can close the book for good and toss it on the fire. How's that for omniscience! And as for time – which is another glaring fault in this writer's bag of poor tricks – what about those time shifts? In one chapter he has the absolute audacity to write *two hours earlier*! Why didn't he just drop it into the previous chapter? Flying back in time a few hours hardly span eons as in *The Time Machine*, and if the writer had a modicum of scientific knowledge, then he might have travelled to a better future (sadly lacking in this tale). This sort of literary trickery adds nothing to our understanding. If what the author offers has no grasp in reality of a situation, then tell me what is the point? Such arrogance.

I also take exception to other breads from this literary smorgasbord. Why does Morris drink? Is it necessary to the development of the story? He brings little humour and I know from my wide reading that drunkenness is often a lazy shortcut to humour. You might ask why this is. A stupid question if ever there was one. Do you think Descartes wrote *Discourse On The Method* while in his cups? I rest that particular case. And other areas of characterisation have caused me to doubt this author's credentials. Not long after her brother's funeral Calvert Makeme jumps into bed with the hero. (Hero? Ha!) I really think not. It is also unbecoming of a young lady of such grace to demean herself in such a fashion. Likewise, when she swears at the duckpond: I think not. And as for punching Morris and landing him on the path? Are we really asked to believe a young well-bred lady such as Calvert Makeme would contemplate such a thing? If I'm totally honest with myself she got under my skin. The fact is I fell for her. How pathetic is that? I was in love with a character created with words on a page and my own imaginings. Not flesh, blood and bone. A woman whose existence lies solely between the pages of a book. How is that possible? I'm a damn fool and a semi-onanist. When I had finished reading the book on the plane I had to go to the toilet and weep. *The End* had taken her from me, had taken her life. I was more than gutted. As I said, a damn fool. I think that we have to start taking these writers to task.

There is a point when an author is simply taking advantage of us and our good graces. As a reader, I have invested not only time, but a great deal of my thought and critical faculties to shaping a character to my understanding, satisfaction and belief. To have them behave in a manner that is outside the parameters of my creation is not only unacceptable, it's damn rude. But manners are, I suppose, optional for the writing fraternity. We might wait for an *excuse me* or an apology, but I fear we would wait in vain.

Time does not, contrary to much opinion, move slowly, and neither is it a river flowing. Time falls from a great height and is smashed to smithereens on the rock of life below. This is what I have brought to his story, and it does not sit easily with what I have read. It jars on me that his perception does not fit snug with mine. It keeps me at a distance, which is hardly an effect even this writer wants to achieve. One moment does not lead easily to the next: it is torturous in its shift; it screams in agony at the loss of another moment; it edges second by second towards its inevitable end. What this writer has to do with time is to make the author its master, and in doing so, control life. I would ask anyone holding this book to ask the question: just what is this writer's intent? And if you cannot answer that, and accept these jumps as natural, then you are no better. How presumptuous! You become, in effect, a co-conspirator. It is all pretence. A hoax played on ourselves, presented as something, but nothing more than a distraction from life.

And there we have it. This fashioning of time attempts to give a shape to life; something life quite clearly does not have. Existence, poorly reined in, is the best that we can expect. Sometimes it erupts and chaos indeed reigns. So, the story that you have just read, that *we* have just read, cannot be realistic or naturalistic: it is a lie. It is nothing more than an illusion; it is there to mesmerise, to let us escape for a few hours from our quotidian monotonous tragedies. At best it will keep us from drugs, alcohol, or suicide for the hours that we are with it. And then what? Perhaps another? The same author? You go to your bookstore or your library and check their name against the author list. You see they have one other book. You look at it, always at the back or on the flyleaf. But what's this? This book bears no relation to the book you have just finished. How many lives does this person think they know? Something – just for a moment – flashes through your mind. It is a judgement. You think you hate this author. You cannot bear to give them your precious time. They have taken enough. You know them well by now, their little foibles and faults. In that we all have something they cannot (although ego mania would drive them to deny this); we have a knowledge of them through their writing that they can never have of us. We, as readers, must hold onto this ace card. They spill themself throughout the work, but they do not see us. We are not really part of the equation. How could one person know so many readers? Quite impossible. Who do they think they're writing for? Not us. It's an exercise in style over substance. The author can toss the literary salad how they like, but at the end of the day it's what's in it that's important. And that's where this author lets himself down.

Not only that, he lets his readers down, and surely there can be no greater charge against a writer.

There is little meat to this tale. One thing leads to another with little rhyme or reason. Is this what literature has become? By a good third of the way through I was beginning to question all of the characters' motivation and the author's moral stance. It seems to me that he has ditched any attempt to teach his audience anything but poor behaviour. I mean, point to one character who is a decent person out of this shower? This is totally irresponsible. The writer must make clear the moral lesson and instruct thereby. I find — and this is a personal point of view — that not to do so is a dereliction of the authorial duty. Surely we read to better ourselves, to sand down the rough edges of our immorality? We do not want to leave a story without having been changed to an extent; made better people. We certainly do not want to exit feeling grubbier than when we entered. And I am sorry to say that is how I felt with this particular tale. How lucky those who did not read it!

How the author keeps our interest in this sordid tale needs to be addressed. At the end of each chapter there is a surprise, something that even you might consider relevant, that perks you up. We might be given a glimpse of a character's behaviour or motivation. We sit back like the cat with the cream. And then, soon after, it comes; the double whammy. What we have learned is thrown aside by a new revelation. He does this constantly, and for what purpose? To play with his readers. There can be no other answer. It's a game of cat and mouse. Why would we want this? To be teased by this psychopath. The jig is up, Mister. We're wise to you. We're wise to your comings and goings; your offs and ons; we're wise to your pretensions. We understand all too well you are not handing us the keys to the kingdom. On the contrary, you hand us nothing. You think we are there to be used.

But who really holds the whip hand in this tale? Let us be

clear: not the characters, and certainly not the author. And if it is neither then it can only be us: the readers. He hands us nothing, but we have the upper hand. That would come as a bit of a shock to this jumped up pensmith. He thinks he rules that particular roost, but he is in fact nothing more than a blind fool. He cannot see that the reader writes the fiction. Let that sink into the numbskull's noggin. I read an interview with the twit and he said that there was nothing new under the sun. Well, how right he was there. This story has been heard how many times before? All he's done is cobble together what many others told many other times. And a poor job he's done if he was trying to hide them, let me say. We have read before of flagellation, so even that crude scene should raise nothing but scorn. Good god, man! Flagellation! Is there nothing this brute won't sink to in order to appeal to the perverse? This really is the nadir of taste and quality. I truly believe outside of literature such things do not exist. I mean that great rapist, liar, and murderer de Sade created such things to encourage perversity in the common herd. We should not be fooled. Nor should we be tricked into practising such an act for pleasure, for let me tell you now, there is no pleasure whatsoever from receiving lashes across your bare hide. Nor, might I add, is there pleasure in performing such an act. Only in the mind of a brute or jackleg reprobate would such actions be considered pleasurable. I am particularly repulsed by this section—and I have read it several times — as there is quite enough violence conducted against the gentle sex without encouraging the masses to whip ladies' arses. This is surely incitement to violence, which the last time I looked, was an illegal activity in itself. I was in two minds whether to write a strong letter to the publishers, or indeed the courts. Reading this filth, I cried for the future of civilisation itself. And do not think that is an exaggeration.

If we are lucky, the book shall sink without trace. If we are not, we might find it in the hands of the mob. One is never surprised when we consider the sort of crapulous nonsense that reaches the bestseller lists. And then there's translations. The spread to other countries as de Sade infected the world with his sickness. This 'writer' should not be allowed to go out on a blaze of glory, he should be simply cancelled out, forgotten, left in the rotten garbage of history. To be ignored, the greatest indignity. To be forgotten for eternity makes a life worthless. Would that this one had not existed. Who would truly give a damn? That is how we should deal with the troublemakers, the shit stirrers: cancel them out. His story is worthless. What does it teach us? What does it give to us? Nothing. And so, what is its point? It has none. It steals from you the hours you invest in reading, but it doesn't reimburse. You do not get the hours back. Eating into your life. For what? A collection of characters that he has made up! I really think that we should all start questioning what we read and stop normalising the abnormal. A hero who we might find out halfway through buggers cats is no hero in my book, and it is a double blow to cat owners. But by this time the author has manipulated you; you identify with them, and it's too late; you are tainted by their filth. Not that this particular author goes that far, but who knows what his future work might sink to?

There is a sexual *frisson* throughout this novel which makes me feel uncomfortable, as it should any normal person. Sadly, there are scenes that are nothing more than titillation for the perverse. The one when Kim visits Calvert's flat for instance: what is that supposed to mean? We watched her, a few chapters before, take out a single stocking and smile as she did so. Cheap and easy. But what of when she raises her skirt and we see the gun in her garter? Is it likely in any circumstances a young woman who has no knowledge of weapons would feel comfortable enough to place a loaded gun in such a place? The damage that could ensue to her private parts should it accidently go off is alone enough to stop any well-bred young lady placing the firearm anywhere in this general region, and this is not a hardened broad in a steamy American detective novel. This is a young woman about to sit her university finals and who has lost her brother in the most brutal fashion. I would ask anyone if this rings true. I have known several women in my days, and this behaviour reflects none of them at any time in their lives. Anyhow, the introduction of a gun at this point is quite ridiculous. Having a gunrunner living on campus is just a dead end as far as I'm concerned. It is an indication of a writer that has run out of ideas and is slipping a bit of danger in in order to enliven the proceedings. These people are not the sort that would consort with hardened criminals. This once again brings us back to characterisation. It is out of character. What started out as a serious piece of literary fiction much of it has been exposed as little more than pornography. And I am sure that I'm not the only one that bristles at the very idea of reading a hoochie-coochie novel.

Now, if this writer is bucking for a major literary prize, it is not in his ballpark, as the saying goes. What a reader wants is truth, an accurate portrayal of people and their actions. Is that too much to ask? If that was indeed his intention, then we have been duped. What is the point of writing what the reader cannot comprehend or identify with in any fashion? Perhaps he was attempting something other than realism. I would suggest he listen to the readers and consider their question: 'What's the point?' I can see no other motive for this work by the author other than pandering to the very lowest tastes.

I will go further in my criticisms and confess again that, once I reached *The End*, I was not a little angry. I seemed to have been promised one thing and given another. Too often in literature I believe we let this go by. We are disappointed, yes, but not enough to act upon it. And this is, I believe, worthy of change. The active reader is what we must be if we are to have any hope of books by perhaps a new Dickens, or

Cervantes, that bring us unending pleasure. I would suggest strong letters to the relevant journals outlining the literary faults. That forum would, of course, give the author ample opportunity to respond to our criticisms and defend the indefensible. The problem with this jackass is he seems to have forgotten who he is writing for. This is a common error amongst today's literati, they think that they are above their audience. They seem to forget who puts the bread on the table and their responsibility towards us. I've not forgotten, though. Their reply to such questions, though, is very telling. They will say "Well, don't buy the book", as if you are supposed to know what the contents are before you purchase the item and get it home. It is a disingenuous response, that reveals arrogance and superiority.

But damn it, is it too much to ask to be able to sit down and get lost in a story? I want relax into it, be able to put the book down, go and make a cup of tea or fix myself something stronger. When I return, I want to pick up where I left off. But this is made more difficult by the quite preposterous structure of this tale. Too many things happen in too short a time. All those deaths! What is it supposed to be – a murder mystery? If it was then I might for the moment accept the preposterousness of character motives. But then, who is investigating the crimes? Every crime story needs the detective, either amateur or professional, to track down and bring to justice the perpetrator. Here we have the implausible reporter turned gumshoe. But he is not in the business of tracking anyone down and turning them over to the law. In fact, this is exactly what this story lacks, any sense of justice. Actions are taken that demand some sort of exposure to accountability. Here, crimes take place but there is no one knocking on doors, investigating. It is as though the whole thing is made up. At what time or in what place does a young man take his life without an exploration of the circumstances and motive? People would demand answers to why a young lad would throw himself in front of a bus or drop himself off a high building. The police might question so many deaths within a quarter mile, I would say. Yet, there is no follow-up, here or later on Gladbody's trip to the Orkney Islands (which I assumed would not end well). The constant chatter of his companion Pie Tait foreshadows his demise. He is a dead man talking. Of course, we might ask how can something be unexpected if it is expected? Only the means of his end are the thing we cannot know and once again the author imagines no apparent retribution. True art can make the reader a better person, but this isn't art.

I would not want anyone to assume from the above that I believe that there is only one way to write a novel. On the contrary, nothing could be further from the truth. I enjoy, as much as the next person, new and exciting narratives. But surely this can be done without throwing out lessons and experience derived from several hundred years of practice? I have always thought that the best novels are the ones closest to the first thought. Dickens' best stuff comes from when he wandered the streets of London with a notebook. Too many revisions sail the boat too far from the shore. Dare I suggest that our particular author knows nothing of the history of the novel, nor indeed its most successful practitioners. Is it too much to ask that a writer perhaps do some research into the history of their chosen craft before inflicting their junk on the reading public? I would suggest that the greatest of our writers are our guides. They are our moral compass in a sea of corruption. The great books instruct us in their fashion to a better way of life and living. That was set in stone many years ago and perhaps we do not want instructions of that sort today, but what we surely must all crave is some inkling of rules to live your life by contained within a work. Our author has clearly had a morality bypass. Take the scene I just mentioned where the Pie character (whoever heard of such a name?) is driving through the north of Scotland. He stops at a pub and drinks a pint of beer before getting in his van and driving. What signal is the author sending out to road users? The issue is not even addressed. I hoped that perhaps an off-duty policeman might have noticed the smell of alcohol and arrested him. A lesson could have been learned perhaps if a crash had ensued to bring home the perils of drinking alcohol and driving. But nothing! It is not even noted by the writer or commented on by his characters. I double checked by reading that whole passage again. I had to double check as I am quite a quick reader and I am, like all humans, quite fallible. Occasionally a phrase, a sentence, or whole paragraph sweeps by me in a haze. I have little recollection of having read it. I am not sure why this is, but I am putting it down to tiredness. It might of course be connected to my other little problem that was dealt with some months ago. I was having hallucinations of one sort or another. Sometimes it would be colours and light much like the Aurora Borealis, but other times it was ill-defined figures appearing in my room, unrecognisable at times as human. I did of course see my doctor. Whether these problems were ocular or neurological I never did find out for they stopped for as little reason as they started. I was correct first time. There is no mention of the drinking outside the actual drinking.

While sitting in *The Dirty Cactus*, I read an interview within which the author reveals that he lives in Paris, even though he has no previous connection to the city. No doubt he dreams of emulating the great writers who lived in that great city in the past. Perhaps he hopes for some kind of literary osmosis, where just by placing himself in the heart of the mighty Proust's home, some of his genius might enter into him as the Holy spirit entered Our Lady. If that is his play, then the game's up. *Talent is born, and genius is earned through hard work.* I thought that if he were sitting across from me I would say that to him.

And what could stop me? *I shall do it,* I muttered. *I shall go,*

The Flaneur

I mumbled. *I shall up sticks and travel to France forthwith*, I said, *and to Hell with the consequences*. This novel is an attack on no less a thing than my being, and I should hold the author accountable. Would that all were as motivated as me and we might not have this trash and suchlike thrown in our faces. Must a reader sit back and take it all? Why? What rules are written that makes the author protected from a reader's ire? *I shall leave immediately*, I announced to myself and my fellow drinkers.

I arrived. Notice the last two sentences? 'I shall leave immediately.' 'I arrived.' None of that nonsense writers often inflict on us about travelling. It is that easy. The journey in our writer's novel between Glasgow and Orkney was interminable, and worse, unnecessary. I reread it on the plane, and I agreed that Pie talked far too much. That is all. It could have been dealt with in a couple of sentences. The more I considered it the angrier I became. I thought of that journey as I tramped the streets of Paris looking for accommodation that suited my purse.

I have come prepared to the land of Proust, Hugo, Camus, Sartre, and Beauvoir. I have come fully ready to the land of Matisse and Renoir. The land of everything I love. I have come with a gun. I have come to use it. I have come to murder. I have murder on my mind and in my eyes…

R D McGregor

1

I settled for a room in arrondissement 5. It was on the edge of arrondissement 6, which was fine. The hotel was privately run and small. Although it had *hotel* in its name, I would have described it more as a *pension*. In all, it had four floors, with me residing in the uppermost part. In most hotels a rooftop view would be deemed a luxury perch, and most would have to pay top price for such positioning. When the establishment is lacking the basics of a guest friendly elevator this pricing is reversed. Luckily, I had recently tried to keep myself in tip top physical condition, so the stairs offered no challenge on my body. On the contrary, the climbing only added to my daily exercise routine. I should mention that this daily exercise routine had only been going for a month, as was my tip top physical condition. I tried to break with past habits and clean up my act. Like most endeavours this was met with some, though not small, successes. Occasional days the mind gives up the ghost before the body has crawled from bed.

The room itself was quite cramped and the ceiling was low. It contained a bed, a table, a sink, and a mirror. There was a toilet/shower room in the hall outside, which I was to share with the occupant(s) of the only other room. My room number was 401 and theirs was 403. It puzzled me that there was no room 402, nor had there ever been such a room, as there was too little space to accommodate such. I resigned to asking the landlord, or should I say the concierge? He was a surly, unshaven man who smelled of sweat. Standing next to him I could easily have gagged. On arrival I told him that I had limited funds but that I was clean in my habits. He looked neither impressed nor unimpressed with this information. Perhaps it was because I spoke French badly, and he appeared to be in no command of English. (I should say that although my French was poor it was, with care, understandable.) He rubbed his finger and thumb together in a vulgar manner to indicate that he wanted paid in advance. I have travelled little in my life but recognise the gesture from unscrupulous bastards in my own homeland. I paid and made my way to my room.

I have a good memory for room numbers. Some are with me for ever. Room 876 that smelled of perfume, books, and sperm, has a particular memory, as does Dorm Room 45, 25 Penrose Avenue, 1052 Cliffdale Drive, 3 Helena Drive. All memories, all in the past. I also have a memory for names. They return to me often as I go through my day. I don't consider them, though. They arrive and depart like some fancy, leaving no impression, asking no thought or consideration. Billy Tusk, Miss Dajbrowski, Darian Broque, William Walatter, Yvo "Sticky" Stickland, Irene Tooth, Bill Petch, Ivan Fish, Father John Berntsson, Nancy Murski, Jane Kowalczyk, Kirk Newton, Clara Pett, the Bump's, Mr John Swinglehurst, Old John, Natasha Lebedev, Emily. (What was your surname, Emily? Did you say? Is it lost?) James Rugman, George Speake, Dan B, Dottie Richmond, and on it goes. How many enter our lives, forgotten, fallen away in an uncertain memory? And yet time is only regained through memory. The senses can be fooled and triggered. Who has not waited for their mother's kiss, Marcel?

As it was late afternoon, I decided to go out in something of a reconnoitre of the area. I changed first into some fresh clothes as the journey had been somewhat clammy in every stage. A crisp and cooling white shirt and dark trousers sufficed to renew my depleted energies. I also took my coat as it had been raining when I arrived at Charles de Gaulle. As indeed it had been for weeks. I didn't want to miss the last of the evening light so decided to forego a shower at this time. I was back on the quiet street fifteen minutes after arriving in my room. The street was as I had left it. Outside were a few trees and neatly cut grass on the road edge. I stood under the hotel awning for several minutes to decide on which direction I should take on my perambulation. Across the road there was a Turkish food establishment which seemed to serve a variety of goodies. I made a mental note to take full advantage of this later.

Meanwhile, I headed left towards the expansive boulevard. I had walked up it when I arrived from the metro not an hour before, and noticed its preponderance of cafés, and a pretty little park across the road, which was home to a scattering of cherry blossom trees, the *Prunus Takasago* and the *Prunis Tai-Haku*, unless I was mistaken. Some years ago, I read Basho and did research on cherry blossom trees. My mother influenced this research. I feel she gave me little but an enquiring mind. My head is a clutter of information.

I walked up the boulevard some way, passing workers, no doubt finishing their days labour, some young people I assumed to be students, and a few other random shoppers. It was unusually quiet for the centre of a major city at this time of the day. Stopping at a corner establishment at the top of the boulevard I sat at a table that gave me full view of the roads running from every part of the compass; the wonderful and wonderfully ornate fountain, and the bridge that straddled the River Seinne. There was a Metro sign and steps that people arrived up from and disappeared down to. I ordered a black coffee and lit a Gauloise. I had pointed to a packet in the little Tabac a few doors down from where I now was. I could have asked but I didn't. Although ordering the coffee was a simple enough procedure, I stumbled over the words. I coughed, unnecessarily clearing my throat, but giving me time to process the language and repeat my order. The cough is rarely given consideration in the etiquette of social engagement. Being outside my usual comfort zone I decided that I would stamp myself on the city. I know a little French but speaking it in the homeland I was noticeably nervous. The public setting put a spotlight on my inadequacies. Like most

28

people, I am reluctant to be thought a fool.

How, I thought, everything had changed in the way I looked at the world. The fact that I heard voices unfamiliar to my ear made me feel slightly giddy. Exhilarated. I felt that I had no responsibilities except to myself, and indeed since I was alone that was in fact the case. It is a curious thing, but I felt younger than my years since my arrival a short time ago. There was something that stripped age from me, and I swear I could have run along to the park if I had wanted. I had not run in many years. I am no longer a young man, but the joy of running cannot be the sole territory of the young. It was at this point I decided to be open to Paris life and gain as much from the experience as I could. Considering my objective it was an unusual decision, but I gave that little thought. If it was possible to return home with this new sense of youth, I considered that I might just join a gym or take a lover. I removed the barely smoked cigarette from my lips and stubbed it harshly into the ashtray: it was foul.

While I was in the process of extinguishing the cigarette, an attractive young lady that was seated a few tables down from me got up and left the café. My eyes lifted from the ashtray to look at her, for I was not inured to the allure of an attractive woman. She was tall and slim with a pale face and the darkest and shiniest hair cut into a bob. If she had glanced at me, I did not notice, but what I did notice was that she had left a small magazine on the table. As she brushed past, my voice spoke to tell her, but was so silent that its softness surprised even me. She did not hear, nor did she see my hand rise ever so slightly. Not one to cause any sort of scene I decided not to reach out to pull at her sleeve. Instead, I let her go on her way. My interest was pricked enough on her reading material that I thought to get up from my table and collect it. I did of course not want to bring attention to such a theft, however trivial it might have been. There was only one other customer: a long-haired young man who was busying himself gulping down pieces of bread and coffee. He had received a beaming smile from the waitress when she served him. Something I noticed that was missing from my order. I ordered another coffee from her, although I felt the last one was enough. The taste of the cigarette was still in my mouth, yet I found myself pulling another from the packet. The waitress brought my coffee quickly as I stared at the vacant seat and the magazine. I was hoping that no one would sit down, but had they, I had concocted in my head a story that would have me introducing myself, picking up said magazine and leaving. What the customer might have done I cannot imagine. As it was, the spanner that was thrown into my imagination was the reality of the waitress picking up a glass and the magazine, obviously fulfilling an important part of her job function. She then laid the glass and magazine on the table next to me and proceeded to clean the recently vacated table with a damp cloth. When her back was to me, I reached out, grabbed the magazine, and proceeded to read what I could not fully understand. Picking up the glass, the waitress looked at me. She muttered something that I could not hear, but even if I had, it was doubtful I would have comprehended. I smiled at her nervously. It struck me at that moment that she might call the manager, but for the life of me I cannot imagine what I would have been accused of. Reading a magazine that was on one of their tables? Preposterous.

I picked up two sugar lumps and let them drop into the coffee.

The magazine was a guide to what was on in Paris that week. It ran from the latest gallery exhibitions to the vast array of cinema presentations. There were adverts for up-and-coming musical events, to circuses, puppet theatres, live theatre, dance, modern and classical, to children's shows, TV programmes, outdoor events of many a stripe, mime, juggling, a magic act that involved live animals (in the street?), to book signings, and readings in various shops around the city. And it was the last of these was the one that caught my eye because one reading event must have caught the young lady's eye, for it was circled in red. I was interested in this, not only because I am a naturally curious person, but because of the name that was circled. Wasn't it just the target of my whole trip to Paris? Some might think such a thing is a coincidence beyond the normal, but it is a fact of life that coincidences are such because they are not normal. Of course, one might ask how many coincidences must you experience in such a short time before you question the very nature of your place in the universe? I have no time for such questions because it has never happened, either to me or to anyone else. So, the coincidence concerned me little. Life chances do interest me though. What interested me in the circled event was that everything was so easy. The date, time, and place that he would be just handed to me on a plate. It was two nights later in a well-known Paris bookshop; I hoped not far from where I was sitting. To be as prepared as possible I would find the bookshop immediately. I would plan my route towards the assassination. There would be nothing left to chance, every step would be rehearsed and planned to perfection.

Often, I have watched films where the great assassin does all the things you are expecting because you have been told that he is such a crack shot, an expert in his field, cold and calculating, with a steady eye, only to find, at the climax, he's like a child with a paint gun. I would not be that man. I was fixed on my target. Nothing would stop me. I stood up from my table, picked up the guide, and left the café.

Across the road, before the fountain, there was a bookshop with stalls outside packed with books. It was getting dark and the lights of the tightly packed shops cast a beautiful yellow hue down the boulevard. A short and light rainfall had lain a sheen across the road which reflected that light. I felt that I

31

could be in a painting of a master like Matisse. I crossed the road carefully, looking both ways, as I had not accustomed myself properly to the direction of traffic.

Under the awning of the shop, I looked at the books. Not surprisingly the titles were all in French, although I recognised a few cover pictures of authors. I picked up a book of symbolist poetry. I had read a lot of it during my teens. Like most poetry lovers I became more fascinated with their lives than their work. As a matter of fact, eventually the work became a distraction from the real business of their lives. This was only true of poets. For fiction writers we had their lives within their fictions. As for non-fiction writers, they were more fiction than the fiction but personal slants in their work were as much as you would need to know about their biography. All novels are part biography. I have no illusions of anyone telling my story. My life, like most, will be dust blown across a dead earth. I was considering the lice-ridden head of Rimbaud when I felt a pull at my arm. I turned to be faced by a gendarme and the waitress from the café across the road. The policeman was a young, handsome man, clean shaven and tall. As he shouted something at me, I noticed he had small, even teeth. I looked at the young man and woman and widened my eyes in innocence. I thought that lifting my arms and shoulders in a shrug would help this picture of innocence, but I immediately thought it probably represented a caricature of a French shrug of contempt. He shouted at me again and I thought I understood something of what he was saying. I pulled the brochure from my coat pocket and kept repeating, 'Pardon! Pardon!' I also thought that causing such a fuss over the theft of a café brochure was unmerited. I was more than happy to offer it to them in order to defuse the situation, but the gendarme pushed the brochure from my hand. The rudeness in those that hold even a modicum of power in society should let us take stock of those that hold more power. The brochure fell to the ground, and, as I bent to pick it up, I noticed that the waitress was clutching my bill for two coffees. My face fell into one of realisation. Again, I could only repeat my apologies in the French I had at my command. I reached into a pocket and pulled a large note out. I then mumbled the word *l'addition*. I knew that the word was part of a sentence asking for the bill but forgot the sentence. (I knew some unusual tourist words and a lot of everyday phrases. I even knew the word for a street cleaner!) Regardless, the word was ignored as she grabbed the money without a by-your-leave. She then snatched at my empty and open hand and thrust the bill deep into the palm. I automatically closed my hand to a fist, crushing the paper. There was a shout from the café, and the waitress turned and walked briskly off into the road. The gendarme looked directly into my eyes and said in perfect English:

'You are a tourist.'

'Yes.'

'You do not pay for coffee in your country?'

At this I realised that he was taking the absolute cunt, but I have found with the law it is better to show due deference and submit to any verbal humiliation that is thrown.

'No officer. It just slipped my mind. The bill I mean.'

'What are you doing here?'

'What do you mean? I'm a tourist.'

There was a silence that seemed to go on forever. That silence was broken by a blood curdling scream, followed by a bang that echoed down the evening boulevard. Was that another split second of silence and life coming to a stalk still? Something of a moment frozen. The gendarme turned his head as though in slow motion and ran onto the road. I could see the waitress lying bloodied before a 63 bus that had Gare de Lyon on its front. I took a few steps towards the kerb and saw, before a crowd blocked my view, the large note that I had given her fly from her hand. Although I quickly

33

considered myself not at fault at all in the accident, I somehow convinced myself that the gendarme would in some fashion try to take it out on me. I decided to depart the area swiftly but not so swift as to attract unwanted attention.

I turned a corner and tried to lose myself in the lanes that lay behind the boulevard. It was as though I had entered a different city. The narrow streets were tightly packed, and the shops snuggled together as though for warmth, it was like strolling through a chest of jewels. The smells too from the pizzas, the kebabs, the fried and baked, the cheeses, the meats. Both sight and smell were being encroached upon and I found it glorious and confusing. Young men stood outside the gaping tunnels of restaurants that held no more than a dozen tables. They smiled and invited me in, and I would say *Non* in as friendly a tone that the harsh word made possible. It was not that I wasn't hungry, it was purely the fact that I wanted to distance myself from the incident that happened moments before.

Walking to the end of a maze of streets, to the top end as far as I could wind, I decided to take a right turn. I could hear water and thought that I must have walked the distance that would have taken me to the river. It was not to be, though. The sound of the water was nothing more than the fountain that I had walked away from some minutes before. I must have walked in a circle. Rather than create distance between myself, the gendarme, and the waitress, I looked to the road and saw that I was closer than ever. I turned my back on all of them and walked towards the bridge some twenty metres up ahead.

The bridge was busy with both vehicles and people of all ages and descriptions. As I passed them, I felt that they were looking at me with some puzzlement, or recognition. I ran a hand across my face to check I didn't have a mark of some such that was drawing attention to me. My scarf, that was tucked into my coat and crossed my chest, I reassembled until it was wrapped around my neck twice then pulled above my chin and over my mouth. This immediately made me feel almost invisible to the throng that passed me by. Looking back, I thought I spied the gendarme making his way up the boulevard towards the bridge. I could have been mistaken in this but to feel safe I took the steps down the river's edge at the far side of the bridge.

There was a boat about to take a slow meander along the river. I felt that would be as good as any escape route. I boarded after purchasing a ticket from the booking box. I then made my way to the upper deck in order that I could look across the river and the bridge to the accident.

I saw the flashing lights of what I assumed was an ambulance. I could not see the gendarme on the bridge or the street beyond. The boat shifted on the water. A mass turning and I was whirled slowly to face ahead. The fall of darkness was met with the rise of lights along the river on the boats canopy. In the distance the Eiffel Tower was lit up like a decoration, which of course is what it is. A giant structure that is to all intents and purposes an ugly construction, but like the least of your children the French have been told to love. I made a promise to myself to visit tomorrow and grab the view like a tourist – something I am certainly not. I am a man with a purpose, a job to do, a killing to commit. There is a time to be avenged. There has to be a reckoning, there has to be a moment where the arrogant meet justice. I knew this not to be true as I have lived long enough to have been shat upon on numerous occasions without any consequences for the perpetrator.

There was a jolt in the boat. Something from below. A chugging sound, silence, then calm. It was something that I do not know what. As I looked down from the top deck, I saw for the first time that the water level was higher than I expected. Although a visitor, I recognised that this was not a normal height. The weeks of rain had no doubt an effect on the water levels. As I thought this a more determined rainfall began. I climbed downstairs to stand with others in a warmer shelter. The boat would make stops on its journey, and I had determined to embark at the first. The first, though, was much closer than I imagined. The boat returned immediately to its mooring and tied up. We, the passengers, were ushered off while several people – two men and a woman – said something loudly that seemed to indicate if we returned to the ticket office money would be reimbursed. I had no time for this as I felt as I was still in the proximity of the policeman and the accident.

2

I walked quickly along the side of the river from the uppermost point. The lower walk was completely submerged. I had decided to make a large circular route in order to return to my hotel without having to pass the scene of my troubles. I walked until I was four bridges away and then took a right over another bridge and onto an area with many small streets, some empty, some holding restaurants and bars. The bridge I crossed was narrow and there were several padlocks attached to the rail.

I felt that to be amongst people would make me less conspicuous than a man shuffling down an empty street. My mother used to tell me that no plough stops for a dying man. These words were on my mind as I walked. I was unimportant to others, as they were to me. Most of us will walk through life unnoticed and with little celebration of our time on the planet. Our insignificance is life's only guarantee. It struck me that all the books written, all the art painted, all the thoughts of the great and clever were just proof of our pointlessness. We search all our lives for home. It is elusive, it is the past. And, outside of fiction, it is lost forever.

I decided to go for a beer in one of the tiniest of establishments, of which there were many. I sat down outside, but under cover, at a table. Although it was raining lightly it was warm and I found myself to be sweating. I have always been disgusted by the human body and its various peccadillos. Sweating was a gross *natural* act to me. I understood its purpose and point but that made it no less distasteful. I removed a handkerchief from my inside pocket and mopped my wet brow and face. Luckily, no one would be able to tell if the moisture was rain or sweat. As I sat there for some moments, a damp smell rose up from my clothes. I remembered that I had left the hotel without first showering.

If the waiter did not turn his nose from me, he was obviously being polite. I ordered a beer without making an attempt at the language. This was not a lack of manners but more a forgetting of where I was. He seemed not to mind and nodded and left.

I was looking at my surroundings and the several people that were passing my table. After a few moments I realised that I was sitting with my back slightly to where I had come from. If the policeman did decide to attempt following my tracks, he would be upon me without a chance to either make my escape or prepare myself for questioning. I stood up to change my seat and position just as the waiter arrived with the beer. With a flourish he opened the bottle and poured about a third of it into the glass. The white foam took up the remainder of the glass. He then looked at me. I muttered something about wanting a different view and sat down. He pushed the beer across the table to accommodate my change of position. There seemed no curiosity in his actions, as though it was perfectly normal to have a customer move seats mid-order. He returned to the light inside. I poured another mouthful into the glass and set the bottle back down.

I don't know if it was my changing positions, but the stench from my coat now seemed particularly bad so I stood up to remove it. The waiter was out again. He rushed up to the table.

'I'm just…' I said, struggling with the coat, which seemed to be stuck to the jacket below. I laughed slightly at the daft predicament I found myself in. The coat sleeve was stuck halfway down my arm and I was jerking it in some attempt at grabbing the cuff with my other hand. It was not working. My other hand could not reach it as the wet coat on my back was giving no leeway to the other sleeve. To top it all I stumbled slightly and knocked the table. It was not enough to overturn the bottle of beer and glass but enough that I felt a wave of absolute embarrassment cross my face. I then stopped and took a deep breath. Or that was what was intended but it came out as more of a sigh.

'Aaaaa…' My shoulder ached with the position my upper body was in. The waiter seemed at last to see or understand my trouble and smartly moved behind me and peeled the coat from my body,

'Monsieur,' he said.

He then turned to walk away with the coat.

'No,' I said. 'No, the coat…'

He turned to me and smiled:

'The coat. I hang and dry.'

'Oh, yes. Yes. Thank you.'

What an absolute fool I must have appeared to him. I sat down and took my first sip of beer. It was chilled and seemed to breathe new life into me. I read the label and then decided to pick it off. Rather than come off in one piece as some damp labels do, it came off in torn pieces of various sizes. Once I had finished that I took out the opened pack of cigarettes. I pulled one out and lit it. A few draws and I sickened of it. I flicked the butt out towards the road. It landed on the running gutter. A little sail boat speeding down the water.

A few people that passed my table looked inside the bar and carried on their journey. There was noise coming from an establishment a few doors down and it got me thinking that I had not chosen well. The sign of a good establishment must surely be how many customers they have. I looked around into the bar and saw my waiter hovering by the entrance. I nodded as though I had done something wrong. He ignored me. Being ignored is one of the things I hate most in life, but he was not to know this. A sharp wind came along the street and blew across my by now cold hands. The warmth I had felt in the air had disappeared. It made me think that I wished I still had my coat. If the waiter had just laid it across a chair I could have put it on again. Many people may try to help us in life but only cause anxiety.

Time passed while I thought of the many things that had led me here. I was thinking of my dead parents and how difficult I found it remembering my mother's face. What started me on this train of thought was an old couple that walked past. Neither looked like my mother or father but their age set me off. I am saying that neither looked like my mother and father but cannot recall my mother's face. What I am really saying is that were you to show me a picture of my mother I could say for certain it was her, and the woman that passed bore no resemblance to her. The man with her bore no resemblance to my father also. But I recollect exactly how my father looked. (A rare thing for me.) They were the only elderly couple that I saw pass the table. Much like my own home, the elderly always seemed to be indoors when darkness fell.

The rain stopped slowly; it seemed to suck all the light from the sky. A psithurism drifted through the leaves on the tree at the kerb. I was thinking that I spent much of my time alone with little contact with the world. Of course, this was partly because I found the world to be a hostile place. This was not of my choosing as such, but something I grew into over a period of many years. I had friendships in my childhood, but my adolescence was a time of great loneliness with little said. It was then that I started reading, and the stories became something akin to friendships. I would read them again and again in the hope of unlocking characters and freeing them from the page. I believed there are some very well-known characters that I could have written more of, such was the extent of my knowledge of them. In this close reading I found that life's lacunae could be filled with reading and study. I had my mind set on some kind of literary critique as a career even at an early age. What struck me was the author as an instructor, which I detested. What the hell was it to do with a novelist to be the arbiter of public morality and judgement? Unless it is, of course, Cervantes. Dickens often crossed that line. I have always thought readers of Dickens have a strong impulse towards the lash. This is not a verifiable thought, of course.

I was never given the chance to properly display my talents, having been set out from birth as a slave to normality. My mother tried to change this, but really, accepting advice from a woman who rarely left her house was no help to my younger self. I felt my station in life was abandoned and nothing came or went or even passed through anymore. There were, of course, moments in my past where I was allowed to glimpse a potentially different future. This was, again, my mother's doing. I must confess it was a cruel trick to play on such as me. I saw, but could not grasp, let alone conquer. My lot was to stand on the sidelines while others grabbed the keys to the kingdom.

I believe I am a curious figure to many. They can sense my oddness, my outsideness. They suspect I am ill mentally and should be avoided. The truth is I make others uncomfortable. This is my lot. I did not ask for such and would not have wished it on anyone. It is a lonely position to occupy, and a painful one to set your days by. This does not mean that I do not or cannot interact with others. I have grown so used to the situation, though, that I now shun company and display none of the outward signs of wanting company. The receptors that open one to others have lain dormant in my life so long that I fear that they have died. This is of no great note. There are many in society like me. The thing is, I became attached to my mother and father the same way that you may be attached to anything that is around you for a long time: a dog, or a book perhaps. But truly they instilled few things in me but the determination to get as far away from them as possible.

The house that I grew up in had many stimulants for a budding literary bon viveur. Mother's library, which was eventually stored in cardboard boxes in the basement, could entertain me for hours. I never saw my father with a book in his hand. Of course, I also had free use of the television, which was both a curse and a blessing in those days. Nowadays, there are no blessings at all, which is why I lobbed the contraption from my fourth story window during one of my sleepless nights. It was offering me nothing. These are the words I told the police officers. They very rightly pointed out that I could have killed someone with my foolish actions. I was lucky to get off with a warning. It was an exciting exchange.

What *ordure* this flash of light that we call life is. It is the most miserable of experiences, of cuts and bruises that leave you howling and grovelling in the dirt. I shake my fist at it all. I curse all those bastards that have gone out of their way to do me down and make my desolate life's trials worse. The scum that laughed and winked and talked in whispers behind my back, that tried to do me down at every turn, I send a plague on all of their houses. And that, if truth be told, is the nub of the problem with the central character of the novel that brought me here. He is part of that vast army that is nothing less than an enemy to life. To set him up as anti-hero is surely a mockery of everything that the novel should be doing. A novel must be there to raise us up as fellow humans, to uncover and highlight our place in life. The author tries to make good of a man that does nothing more than add to our foul existence. He in effect ruins lives. He takes lives. This is no longer acceptable. Is this seriously how the author feels life's hours should be filled? As Humpty Dumpty said to Alice: *neither more nor less*. We live in dangerous times. Our breath might be stopped by stepping out of our front door. Is this sort of writing offering us anything to cling onto? The world is in turmoil, people fleeing their homeland and bodies being broken. It seems all of it is the result of ego and rapacious unfettered greed. The global body fights, the man

42

in the street fights, and it is a fight between two heads of the same monster.

When you have chosen a solitary life, you have time to think.

While I thought, the rain came on again. It was splashing down on some tables. Luckily, I was further in, but the wind was whipping up so much I thought I would be soaked in a matter of moments. No matter, I was cold anyway. My beer was down to the bubbled watery end. I lifted my hand to the waiter and left some money on the tabletop. He brought my coat out and helped me on with it. Some might see this as being helpful, but had you been there you would have understood that he was ushering my exit. I hoped he gets cancer. As I walked into the rain, I could feel his eyes upon me. I believe he thought I cut a comical figure.

Some yards up the road I found that I had been walking in the wrong direction. If I turned around I would have to pass his sad bar again. There was a shop that sold tourist gewgaws and gimcracks; ornaments, posters, cups, scarves, lighters, playing cards, jigsaw puzzles, shorts, tee shirts, and all the other paraphernalia of the tourist industry junk. I entered to collect my thoughts, and near the far end of the store I tried on a beret. Although it is known as the hat of the French, I had not seen anyone wear one since I arrived. Sitting back on my head it looked quite smart and would, I thought, serve the double purpose of keeping my head warm and offering something of a disguise when I passed the bar again. If the waiter was inside he might not have seen me passing, but if he was again standing at the entrance, he might not recognize me. I could have put my head down, my chin tucked in, and walked quickly by. He might, of course, have noticed the coat. If, until I passed him, I rolled the coat up and held it under the arm closest to the road he would not think of his last customer. I decided this was an idea worth following up. I paid for the beret and left the shop. Outside, I quickly removed my coat, rolled it up and shoved it under my right arm. I only had a light jacket and my tee shirt on underneath. It was a cotton shirt, blue, with a worn brand name.

As I approached the bar, I saw that the *serveur* had climbed down the few steps at the doorway. He had cover under the awning which jutted far out into the street. He was standing at the very end of it, smiling and gesturing to potential customers. I tried to pull a face that was not abnormal but would disguise the features of the man he had just served. I did this by tucking in my chin, pursing my lips, and squeezing my eyes to almost closed. His eyes followed me. It was then that I realised that he had seen me longer in my jacket and tee shirt than in my coat, and so, while still walking, I let my coat unfurl and held it over my beret covered head. I was determined not to make eye contact with him and so fixed my gaze on a distant point. As I was almost upon him, I could feel his eyes staring. The moment I was passing he cried out:

Rat!

My pursed lips fell to their usual sloped position, the eyes lost both their screwed-up look and the distant gaze. My face gave the immediate look of shock as I followed his eyes to a rat about a foot long running along the gutter. He rushed indoors, no doubt to tell someone that he had seen a large rodent. I was happy for the distraction, as I passed easily and put on my coat again. At the corner, I dashed across the road and made my way into a park. If I continued to the far end I could walk around its perimeters and make my way back to my area and my hotel. As I walked, I thought of Proust. Is anyone's mind quiet for an instant?

The Flaneur

3

The rain was coming down heavily. I took some rest and shelter on a bench under a very large plane tree that had not been pruned enough to take away its cover. From where I sat, I could hear noise and laughter up ahead, further into the park. I listened carefully as I did not want to walk into a group of revellers. The sound faded and I closed my eyes for a moments rest. The moment that they closed I felt that someone was beside me. I heard nothing, but I felt a presence, as though someone was staring at me, examining me. I have felt this before, but I have refused to open my eyes. That is the perversity of fear. I was thrilled by the fact I was maybe being watched, or at this proximity, examined. But I have felt it before. I have felt that since I was a child. I was spoken to by a school doctor who asked who could possibly be looking at me when my eyes closed. I answered him with the innocence and lack of fear of a child.

'I don't know.'

When you are a child what you don't know is something you can understand, and it is not something that is feared. The doctor for some reason believed me to be faking illness, although I did not feel ill. He told me to snap out of it and stop spoiling for attention. I was wise enough to feign shame and apologise to everyone. It was a cry for more attention my mother said. My father said that I was a spoiled brat. To be fair he did call me that and other things long before I informed people that I was being watched. He would mock me at every turn; mocking how I walked, he told me that I was pigeon toed. He told me that my hair was too long and I looked like a girl. I would chew the end of my hair in the classroom and was always surprised I didn't end up with a fur ball like a cat might. My father also said that I was too skinny, and should I get seriously ill I would surely die. He believed that carrying extra weight was a great medicine for sickness. The weight, though, had to be muscle. I really do try not to dwell on my life but fail miserably on a daily basis. Every day I seem to relive every single year since my birth. I'm sure this must be a psychiatric condition. If it's not it should be considered one.

The moments rest that I closed my eyes for turned into a full sleep. We are always aware of our waking moments, but the moment of sleep is upon us before our consciousness can give the moment consideration. We say that we *fall* into sleep and that seems correct, but there is also a net there that catches that fall. It rescues the mind and offers it different avenues of escape. I used to think that death was that fall into sleep but without the net. And my own forsaken cry. I hold out no hope of an afterlife. Even the absurdity of metempsychosis left me not only cold but horrified. I cannot fight the inevitability of death. I cannot fight the inevitability of life.

I awoke shivering in the cold morning air. It must have been the cold that forced me awake. I had pulled my legs up to my chest, but as the rain was blowing my clothes became wet and my body was shaking. My clumsy foetal position made no difference. As I sat up, I felt ill. My thighs were stiff and had to be rubbed vigorously in order to get the circulation going again. I could feel the blood infuse the legs with a tingle. The body stiffens as one gets older. It must be something to do with inactivity, although I'll be damned if I don't walk more now than I did as a child. I did not feel well. My mind was made up to get back to the hotel pronto and have a hot shower. After that I would slip under the welcoming sheets and fall into more sleep. The very thought of this got me standing and setting off.

What happened the night before I know as much as I said. But what was on my mind, in my thoughts, when I placed my feet on the bench seat and curled up? That part of my story must be left a blank for that is what it is for me. Certainly, I could imagine a particular scenario and relate that as though truth, but it is my intention in this story to record only that which I remember. Fictions are for escape, and my intent is the whole truth, and therefore reality.

As I walked through the park I saw only one man in the distance. It was a gardener, I believed, although the distance made certain recognition difficult. Why I thought that it was a gardener was that he seemed to be pushing a wheelbarrow. Of course, it might have been a man pushing a wheelbarrow through the park to work. I have never seen a man push a wheelbarrow to work before, but I reckoned it was not beyond the bounds of possibility. As I went around the outskirts of the duckpond my eyes kept the figure in view as long as was possible, without turning my head. It struck me at the last that it was possibly not a man pushing anything but a woman pushing a pram. My sexism no doubt kicked in, for it could have been a man pushing the pram. Let us settle on *a figure*. I had almost done settling on this last idea when my stomach quickly went into a knot and my body jack-knifed. I felt a surge of my stomach contents, I fell down immediately to one knee and began vomiting. The little I had in my stomach came up and splashed on the duck path. As I retched two things came strikingly to mind. One was the waiter from the bar the previous night, standing, smiling at me from his post just under the bar awning. The other was the scene from the book where the character is sick on the ferry. Although the author does not describe the actual process the character went through, I thought that I was positioned in a similar posture that he must have been. I looked to the distance as I stood up and saw that the man with the wheelbarrow, or the woman with the pram, or the man with the pram, or none of these, let it go, and it rolled a few yards before toppling over. I then thought that it could possibly have been a woman with a wheelbarrow. My mind is constantly in a state of flux about what I see and what I hear. Creeping into my thoughts are often different interpretations. I consider these interpretations and while doing so wonder if others experience the same thing but just don't discuss it? There is much in life that we all keep secret, not the private things – which is another thing all together – but the day-to-day public happenings. I would imagine there is an unspoken etiquette on this matter. If we all discussed our daily ruminations at every turn society would be running backwards.

The novel that I have related and that sent me travelling from my home would have no such uncertainties, as the author would have painted a picture so detailed and exact that the reader would know exactly what to think. Rarely do people have such exactitude on the everyday. Should an author allow his reader to have any imagination? Where would the story go? It would meander down dead ends and blind alleys, everyone seeing something different. There would be no story proper, and everyone would have their own imaginings. With the description of character this was appropriate, but with the line of story would be impossible. No, not impossible. There are ways.

It was with these thoughts in mind that I found myself at the south end of the park. The gate was closed. Obviously, one must have been open for the figure that I saw to have entered, but I could not be bothered walking around the perimeter until I found an unlocked gate. I decided instead to climb over the cast iron railings and drop on the pavement outside. My limbs were not as flexible as they once were, and I struggled to reach the spiked top. Tip top condition has its limitations with age. At the top I tried to catch my breath while my arms pushed to hold my bodyweight off the spear-like heads. It was at this moment that a park-keeper of some sort arrived carrying a large bunch of keys. He obviously could not help but notice me and in the softest of voices spoke:

'Maintenant, descendez doucement et gentillement!'

My arms, locked in a state of rigidity, began to shake uncontrollably. If I had let go I would have been a goner. This thought made me decide to push out forcefully and by doing so cast my body away from the gate and drop, hopefully unharmed from the perch. This plan would have worked had I not been wearing such baggy trousers. One of the trouser leg material got caught on a spike and was torn from knee to ankle. The sound of the tearing told everything about my clumsy manoeuvre as I landed heavily and awkwardly on the ground. My right ankle twisted and I gave a cry of pain. This was immediately followed by my left knee grazing the gravelled pavement.

The parkkeeper said some more words to me, but I wanted to be far away, and so started limping towards the morning traffic. I could feel his eyes following me as I tried my best not to cry with each step. I knew that I would have to sit down and rest, for the pain would not permit me to make straight for my hotel.

Crossing the road was easy as the traffic was light. I made a promise to myself to rise early every morning, for with the soft rain, and the air cleaner than I had felt in my life, it was something to be desired. A change in my routine was necessary for me to reach whatever potential I had, and in whatever area I chose to live my life. No sooner had this thought run through my mind than the freshness disappeared and was replaced with a stench like I had never experienced before. It was much like raw waste, a sewage farm before the sewage was treated. From the running gutter a drain exploded with filthy water. A piece of carpet placed just outside the gutter outlet was meant to direct the water that comes out into the gutter. The strike by the water workers meant there was a lack of fresh water. The rolled-up carpet was pushed aside by the filth. Looking down towards the embankment I saw that the river had covered the bank below.

Some distance in front of me I saw a man and a woman. They appeared to be dressed in old fashioned attire. From the shoes up they were dressed in 19th century garb. A fancy dress party? The man was happy, dancing, laughing, in front of the woman. She was giggling at his antics. Were they married? Were they friends? His hair was long and grey, pulled back and held with a velvet ribbon. The girl had a rolled parasol, big ballooning skirts, a hat with a brim, ludicrously wide. She gave a fake curtsey then ran on past him. Past me, laughing. She came close to bumping into me, but I moved ever so slightly, and a collision was averted. And then he came towards me. And he did the strangest of things: he stopped and just stared at me, as if I were the curious looking one. As though I were walking the streets in fancy dress. He was older than I thought; an elderly gent, I'd say. But so pale and thin looking. Was he wearing makeup? The pallor was quite sickly. A gentleman going to a party with his daughter or young wife. Stopping to stare at a man that was staring at him. He was no longer laughing, though. Maybe he thought I was about to do him harm. I decided to speak to reassure him:

'The weather…' I said.

He did not move. And then she shouted, *Allez*. He snapped as though caught in a trance, turned and rushed towards her. I watched them walk away. She had her arm around his waist. He looked feeble. They disappeared into the distance. My eyes followed them until they were gone.

My hands were shaking. I put it down to the cold.

4

I was exhausted. I needed a coffee. I would not make it back to my hotel before collapsing with exhaustion. I knew that I must sit and get sustenance. Coffee. Some bread. A café. I saw a café up ahead. As I walked towards it the rain came on heavier than before. I would get in and dry off. Into the warmth. I would get breakfast, a *petit dejeuner*. I would have bread, and eggs, and hot black coffee. I would feel better. The smell of the coffee would permeate the place. The tabletops would be clean. The coffee machine polished chrome. I had it painted, line and colour, in my mind before arriving. The thoughts alone carried me over the road. I tried to skip over the running gutter, but my leg hurt so I missed the jump and kicked the top of the water. The water entered my shoe but was not cold. It was warm on my foot. A pleasing moment. There was a comfortable rush to my brain. We take what we can. Little moments of solace; little moments of pleasure.

Inside the café, which was exactly as I had imagined, I slumped into a chair. I was dragging my arm across my face when the waitress pushed through the swing door which led to the kitchen. I couldn't imagine the kitchen. She was shouting back at someone that might have been the chef, or another waitress. I tried some small talk with her, in French and English. Mostly the latter. I feigned joy at seeing her and being in Paris. If I was in something of a state, she appeared not to have noticed. She told me that she was born in the city but now detested it. She wanted to go live in the country by a stream and tend to her garden all day. I smiled at this, for it's impolite to argue with residents of a city you are visiting. She told me that the city was stifling and was killing her. She told me that she couldn't afford to strike, and that even the strikers and protesters need coffee and cake. Her English was broken, but much better than my French. I complimented her on her English. She told me she learned most of it from serving tourists. I told her that I am a tourist and think that her city that is killing her, is beautiful. The river is overflowing she told me. It stinks. She goes further and told me it was putrid, and the smell comes in her window at night. She blamed the council. They should have given the workers their pay rise. Corrupt bastards, she told me. They steal the food from the mouths of workers. They will drown in filth. The police too are refusing to work overtime. It is illegal for them to go on strike, but they can refuse to do overtime. The city was falling, she told me. Nobody signed up for this. It was a curious statement. Finally, I asked for bread and eggs and coffee. She told me that there was no bread to be had in the whole of the city. There were no deliveries. She was a tiny woman in her late fifties, sporting frizzy red hair piled up high on her head. I asked her name and she clearly saw it as a line to getting more friendly. Her name was Collette, she said. I laughed and said Collette was a great French writer. She told me that she never read and that all books should be burned. She told me that the Nazis had the right idea. She was now another person to me, and I will admit that I suddenly feared her. I don't know why I asked her name. We judge people in a moment and change that judgement in an instant. She was at that moment a stupid person. She was poorly educated, her beliefs transient, she knew enough to know that there was something wrong but was confused as to what exactly it was or what could be done. The workers were being exploited but the Nazis were right to burn books. The city was falling. Dreams of Eden. Another one dissatisfied with life who would grab onto anything that offered a difference. Until that time, she would serve bread, eggs, and coffee.

There was a lull in the conversation and as usual I had to fill it. I don't know where this need to fill silence came from but I have had it since a child. My house was a place of silence, but for my father grunting. Tomorrow I might forget about

Collette, but right there and then she was all. Unless I wrote about her. The chat might be seen as research. If I was a novelist I would definitely research. I would be open to people and to ideas. I would share people and their experiences. I would not be one of those internal monologue writers who write the stories where the weight of the authors self is pushed against the door. Of course, that is not the only way a writer betrays his audience. Like my future victim. His betrayal was very different. He let the reader in, but there was nothing to see. He talked down, not up. Let me say that nobody talks down to me anymore. It was like once I had a boss; well, one time I just let go at him. Verbal of course. In those days I wouldn't contemplate violence. But those were the days that I saw a doctor. She had told me that she worried about me. The lack of control. It was the spontaneous bouts of anger. But this time is, of course, different, because this time I am in control. This time my actions are planned, slow, and premeditated.

On that thought I understood that I had to return to my hotel room, for that is where I had left my gun. I was surprised that it passed the customs check as it was just lying inside my suitcase. Obviously, the strike action by airport workers affected their ability to check every bag. There were few people at the airport. If I could get back to the hotel, then I could shower and get cleaned up as well, I thought. I needed a change of clothes and a wash. Maybe Collette thought I was nothing more than a beggar. But would she serve a beggar eggs and coffee? She would be suspicious and tell me to leave the café. She would say she had to shut up. I would say *but it's early*. She would get angry and threaten me with the police. She disappeared through the swing door she had appeared from. She could not have thought me a beggar. I looked through the window at the low sky and rain.

I feel that I should say something of the weather, which must be of concern. It had taken an even greater turn for the worse. The rain that had hardly let up and since my arrival had developed somewhat. It was coming down in sheets. With the rain arrived a wind. The wind was not gale force, but was discernible and had picked up some speed and strength. Added to this the extreme river level, I was concerned that there might be more serious flooding. The sewers were already spilling onto the streets through drains and gutters. There was also, as a result, something of a stench that was unpleasant. The ongoing strike by the municipal cleansing department hadn't helped matters. Much of the unrest started over a wage dispute three weeks before I arrived. Outside, restaurants and bars were piling up their rubbish in plastic bags. After so many days you can imagine these piles. They were built up like pyramids, some around fifteen metres high in places. Newspaper boards announced something about unions – the CFDT, the CFTC, the CGT– but I did not plough through any paper to get the details. Not that I could have gleaned much with my lack of language. There was certainly something of a national strike in the air, and student leaders also lent their support to the cleansing workers by organising a national march. This is as much as I knew solely from headline boards outside shops. Earlier, when making my way to find a hotel I saw much to-ing and fro-ing outside the Préfecture de Police. Normally none of this would concern me, but what with the political disruption, the weather, and the looks on people's faces, it created an atmosphere in the city that I found slightly unnerving. It did not dissuade me from my task in hand, but it did set me on edge somewhat. I felt that everyone was ready at the drop of a hat to either man the barricades or storm the barricades. It could be read on the faces of those that passed me on the street. There was a palpable tension in the city. People, I am certain, were waiting for inevitable unrest. If I can get back to my room, I thought, I would have time to contemplate how I might work social disturbance to my advantage.

The Flaneur

Collette returned with my eggs and coffee and placed them in front of me. She had a knife and fork wrapped in a paper napkin in her left breast pocket. She removed them and set the cutlery down beside the plate. Before I asked for salt, I saw it standing by the pepper in what looked like small porcelain containers modelled in the style of a man and woman from a Lautrec painting. The lady was dressed in a Moulin Rouge outfit and the gent looked like Lautrec. The lady was salt, the gent, pepper. Picking it up I saw the salt said *La Goulue*. I thanked Collette in English and in French. She showed no reaction and returned through the swing door. When she was gone, I noticed that she had not left me milk for my coffee. I cannot remember if I asked for the coffee black or white. I drink both. Tea, though, I only have black. Rising, I went over to the swing door and looked through the porthole window. I saw nothing so pushed the door slightly and said *Hello?* There was no sound. I opened the door tentatively and again said, *Hello?* There was a sound coming from inside. It was a high-pitched hissing. I coughed loudly and entered. The kitchen was small and empty of people. Of the two sinks, one had water running. I went over to it and saw the water running over a vacuum-packed steak. I turned the tap off and looked around and identified the high-pitched sound: it was an electric kettle reaching boiling point. I left it and crossed to the fridge. Inside, I removed a carton of milk and returned to the dining area and my table. The milky coffee was good, but the eggs were dry, overcooked, and tasteless. When Collette returned, I said nothing of this. I smiled and ate as though it was my last meal. She stared at me and then picked up the carton of milk. *Milk*, I say. *Au lait!* It sounded more like the Spanish *Olé!* She returned to the kitchen. I wondered where the chef was. Or the cook. Could she be doing all of this herself. Maybe he was outside the back with her having a cigarette. It is the only reason I could conjure up as to why the kitchen was empty. Although I'm sure there are a hundred reasons. I finished the egg and removed another foul cigarette from my inside pocket. The Gauloise were as horrible as I remember from the day before. I had in my mind, as I lit it, that they were known as the ladies' cigarette. I was at a loss as to why they were known as the ladies' cigarettes.

While smoking I thought about the book that brought me so far from home. It was clear that I would not be here without that novel being in existence. So, I can say that it guided me, or created me, for this place. In this city, at that moment, I was as much a product of that book as the book was a product of imagination − or should I say imaginations? If we, the readers, can make any book we read from our own life experiences then surely those pages also create us. Every reader enters into a pact with every story. We arrive as equals. But what happens when one side of this pairing betrays the other? If the story comes with false promises? If the story lies? If the story cheats on the reader? Should the abused partner not demand some justice? A recompense? Is a literary betrayal less than that of a lover's betrayal? The time put in; the energy given? The hours of attention? The reader gives himself or herself; they have surrendered themselves. Blinded at Gaza, left scrambling around at the mill of slaves. We, the reader, become dust in a land arid of story. Who should we turn to when the characters have gone? Who or what should we hold on to? Our past? Who does the reader use as their guide when the author betrays them? Our own memories? It was as good as anything at that moment. While I smoked the cigarette and drank the coffee.

I was a clever boy. Never a troublemaker. If I had faults, they were that I missed out on friendships and adventures that I have been told are the spine of childhood. I climbed no trees, rode no bicycle, swam few waterholes, exchanged no secrets; I ran rarely, unless being chased by bullies; I only hurt those that attempted to hurt me, and only then when I was trapped. My time was spent reading the classics, and critical works that would help me understand fully the great writers. Being an only child, I could devote many home hours to study. Which is what I did. I won every school prize except attendance. I was often ill with headaches, and what my mother called *the melancholy*. Sometimes, for no reason, and at the most inappropriate moments, I would collapse into a heap of tears. When the character, Holly, in the novel, broke down in the gallery, I had a moment of recognition, for I had suffered such an incident. I was about twelve, and out with my mother at a city gallery when I collapsed in a heap crying, after leaving a Dutch master's room. It wasn't any particular painting that provoked the emotion, but more the use of paint on canvas. I have always been emotionally attached to any act of creation. My studies often brought me to the door of emotion.

I am often engaged in study of one sort or another. I often make notes thinking that I might write a paper on my enquiries. Most of the time these enquiries and notes taken result in nothing but expanded knowledge, which in itself is a success. I spent some months last year researching the history of Indian theatre in which I learned a great deal. Sanskrit theatre is as old as Greek theatre but is rarely mentioned in theatre compendiums. Study is not time wasted.

Collette was standing over me. So lost in thought was I that I didn't hear her approach. She slapped the bill down on the table and said in a heavily accented voice:

'Pay. And leave.'

Her tone was one of anger, but I had done little to anger her. Perhaps she didn't like the fact that I had entered the kitchen and removed the milk. This was possible. There are rules for a customer and there are areas in a restaurant that are a sanctum. Entering, I trespassed on the holy.

I paid and left. But not before I pocketed the salt cellar. *La Goulue* slipped easily into my coat. Old habits and all that.

Outside, I heard nothing at first. I felt nothing. But, turning my head, I saw it. It came tearing out of the shop next to the café. It was a blast of flames and glass that blew tables and people onto the road. It was then, for a split second, one fraction of a moment, when my head was turned, I heard the sharp bang that muffled my hearing before closing it off completely. Like someone had hit the mute switch on life. Two men, their shirts soaked in blood, were running, and screaming out words. But all was silent to me; the patisserie next to the café seemed to swell in the mayhem, before the window collapsed like water; a child, no older than ten years old, lay quite dead in the running gutter; a car was ablaze some yards from me, but I heard nothing of the fire. Nor did I hear the sirens arriving how long later? I was wandering around amidst the chaos, confused and lacking any coherent purpose. A small, nut-brown man, wearing a white apron, appeared from the café doorway; he was carrying the limp body of Collette. If she was not dead, then she was one tick away from it. The image brought to mind Caravaggio's *The Entombment of Christ*, which I had seen in the Vatican Pinacoteca some years before. In my obviously confused state, I felt that I had to remove myself from the situation. A blue scarf shifted across the ground, although I felt no wind. It got caught in an overturned table. I walked on through a crowd of onlookers who, if they looked at me, I did not notice. I don't know how long it took for my hearing to return but it brought with it a feeling of extreme cold. I reached in my pocket for my cigarettes and lighter but realised that I'd left them on the café table when paying my bill. Perhaps my mind was distracted by my small theft. I was dog tired and really wanted to sleep. Down some dead end was a row of refuse bins. I pulled three black rubbish bags from inside one, pushed the bin on its side, crawled in, and pulled the lid shut. I fell into sleep listening to the rain hitting the plastic container. I felt that I would have to take stock of my situation, but sleep would come first. I had only been awake a couple of hours.

My dream was my explanation should I be questioned. I knew nothing. I had eaten eggs, drank coffee, smoked cigarettes, and then left the café. I was a tourist. I knew little about anything. Of course, other dreams came in the fug of the unconscious mind. My mind has always tossed over many imaginings through sleep. One involved me confusing *Combrey* with *Llareggub*, *Little Willy Wee* six feet under *Swann's Way*. Imaginings…washed up on the shore again and again, waves of oblivion…

Late morning arrived with the same tapping of raindrops on the plastic bin. Water had entered my shelter and soaked one whole side of me. I was shivering; I smelled of rotten vegetables and piss. One trouser leg was torn and hung down. In the gap in the material my knee showed a cut and a patch of blood. I made up my mind to go straight to my hotel and wash. If I was stopped, I would tell them to go to hell. I had done nothing wrong. I accidently left a café with an unpaid bill on my first night. That was the sum total of my crimes. I did not knock the waitress down. I did not plant a bomb and cause death and destruction. I was innocent. Then my hand gripped the salt cellar in my coat pocket. I pushed the lid of the bin open and started to crawl out but stopped as I saw two people above me: a young man and woman. The young man was wearing a pair of brown and cream coloured brogue ballroom shoes; his trousers were black with a shiny black stripe coming down one side. They were undone, as the couple were in the act of sex. His suspenders hung loosely down to his knees, and he had a black tailcoat. It struck me that he had come either from an upmarket party or perhaps some kind of ballroom dance competition. His hair was slicked back and short as is the style today and as it was many a yesterday ago. As for the girl, I saw little of her. She was shielded by the young man's body. Her bare arms were around his neck and her black stockinged legs were tightly around his hips. Only when I pushed the lid of the bin fully open did they disentangle themselves. They appeared to ignore me totally and fixed their attire. It was at this point that the young woman was clear to me. Her dress was a silver concoction with small feather decorations around the hem, which swung loosely just about knee level. Her hair was short and blonde, and her face was pale, set off by the bloodiest of red lipstick. As I crawled out of my bin the young lovers walked slowly and calmly away from me. I had heard often about continental loose morals, but not even in Rome had I witnessed such a disregard for public etiquette. I pulled myself from the bin and exited the lane.

I stood where the lane met the main street and looked around. Bags of rubbish, bins, and some windows, boarded up, greeted me. It was still early. There was little traffic and no people around. Every day seemed to bring a new disaster. If not a personal disaster, then one for the city I was in. I started to query whether it was indeed later that morning or I had slept through a whole twenty-four hours. Was that my third day? My second? Time and memory seemed confused. Of late I have had many doubts about time.

5

I was walking back towards my hotel. A wet, pink petal fell and landed on the back of my hand. I stopped and look at it. Thoughts and memories often bring me to a standstill, for I could just as easily walked on and examined it. I am in rapture much of my time. Our losses come in the most natural events. I brought my hand up and levelled the petal under my nose. I breathed the essence but smelt nothing. I then wiped my hand on the side of my coat and continued on. It is the only way.

The rains of summer...

I was brought again and again back to the novel. This was no surprise considering my plans. Going over what I remembered of it helped my movement. When I walked with no thoughts, the area that I covered seemed to have been done so in slower time. But when I thought of the novel, time seemed swifter. I was of course moving no quicker. I was considering why the author decided on model ship building as a hobby for his main character? Was it that it is such an unusual pastime, or was it to reflect something else about the character? If I said that it would be impossible for such a character to have such a hobby, I would then have to say that no one builds model ships. That, of course, is a nonsense. But what first struck me about it was its unusual quality. I would have asked the author why he could not have had a more ordinary pastime, like reading. If it had been reading, that might have fitted with his later skills for writing, for every writer must surely be a reader. I have no interest at all in model ships, so I found those few sections tiresome. If he had been a reader, then Calvert, his lover, might have something more to discuss with him at the start. It might have set things up for the attraction. I was not suggesting that every writer bows to my ideas of what does and does not make a good novel, but a novelist that does not listen to his or her readers is a fool.

I came out of my thoughts and walked in the moment. The faces, apparitions, came at me as brush strokes of a Renoir, forever pushing to demand their reality, their existence. What if, I say, I came across the author? Say, in a public square, a quiet boulevard, a park or café? Would that moment be too great to contemplate? Would I continue on my way and return to my bed to consider another day? To make excuse after excuse from cowardice or fear? His life I wanted so much to end became a reflection more of me and my being. A reflection of my truth and my hypocrisies, my own lies and contradictions? I asked myself who wrote the story and who read? Am I the same man that I was then? Is he? Maybe we are both someone else.

I was following the river from above as the lower level was flooded. The wonders of the living earth. A river that overflows is a powerful beast. It surely looked untamed and wild. I am not sure what the authorities were doing to stop the water, if indeed they could do anything. Unless the rain let up, I couldn't see how it could be stopped. Of course, sandbags along the perimeter would block the movement of water onto the roads, but those responsible for executing such a task were on strike so the water flowed unhindered.

As I walked along the embankment people came towards me, their head down. Some had umbrellas, some hats, all with coats buttoned high up to their necks. The beret I had bought sat on my head. It was only when I had come out of my thoughts about the author and books that I started to feel the cold. Some thoughts, I deduced, must keep you warm.

A woman blocked my route.

'Pourquoi me regardes-tu comme ça?'

I didn't understand her but keep staring in the hope something would click. I knew these words but my mind was muddied.

'Pourquoi me regardes-tu comme ça?'

I still hadn't a clue what she was saying, so I just stared. She appeared angrier with each repetition. I should have informed her that I was a tourist who was uncertain of the language.

'Pourquoi me regardes-tu comme ça?'

'Toureeest!' I said, hoping the elongated latter part of the word would somehow make clear my position in her country. Her words, meaningless to me, however, planted themselves in my mind.

'Pourquoi me regardes-tu comme ça?'

They didn't however grow to translation. Not to be understood is surely the most tragic of circumstances for any human being. I think that is the thing that I tried to instil in my students over my many years. Communication is all we have that can save us from the abyss. I have little doubt, though, there are those who believe that the abyss is God's plan for us all. Why would he be so upset at the inhabitants of Shinar trying to reach him? Isn't that the purpose of prayer and other such desperations? Although, I confess, misunderstanding is part of that same problem. It is part of being human. I tried to discuss this very point with my department head, Professor Darian Broque. I told him that I thought that there was a lack of humanity in humanity these days — we had been discussing a particularly distasteful crime of cannibalism in Upstate New York — Schenectady, if my memory serves — and what brings a human being to eat his neighbour. As I remember it was also at this time I stopped him mid-sentence and said, *I think you matter.* Well, that seemed to shock him more than my comments about cannibalism. He suggested that I go on a short sabbatical: I settled for a couple of weeks in Rome. It was like walking through a gallery. But I still wasn't understood.

The woman in front of me was not giving ground, so I relied on brute force. I pushed her to one side and walked on.

After I had strode on about twenty yards, I looked back and saw her lying half in the gutter. I'm not sure if I pushed her too hard or she slipped afterwards. I was not waiting around to find out. A church up ahead offered, if not sanctuary, then some respite from the rain and harassment. I crossed the empty square and looked up at the magnificence before me. I find churches in Europe much more sombre and dignified affairs compared to my local den back home. The weight of history alone would make kindling of our little town's structure. That's not to say that one might be less prayerful than the other. Surely no god would complain about the real estate erected in his name. Having said that, we have a choice between prime steak and a frozen burger.

I entered through an archway that has welcomed kings and paupers for nearly a millennium. Back home, my town church was built in nineteen sixty-four, after the previous one had been demolished to make way for a car park. To be honest, the car park drew fewer visitors than the church over a week, but it was all part of the town planning committee assuring council leaders that a megamarket was going to be built and that would be a magnet for people in satellite towns. The megamarket came to fruition, in Ae, a town seven miles down the road. Now families go to Ae for their monthly grocery needs. Personally, I was happy, for I like the quiet of our own town. We have never, as far as I'm aware, been visited by the good and the great of society, although we have our fair share of paupers.

I shuffled down the aisle until I found a pew that I liked. All of the seats were the same, but it was more the position of it that suited me. It was about halfway down on the left. When I got settled, I lowered my head as though in prayer. I was not in prayer, but in thought. From the church I was only about fifteen minutes from my hotel room. As a matter of time and distance this was nothing, but I felt that I was being, in some sense, hunted. When I tried to reason this out in my head, it was plainly nonsense. I was an innocent man. I was not a criminal, so why would anyone be hunting me? Sometimes reason does not settle the mind, it just throws up more confusion.

Silence often provokes a storm of thoughts. They batter at the door of the mind with little connecting them other than other thoughts. For some reason I started to think about the fact that I had never married or had a long-term partner. This has nagged at me all of my life. I am not against long term relationships. As a matter of fact it is something I have sought, but all my attempts have come to nought. Those few women I have gone out with have not been suitable for my temperament. As I have said, I am something of an academic, so a shop worker is unlikely to have much in common with me. I did once go out with a checkout operator in the local sporting goods shop. She was a nice piece, but unfortunately also a piece of work. To cut a long story short she drove her car, at speed, into a wall, with me in the passenger seat. I was also, for a few months, enamoured of a more mature lady who joined the department some years ago. Standing next to her perfume made me dizzy and I was struck by the beauty of the lines at the sides of her eyes. It was clear, though, that she had little time for me. When I stood next to her, she would give a little sniff, lift her head, and remove herself from my presence. A colleague told me that what I was doing might be construed as harassment and so I made a determined effort to ignore her. Eventually she left to take up a post in the city. I missed her, even though I was doing my best to ignore her. It had been good knowing that she was there. Two years after she left, another colleague, Jane Kowalczyk, informed me that she had died in a fire. An *In Memorium* had been placed in the obituaries column of a national newspaper. I read her full name several times: Luiza Michalina Dajbrowski. When alone I wept for several moments and said softly *Miss Dajbrowski*. To this day, I can smell her perfume. I think about her often, as I think of much often. The mind seems to be a storeroom whereby nothing has been given its proper place in time or in subject. Can thoughts be catalogued like the Dewey System? I can think of Miss Dajbrowski and in the next moment think of something completely unrelated, as much as anything can be unrelated. And so it was then and now.

I turned again to the book that had brought me on my murderous quest. Art is all. All art is about trying to understand the world. Both the reader and the writer. It is now out of fashion to talk of art as a life blood on its own. It seems that we constantly discuss the financial capital of a work as a measure of its worth. This of course cuts out the need to engage with the work on an emotional or intellectual level. The grading of a work on financial terms makes it easy to judge its success. On that level. It is not a level that I adhere to. Trash will always be trash. Our standards haven't lowered, they have collapsed. I would suggest they are in urgent need of a defibrillator. Year by year the intellect has been rejected for the quick fix; junk art reflected in every area of life. Maybe it's time all writers had a bit of self-respect. Maybe my actions will bring them to their senses. My actions become the art. The assassin becomes the artist. All art inflicts wounds. Jesus, look down on me. Father, I am the one you let go; the one that you will never really know. No response. No surprise. Pah!

A door banged behind me and I heard murmurs of quiet voices. There is nowhere quieter than a church. I turned my head to see a young woman with three children. The woman was wearing a worn brown coat, a small hat, and a veil covering her face. The children were two girls and a boy; the boy, nine or ten years old, wore a flat cap, and jacket, and trousers far too small for him. He was pale and black-eyed. The girls were younger and looked like twins. Both wore dirty blue dresses and, on their feet, brown boots that had seen better days. They looked like they had been weeping, but that might have been the rain on their faces. They all bowed their heads in prayer. I wondered about them. I tried to create a history for them, but nothing seemed right for they did not seem to be connected with the time and the place. I'd had enough and felt that I should leave. As I passed them, slowly, the boy reached his hand out to me, but the mother gently moved his arm down. She did not raise her head while doing this. I continued to the nave and exited.

My head was down as I walked, chin tucked in low and deep. It struck me that was always how I walked. I never caught the eye, never acknowledged another. Since I was a teenager this had been my gait. The introversion of the teen might account for the start of such a way about life, but later? Shaped forever by childhood. The manners have set, the body language that we present to the world, the gait, all hardened in our genetic code. We are who we are. Our minds too have their limitations. We cannot capture the past. No word or pictures. It can flit through the mind or lay on the mind, not to be held, but just to be noticed. But always enough to cause pain or grief of what has been. We are without hope of saving. Our lot is to lose everything. The greatest tragedy. Damned to memory. Capture the essence. Here and gone, here and gone forever. But a spectral mark left.

I am lost. That is the truth of it. I am lost and I am falling. What happens when everything you hold as true is turned to ruins? Pah! Thoughts rattle around like farts in an oil can.

I constantly feel as though I am being watched. Not by security forces, but someone else watching my every movement, listening in on my words. I feel that I have to recognise something in order to shake off whatever it is I appear to be caught up in. Something exceptional must happen. Thinking these things through doesn't make them clearer or more normal. Talking about them does not normalise them. That's something I've had a lot of in the last few years: talking. Or rather muttering to myself. I have been picked up on it. Someone might say 'What?', and I cough and say 'Oh nothing. I was just thinking out loud.' But that is never the full story. It is more involuntary. I have a lack of control, or even consciousness about any of these things. I've tried to pinpoint exactly when my mutterings happen and if there is a pattern to them. At first, I believed that they were just suppressed anger, as when Dan B ran up to me and straight out accused me of stealing his cigarette lighter. I listened silently while watching a glob of collected saliva in the corner of his mouth. When there was a break in his verbal attack I said quietly, *It wasn't me, Dan.* The denial seemed to inflame him more as he then threatened to punch me on the nose. I wasn't having it. I walked away, my mind racing with words that I could have thrown at him. One of the things that went through my head was *Try it, Dan, and I'll knock you down.* This thought was not given expression, but I ended it by saying aloud *Yes.* Now, in that kind of situation, it might be understandable to mutter in anger. But several times I have been in a shop and done similar. I was in *Bump's Bookshop*, a local family business run by Peggie Bump and her daughters, Merrie and Mackenzie, when I pulled a book from the shelves about the works of Nehemiah Grew. An involuntary *Yes* escaped from my lips. Merrie, or Mackenzie, said *Aaah, you found it, Mr Page.* I answered that I had, but I did not correct her on getting my name wrong. The only Mr Page in town was Will Page, the barber, and he looked nothing like me. For some reason I was embarrassed by this error and so replaced the book and left the shop. How it could have happened I don't know, as I have known Peggie's daughters since they were babies. I had come back to town to stay a while and commuted the few miles to work. Mother needed me, although she never asked directly that I return. Of course, it might have been that at that time I needed her? Running from and running to. Like every other poor mutt. Yes…

So, my speaking my mind aloud seems not to be dictated by the situation or at any time of the day. I then tried to consider when it started, though, but I really can't remember. I know I certainly didn't behave like that as a young kid, so it might be an age thing. I never had an invisible friend when a child, unless you consider books and characters contained in them to be invisible. I might be spending too much time on my own. I don't know that is such a bad thing in and of itself.

People often cause most of your stress and discomfort. It can have a real effect on your body as well. The worry and concern others have brought to my doorstep have had physical consequences for me. I have been losing some hair in the last few years. When wet, and I comb it, there are bald spots. Thinning, I suppose. But this is not an age thing. It can be an age thing, but in this instance it is not. It is stress. Just the last couple of years, when I started to feel not right, I'd be outside when I'd just stop in the street and wonder what was really the point of being outside in the first place? To be perfectly honest everyone should try this questioning of their behaviour. Not constantly, of course. Too much questioning makes you appear odd.

My thoughts of then and not now were interrupted by my having to negotiate a large puddle that stretched from the riveredge where it had risen to halfway across the street. Its dirty brown water had spilled out and overrun the bank below me. I had been told before I arrived that flooding was imminent, and so it had come to pass. The only time the rain quietened was when it seemed to gather strength prepared for the next deluge. It is as well that I had not arrived as a tourist, for most of the sights to be seen were closed because of flood or strike action. Strangely, the cafes and bookshops have remained open, some of them with their own sandbags piled up outside hoping to stem any encroaching flow. Of course, business must go on. Money has to be made, wages have to be paid, people must be served. Outside a café next to the church one fellow was perfectly dressed in his waiter's uniform, apart from the Wellington boots to keep the wet from his feet. I look at people when they are not looking my way. Catching the eye of a stranger can be challenging.

For a moment I went off course. I seemed to have lost direction and I found myself in a quiet street with the buildings pushed up close together. It was an attractive little spot. Tucked in a corner I saw a stall packed with books. I had, totally by chance, happened upon the very bookshop that my victim would be visiting. I do not believe in precognition or any of the heebie jeebies, but in a city as large as this what really are the chances? I could only conclude that I was drawn here by some force of nature, or science? A chalkboard with different coloured letters spelt out his name. It was billed as a Q&A, about the mechanics of fiction, with emphasis, obviously, on his novel. I felt a jolt, not of excitement, but of a realisation so profound that my task would indeed come to fruition. Visiting the church seemed to sort out my confusion about time. The event was two days away. That gave me plenty of time to prepare, so that I would have no excuse for failure. I have always held on to some reason for not completing business, should I not complete business. This, I am now certain of, is a flaw in my nature. My Hamlet syndrome. It reflects a personality unable to accept responsibility. Let me reiterate, I am fully aware of my actions and the consequences of those actions.

A large puddle had formed over the pavement and most of the small road outside the shop. Boards had been laid out from the doorway to the pavement edge, and from there, on the road, were planks of wood. I walked the planks carefully, onto the boards and into the shop. I was immediately overwhelmed by the smell of paper. It has been one of the few joys in my life: to enter a bookshop selling second hand and antiquarian books and manuscripts. From large format cartographers' volumes to faux leather Bibles and religious sutras; from heavy and torn leather-bound tomes on ancient travel, to slim cardboard guides on sea birds and their habitats; from parchment like treatises, yellowed with age, to a composer's opus in manuscript form. All and much more always holds me in an olfactory haze, as I succumb to the vanilla scent of lignin. I can spend, and have spent, many joyous hours flipping pages, reading random sentences and paragraphs, and, when no one is in view, I have brought those pages to my nose to complete what appears to be some perverse act of osmolagnia. Shelves, floor to ceiling, packed with wonders, offering both escape and education.

The shop floor was carpeted, and it bore witness to the many who had wandered between the cases. The middle section of the first room (there appeared to be another room at the far end via a narrow aisle) seemed dedicated to new volumes, face up, most of which were colourful, and beautifully designed paperbacks. And then I saw it: a stand devoted to the book and the author that had brought me so far from my home. A wave of nausea came over me and I felt as though I might vomit. I made my way towards the front of the shop to be nearer the open door and the chance of fresh air. A young woman was perched high on a chair beside a till. In a very distinct southern Californian accent, she asked me in English:

'Are you okay? You look a bit pale.'

I pulled myself up straight and summoned all my energy to answer confidently, even though I felt like throwing up.

'It's just the smell outside. The river…the gutters…'

'It's no fun.'

'Yes. The writer giving the talk…'

In my rush to appear fine I switched the conversation too quickly. A panic seemed to grip me.

'The writer…?'

I motioned towards the stand of books.

'Yes. We're very pleased to have him. He isn't known to do these sorts of things.'

What are *these things*? Public readings? Don't all authors promote their books and build their profile through *these things*? A complete waste of time from the reader's point of view. Who really cares about the writer's interpretation of the story? It is each reader's understanding of it that brings clarity to the text. My life in academia gave me some understanding of the story's place. I considered this book's place was by the hearth for kindling. Although my experience has been through a very minor university in a very small town, the general backdrop of the story I could identify with. Certainly more than if I was a checkout operator in a sporting goods store. The reader's life experience, what they bring to the work, is more important even than the writer's intention. What good are intentions if the reader disagrees? I really am done with the reader placing themself on the footstool of the gods.

'Do I need a ticket?'

'No, it's a free event. But I'd get here early; there's been a lot of interest.'

'George!' A female voice cried out my name. To be shouted at in your hometown can be something of a shock, but in a foreign land the feeling you get is one of immediate guilt. It is as though a character in a Victorian Penny Dreadful had called out *Stop thief!*

'George!' Again. My immediate reaction was to run. But as I turned, there was Clara Pett, the college librarian, dressed in a grey and pink two-piece wool suit, and clutching a shopping bag.

'I didn't know you were here.'

'I'm here.'

'Of course you are. Are you with a party?'

'A party?'

'A group? You know at our age...'

She let the end of that offensive statement go.

'I always travel alone, Clara.' It was curious that I called her Clara, as I usually call her *Mrs Pett* in the library. It didn't sound quite right.

'You do. What the hell have you been doing with yourself?'

'What do you mean?'

'You look like you've been sleeping in the river. And your knee...'

'I fell in a puddle.'

To lie about such a thing is to confess the guilt that you carry around, a weight that drags you into the earth. I could not tell her of my having run away from a policeman, a waitress, a parkkeeper, a barman, a lone woman in the street, of a night sleeping in the park or in a bin. Just one of these confessions would condemn me surely to the mental hospital. But it is only when taken out of context. Of course, sleeping in a bin might be questionable to many, whatever the context.

'Are you sure it wasn't the sewers?'

For the first time I got a whiff of myself. I took a step back. She continued:

'The way they're rising to the surface I wouldn't be at all surprised. What is happening? I heard the students are calling for an all-out strike, and march later.'

'The freedom of others extends mine infinitely,' I mumbled unheard.

'The weather might have an influence on the numbers. An exciting time to be here. We can tell our grandchildren.'

Clara seemed to be ignoring the general feeling of lawlessness that was sweeping across every nation. People seemed to believe that freedom was absolute, not that it would lead to a slow break down of the norms of society.

'Our grandchildren?'

'Well, yes, but I will tell mine. You're a funny old dog, George. Even abroad. Are you still staring at things?'

She was referring to a habit of mine which had gained

something of legs as a story. I liked to look at things. When I did it wasn't in any dreamlike state, but perfectly focussed on the object of my interest. I found that the more I stared at something then the meaning of that thing fell away and I would be left with the thing itself and nothing more. It was therefore born afresh in my mind and closer in every way to its place in the world. This *uncovering*, as I called it, had serious consequences for my understanding of ourselves. Unfortunately, there were those out to put the kibosh on my understanding, on my progress to higher things. Constantly staring at people and objects led to mutterings about my mental health. These mutterings were not out of concern. Tittle-tattle and barely disguised snickers in the college club led me to resign my membership of that particular establishment. This was a shame, for I had taken something of a shine to the bar manageress, Maisie Heilbrandt. My reasons for resigning were not, of course, what I had written in my resignation letter. I certainly was not about to write to such an establishment and tell them several members were being absolute cunts and laughing at me. I told them that I had a liver disease brought on by an overindulgence of alcoholic beverages, from which they made their profits. I went further and told them that my liver would protrude through my anus unless sobriety was grasped immediately. Medically, I don't think this is possible. Though, having nailed my alcoholic flag to the mast I had to find a new watering hole. This was sometimes *The Dirty Cactus*, and sometimes *Molly Malone's*. Neither of these places would have seen Clara Pett any day of the week. Which was surprising since Mr Pett had been trapped in a coma for three years. Maybe libido or even companionship would have pushed her to seek comfort elsewhere. Her work seemed to fill these desires. In my wilder thoughts I considered she might have been abusing Mr Pett's vulnerable state. Her refusal to switch off life support was not, I felt, driven by love, but more control. She ran the library as a tight ship.

'Is your husband travelling with you?' this question was asked purely out of spite.

'What? Of course not. Mr Pett can't travel.'

'Oh, I'm terribly sorry. I had forgotten about the accident.'

'There was no accident.'

Indeed, this seemed to be true. The story that went around was that she awoke one morning, and old Pett didn't. What had he dreamed of that was so pleasurable he decided to stay with it?

'Well, I have to be on my way.'

I don't know why I said this, but it might be worth analysing. I was not prepared for meeting anyone that knew me in a foreign country. It was more than disconcerting; it was deeply troubling. This was not because of the task that lay before me, and to be recognised or not was of no significance. The idea of me escaping after the completion of the job was neither here nor there. I really had no interest in the aftermath, or I had never thought it worth considering. Up until now I had always considered that I would die in a hospital bed. I would watch my life end behind a broken camera shutter. The shutter would get stuck halfway closed. The last shard of light would close, and that would be it. The mind would continue for a few moments, and it would consider the life in a flash. What memories would make that final cut? What memories sidelined forever? Until the formulation of my current task that is what I thought. Now? Do with me what they will, I didn't give a tuppenny damn. Most who kill do not consider the escape. So, Clara Pett recognising me was troubling for a different reason. It seemed to me to be too much of a coincidence. All coincidences might be described as "too much", but that seems to be the very nature of coincidence, of course. At some point, though, coincidence must legitimately be called into question. Here was I, many thousands of miles from home, from a small town in a country with many millions of citizens, to a country of many millions, in a city of several million, within an area with a population of round sixty thousand — not counting the tens of thousands of daily tourists — and I ran into a woman who worked in the same building as me? What is "too much"? Chancing upon each other in that particular bookshop at that particular time? Life lived never ceases to amaze.

'Where are you off to?'

I was quite enjoying my consideration of random encounters so her voice came as an intrusion. I have always found it difficult to conceal any annoyance that might trouble me. I am aware, and it has been pointed out, that my lip curls slightly, close to a snarling gesture. To cover this, I raised a hand and pinched the tip of my nose, as though stopping a sneeze or a potential run of the nose, or an itch.

'Oh, I'm just going back to the hotel for a rest.'

'A rest?' She looked at her wristwatch. 'It's still morning.'

'Is it?' This was beginning to sound like an interrogation. Some people are like that. They think that they have a right to keep on pushing. Maybe she saw that, as she offered a way out.

'Look, I've got to meet the rest of the group for lunch, but do you want to hook up for dinner?'

She had barely exchanged a few words with me in four years and now she wanted dinner? Why would anyone think that you travel for hours, get to another country, only to consider dinner with someone you see almost every day at home? Those people that hear a voice from home and zero in on it as though it's a welcome intrusion. Fuck that.

'Dinner? I don't...' I was going to say that I don't eat dinner. There is a truth to that. I don't eat at particular times. This might have extended the conversation while she questioned this habit. She would have thought it odd. She would have said so. She would have made me feel abnormal.

I eat when I'm hungry, and that's getting more infrequent. Before I knew it, she had a piece of paper and pen and was scribbling.

'I'm going to leave my hotel number. You call mind.'

And then she was off. It crossed my thoughts that there were enough bullets to take her down as well.

'Are you going to buy that?' The girl with the Californian accent leaned over the counter indicating the crushed paperback book in my hand. I looked at it. I had no recollection of picking it up. It was a book on Yoga.

'No, I have it.' I lied as I passed it to her and exited the shop.

6

From the moment the shopworker spoke to me I knew she disliked me. Of course, likeability has always been a quality to take with a pinch of salt. To be disliked by some is of no real consequence. I felt that I was usually liked by those that mattered, and since very few mattered that was enough. Beline Doughty, a local *artist*, thought me a bore, as most ill read cretins must have done; likewise, Earl Cobbler, the man who, in his college yearbook, was considered "the boy least likely to". Prescient to say the very least. The last I heard of him he was in police custody for stabbing puppies. There was also Gary Bonnie, a man who could strip an engine but had trouble writing a sentence. Engaging any of these people in conversation about the finer things in life was tossing pearls before those proverbial swine. This was not snobbery; it was a tiresome activity. There were many more people that disliked me, but my memory is poor these days. Or perhaps it cannot rise to the subjects on offer. The sad bars of my memory, playing minor notes with my past.

Outside the shop I walked through the dirty water. It was above my ankles. This was not deliberate. I had forgotten for the moment about the flooding. Mrs Pett had distracted me. The girl from California had distracted me. I had forgotten about the conditions of the streets. Apart from stealing and staring, I have also been forgetting much of late. Well, the last year or so. I had been in the car and trying to manoeuvre a U-turn on a normally busy, though at that moment quiet, road. I had turned approximately 90 degrees in a clockwork direction when another car was upon me. I stalled, and started jamming, pulling and pushing the gearstick wildly, for I had no understanding or recognition of the stick's purpose. Now this, you might think, is close to staring at an object until it loses meaning, but I was engaging in a driving procedure. All of this seems to point towards some malfunction in the right side of my brain. Strangely, it is the side on which I am totally deaf. I do not think the two things are related, but I have not seen a professional to have it checked.

I retraced my steps back to the church in order to set my bearings. To lose one's orientation can lead to panic. Among my other quirks of mind and body I have experienced panic attacks for the slightest of reasons. Queueing in shops, preparing a class, ordering food in a restaurant, lying in bed. I have also had panic attacks in my sleep. The last of these is akin to having an electric shock. I experienced an electric shock once whilst trying to repair a television. I had left it switched on. I know what I speak of.

The small street that housed the bookshop looked like a hundred small streets in the city. It offered no clue to my planned route. I knew, though, where to go in a couple of nights time.

While walking, something struck me about Mrs Pett in Paris that seemed to be different from the Mrs Pett at home. It was not her manner, although that had certainly changed. It was a physical difference. Mrs Pett at home had a small mole on the right side of her jaw. The kind of thing that women in another age called a beauty spot. I did not see that in the bookshop. Could she have had a cosmetic procedure to have the offending black nevus removed? If indeed surgery was involved then she might have wanted to go abroad; less to recuperate, than to allow the healing away from knowing eyes. But surely there would be a fresh scar, and I saw none. If I noticed the lack of a blemish, surely I would have noticed a crater, no matter how small?

Possibly none of this would be suitable dinner conversation, should I have decided to share a table with her, which I hadn't. Indeed, I found the lady a trifle presumptuous to the point of pushy with her invite. It was less of an invite than a demand. It has always irritated me that women find a man alone in need of a companion for dinner, or for life. I decided before I reached the church that I would not be appearing. Cheek of the woman, I muttered aloud. I need no one, nor have I for a long time. Obviously in the throes of childhood to be fed and clothed. We all need this, though not all receive it. The love of a mother; mom; a mama, a maman; ma; momma; mum; mummy. To clothe with love. To protect with love. Aaaaaah, mammy. As for romantic love, I confess that I have become cynical of it; the one that we are told of constantly in books and cinema. Time and experience eventually knock that nonsense on the head. I had met no one yet that I wanted to spend more than a few days with. Apart from Emily. Who I spent an hour with. What would a lifetime have wrought? Contempt? Hatred? Boredom?

As a child my parents called me *Babe*. I can't remember how that started, but I imagine it was from babyhood and no one could be bothered changing it when I grew. My mother was always *Babe* this, and *Babe* that. She told everyone that I would be a great violin player, or piano player, or whatever the hell lessons being tortuously taken at that given moment. I became none of these things, but I did close my bedroom door on the world from a young age. I had few friends, and the ones that I did have left me early on. As a result, I have not only been alone a lot of my life, but if truth be told, lonely. I have learned to live with this loneliness until it became the perfectly natural state of things. So, when a Mrs Pett encroaches on my natural state, it is not appreciated at all. There was a point that I cried from loneliness, because I was taught that to be alone all the time was bad. I didn't want to be bad. I wanted to be good. For others. But the more you're alone, the more you accept that aloneness, the more normal it becomes; the more it sits easily on your mind. My mother often said that real writers enjoy being alone, but not everyone who enjoys being alone is a real writer. It is strange that in literature and in the movies the lone figure is often the hero. He is his own man. He is not part of the common herd. He has his own mind, and for these things he is considered better. He is looked up to. In reality the loner is shunned, mocked, despised, attacked, suspected. So, I am now alone but no longer lonely. I get out and about and I have colleagues. I am often turned to for information on various subjects because of my wide reading. I am part of a community, although if truth be told I care little for any of them. I think I see myself as some kind of bohemian, but truth is that I fell into the rat race at a pretty early age so am just kidding myself. How many lies do we tell ourselves to get through another day? How many thoughts to cover more ground?

Crowds were building outside the church. They had umbrellas and were dressed in rainproof clothing. A good pair of Wellington boots might be an idea what with the rising water levels. I walked through the crowd as though I had a particular goal or destination. I can say that my destination was vague. Of course, I wanted to get to the hotel, shower and shave and change my clothes. I also had a gun there, which even if I was not about to commit an assassination, should not be just lying in a hotel room. Maids come into rooms. And the concierge. He was a surly looking fellow, and finding a gun would open me up to blackmail, or arrest. If anyone looked like a blackmailer, it was him. Should we judge a person's moral standing by their physiognomy, that debunked early 20th century idea? The point is that it would not be safe for me to leave the weapon lying around where any fly by night might come across it. Obviously it was not declared as I came through customs checks. I had broken it apart. Most of it had gone in my hold luggage and the rest in my hand-held bag. It was surprisingly easy to enter a country with a weapon. My original thoughts were to just buy one from a member of the criminal fraternity, of which I imagined there were many. That, though, would bring me into contact with others, something I had no wish to do. Lone gunmen may be considered crazy, but a lot of thought has to go into their task.

As I walked amongst the gathering protesters – for that was indeed what the gathering was – it struck me that to march with them might be my best bet of getting back to the hotel. The demonstration would almost certainly go down the Boulevard that was close to where I wanted to go. The breakdown of any society begins with the individual. In rooms across the world someone is thinking new thoughts, new ways to run the world. The first action, though, is to gather in a group. A lone voice needs its echo system to be heard. It always comes from the young. It is the young who first get ideas of freedom and equality. Those ideas will, of course, be eroded when faced with 2000 years of a structure denying these very things.

When one thinks of a good idea there is a physical excitement that gives you a new energy and focus. Such is how I felt outside the church. A young man gave me a placard with the words *lutte des travailleurs: continue constituez vous en comité de base*. I smiled and accepted it, although it did seem a little wordy for a slogan. I must confess my French didn't stretch to a translation. The flimsy board had been poorly glued onto a short length of wood which, unless I was careful, could have resulted in a sliver of it piercing my skin. To avoid the possibility that someone might try and engage me in conversation I thought I'd best do something. I do think it is the height of bad manners to visit a country and take to the streets protesting about that country's government. But desperate times call for desperate measures as we are oft told.

To make myself appear occupied I busied myself with my clothing. My coat, I buttoned up to my neck, and turned up the collar. My beret, I removed from my head several times, stuck deep in my pocket, fished it out, placed it back on my head, removed it, put it again deep in my coat pocket, fished it out again and set it at a carefully placed jaunty angle. To do this, I stuck the placard tight between my knees to stop it falling on the rain-soaked ground or being blown away in the gathering wind. Outside the square where we stood, several police vans cruised by observing the group.

It was interesting to note the demographic of those around me. There were many young people — teenagers and early twenties — some possibly students, but it is hard to tell in the modern world. In my younger days, students tended to have a uniform of sorts, the college scarf thrown around the neck to show that you were part of that elite. It seems they dress today to hide that, to try and fit in with the general populace. Having said that, certainly all walks of young life were there. There was an older group — perhaps between the ages of thirty and fifty — some of whom held young children, some of whom had a pained expression, as though the wind and rain were a new phenomenon, and one they couldn't cope with. Of this group the older ones looked betrayed, perhaps less by the government and more by life. Those just younger had a look of realisation on their faces. The oldest, certainly over sixty, looked focussed and intent, and their eyes more sparkling than the youth. Was it that ambition had gone? Or perhaps I was reading too much into their faces. Maybe it was the onset of cataracts. Of course, I might have got everything wrong about every one of them. Perhaps all the young were students. Perhaps those between thirty and fifty were lecturers, and the oldest were retired academics. Perhaps there was a scattering of police agitators in the crowd also. Perhaps none were students, or lecturers or retired academics. Perhaps they were all like me, and just wandered into a situation. People were bored with politics. They were bored with the voices. And so they took to the streets. The boredom hadn't quite driven this country to war, but that might have just been a matter of time. I thought of future history books: third world war broke out due to boredom.

That's got to cause a cosmic laugh.

A whistle blew and, as though rehearsed, the crowd organised into a more coherent group. Young people tended to move toward the front, near where the man with the whistle stood. He was shouting something, as though herding cattle, and everyone was following instructions. As for me, I found myself in the centre group, but on the ragged edge of it. I held tight to my sign as we all began to move. I was part of the movement and was momentarily thrilled with being such. The mass movement was a slow affair, no doubt to guarantee that those slow of gait could keep up. I was glad of this as my knee was aching and I had little energy for a quick step. From the front chants began. *Liberté du pouvoir*, they chanted. The chant spread through the marchers and I joined in. Although my French was poor, I understood this to mean *Freedom from power*. Perhaps, like me, they had read books about May, 1968.

Before the bridge, a line of police vans and motorcycle cops sped past us. In a fleeting moment I could see the windscreen of one of the vans. One policeman caught my eye. It was the policeman from the night of my arrival, the one that I had run from after the waitress had been knocked down. And he recognised me. As the van passed, he turned his head to keep me in his sight. I decided that being part of a protest group was not beneficial to me. I handed the placard that I had been holding high to a young woman walking to the inside. I feigned an illness by twisting my face, rubbing my belly, and groaning. If I was going to be arrested, I thought it better to be caught in a more common activity than public protest. A small act of pilfering, perhaps a chocolate bar or some tourist trash.

As much as I could race, I did so towards and over the bridge. Such a simple journey that had somehow been beyond me since I arrived. Once over the bridge, I kept walking down the boulevard and stopped at the first café with outdoor seats.

I placed myself and motioned a waiter from inside. As he was walking towards me I realised that I had chosen the same café and the same seat that I had on my first night. Would he point and cry, *Meurtrier!* To leave now would be suspicious, so I greeted him with the largest smile I could muster. If I had been him, I would have run a mile. He removed an order book from his short jacket and wrote down my order. I was soon left alone, apart from the people at two other tables. One was occupied by three very loud English women, and the other by a young man and woman who were speaking too quietly for me to discern their nationality. The young man's hands were buried tight and deep in the pockets of a long dark coat, and a hat was pulled low over his eyes. The girl wore a wide-brimmed hat and a coat buttoned up to her neck. They looked like they should be part of the march. Perhaps they had been and exited like me. Perhaps they were tourists and joined for a laugh, and then thought better of it. We can create scenarios for any strangers. Often the imaginings could not be further from the truth. Reality often lays flat a soaring imagination.

From over the bridge the throng came. The police that had moved ahead earlier were now organising. A horse brigade of perhaps a dozen fully armed riders spread themselves across the road about a hundred metres away. Batons were swung above their heads in a gesture that was no doubt meant to frighten and disperse as many protesters as possible. This was successful, to a degree, for even at that distance twenty or so protesters broke off and quietly sat around the fountain. The vast majority, though, stood firm with weapons that, as they got closer, I could see were flag poles, wicker chairs and stones. The first move of aggression was from the officers side. Three policemen stepped in front of the horses and fired tear gas into the crowd. This resulted in some panic. A few of the cannisters were picked up and lobbed back along the road. They bounced harmlessly and came to a stop some distance from their intended target. The immediate reaction to the tear gas was a surge of people from the centre outward. The crowd appeared to swell and then shrink. From my safe seat I awaited my black coffee and madeleines. Events seemed to be happening quickly. The news had been rolling on café screens since my arrival. The police started to move forward slowly, clutching shields behind the horse brigade. They were beating the shields with their truncheons, the sound of which thundered along the boulevard. Stones from the protesters started to fly. Through the rain a few reached the police. Some horses were startled and had to be brought into line. My coffee arrived in a small cafetière, with a cup and saucer, and a plate with three madeleines. A bowl of brown sugar lumps was on every table. As I dropped a couple of lumps into my poured coffee, the horses charged. Such was the spectacle that the three English women jumped to their feet and clapped and cheered.

'It's the charge of the Light Brigade,' shouted one.

'I bloody hope not,' cried the second.

'Death or glory!' the third screamed out while punching the air.

All three wore puffed skirts down to their shins. On top they wore white blouses. All that distinguished their dress was the different coloured scarves tied about their necks: one white; one blue; and one red. As the horses galloped, they looked fearsome and magnificent. What wonders they are. The nostrils were flared, and the reins and bits jerked the mouths open. I could see their large teeth, the inside flesh of the gaping mouths, the hot breath steam through the rain. The beautiful smell of coffee reached my nostrils. As I was dipping a madeleine into the liquid a rock was thrown from the crowd of protesters. I shall not describe the madeleines for that has been done to death, but I followed the projectile through the air and watched it connect perfectly with the helmet of one of the riders. Although it easily bounced off there must have been a moments loss of concentration, for the horse turned sharply and ran blindly, pell mell, for the café. The canvas barrier that corralled us off from the street was destroyed as the animal came lumbering and crashing through and into the tables, twisting, and clattering. The rider was thrown out of the saddle (a rather nifty light brown leather affair,) and headed towards my table. I threw myself to the ground, deserting the small sponge soaking up coffee. The helmet strap on the officer broke and the head gear flew off. I was no sooner on the ground than I was lying face to face with an unconscious police cavalry woman. She had blonde hair and a bloody nose. Looking down I saw that her tear gas mask was still clinging to the helmet and noticed that her holster catch was undone. Whether for ease of drawing during the charge, or it was broken in the fall I don't know. I do know what went through my mind and I needed no second chances: I removed the pistol and hid it in my coat. I stood up and looked around. The three women were nowhere to be seen, and the young couple had also disappeared. I left the café quickly for the second time. The moments before were played out in my immediate memory. The horse falling without grace or elegance, crashing through tables, the head twisting and pulling on the rein and bit, upwards, while its unwieldy body collapsed with saddle and rider. I fell to the ground breathing in the animals hot, panic-breath before the policewoman faced me. Moments before were already being constructed differently in my memory.

Once again, I did not pay.

7

The past is indeed prologue. What brings us all to a point? What hands held, words said, tears shed, bring us to where we stand? I walked in the direction the police had come from. I did not look back but heard the cries and screams behind me. Before long the sounds were far in the distance. I had walked much further than I had intended. The intention had been to take the left turning a block up. Instead, before I realised, I had walked at least five blocks along the road. My eyes were irritated from the tear gas, and the stink of it was still with me as I arrived at the boulevards end. The smell reminded me of the strips of fly paper my mother would hang from the window frame above the fruit bowl when I was a child. I stood dead still on the road. There was no one in sight. Through the rain I could see a distant patch of smoke in the skysill and I heard a firecracker sound somewhere behind me. But there was no one. No cars, no bicycles, no people in any direction. Some bin bags had been blown or dragged onto the road. Weeds, I had not previously noticed, appeared at the edges of buildings and between the cracks in the paving. The brown sky was as low as the rooftops. As I watched, a small tree fell over, spilling its branches onto the road. I turned and walked eastward, towards a livelier looking area.

I felt cold as I walked, clutching the newly purloined weapon in my coat pocket. It was very unlike the one that I had smuggled into the country; larger, heavier. A week ago I had never owned a gun, now I had two. I have always been anti guns, but what extremities of the mind push us to the unthinkable; that which could not be contemplated will be embraced. How everything can change.

The lights of a cinema were on and the advertising board of a current Hollywood blockbuster loomed over the street. Or rather the actor loomed, blown up a hundred times his size. This way he could be seen as he is in his mind's eye. He had been in many things since his rise to fame a decade before. His smug, square jawed, lightly tanned and unshaven face was losing some favour with the public. In fact, trips to the cinema to see rich self-satisfied bores was slipping. Questions were starting to be asked from politicians at the behest of their constituents. This was no doubt as a result of some very high-profile killings. At one award ceremony the recipient of Best Actor was shot in the face while thanking his mother and God. He survived, and after much cosmetic surgery returned to the screens with the voice of a stroke victim. It flopped at the box office – one particularly acerbic critic suggesting Robert Charging (the failed assassin) be released for another crack at it. Other stars of the large and small screens were targeted and as a result spent a good proportion of their large earnings on security. It was not just the thespians that were on the kill list; it seemed to be the wealthy in general. Clearly the poor had just about had enough of the rich and the control by an establishment made up of the law, the armed forces, the media, and big money. It was always a precarious balance and guaranteed to tilt the other way eventually. My task had nothing to do with any of this. My target was earning little. I was propelled by much more noble sentiments. My task I would describe as extreme literary critique. I felt that the killing of someone solely because they were wealthy was rather vulgar. It might be understandable to rail against the privileged, but to end their life is rather an inappropriate proposition. Of course, many of the poor are in untenable positions. I have little interest in politics, and less in the rich and powerful.

My thought of entering the cinema to pass some hours were dashed by the fact the venue was obviously closed. The windows were covered with wooden boards and the entrance was shut off by drag railings. It was possible the lights were left on because it was only closed for the duration of the protest march. Like much of the city establishments, sandbags had been placed across the entrance – three high – to protect it from the rising water levels.

A group of about seven or eight children were passing on the other side of the street from the cinema. They watched me for a few moments before throwing missiles in my direction. These were small, though dangerous, stones and bottles. The children did not bend to pick up the ammunition but had arrived fully armed. Perhaps they had seen the street violence earlier and decided to copy it. I ran from them, but not before several stones had landed blows to my shoulders, back, and legs. Perhaps I should not describe my escape as a *run*. It was more of a speedy limp. Had I been several years younger I would not have hesitated on taking on the ragamuffin bastards. My strength, though, was poor, and my mobility severely limited. It crossed my mind that I could have shot them, but I feel retribution should be appropriate to the damage inflicted. They decided not to follow me. I wasn't worthy their time, their energy, their attack. I was there at that given moment and so was partly responsible for the assault upon me. I held no grudges. This is the world that they know, and the only one they have known. The television screens bursting at the seams with images of horror around the globe. The fires and floods, the extremes of weather inflicted on communities woefully unprepared. It was a matter of survival. It was left to the children to tell the adults, to warn the adults. And it was left to the politicians to do what amounted to nothing. And so rains hit suddenly, caused carnage, and then just stopped at the next break. And droughts descended on war zones and the movement of people that pressured other people. And so it was repeated. Circling the drain. If ever there was a desperate age, this was it. Travel bans put in place for short periods of time, the stock market pausing for fifteen minutes in order to contemplate the full horror of a crash. Of course, tourism plummeted. Oh, for the times that I wanted to travel and could travel without restrictions. I jumped at a gap in recent weeks of travel bans, and an unexpected break in my work duties. A voyage called. This is not the absolute truth, other reasons prompted my decision to travel, of course, but this is what circled my mind while making my escape, until my empathy snapped. What had throwing stones at a member of the public to do with climate extremes? I draw a full stop after my defence of the little bastards.

No sooner had I distanced myself from the young rascals than I was gripped by a fear and panic. I was overwhelmed with a feeling that I must return to my hotel room. It was no doubt the urge for protection, and I had made too much of my not being able to go back. The plain fact is that I should not have had to sneak around corners or take longer routes to a destination. I understood that I created my own problems by doing so. Much of our problems are created ourselves. In this I am no different from the common herd: a fool. That the mind could only take a stance when foolish deeds are contemplated: *Take heed, sirrah – the whip!* Alas, no.

I had now walked so far that I was further than ever from the hotel. If I had taken a left after leaving the café I would have been back in my room. Instead, I carried on to the end of the boulevard and then took a right. I would guess that I was just under a mile from my intended destination. If I was Marco Polo I would still be on the Silk Road and *Il Milone* would be mere thoughts on truths and lies.

The metro had been shut since before I arrived. It had been flooded out for a week, but the city's buses seemed to be running some kind of a skeleton service. I stopped at a shelter and took an uncomfortable seat. The timetables at the bus stops were useless and I could only wait and see what turned up. After nearly an hour I realised the service was less frequent even than on a Sunday. I sat in the shelter and took stock of my situation.

To return to my hotel would allow me to have a much-needed wash and change of clothes. When you can smell yourself you know that things have gotten out of hand. I was foul smelling. A stinkpot. (A flashing image of my father lying on a bench press pushing his own weight.) I thought I might have pissed myself but could not recall doing so. Perhaps it was while sleeping on the park bench or in the bin. Thank God that I had not eaten enough to defecate. The body really can be a sewer. Our stink really must call into question a loving god.

My knee hurt badly. It was only now that I was sitting and thinking about it that I felt the pain. I thought I might have cracked my kneecap when I came off the park gate. Normally I would visit a clinic, but I didn't wish to draw attention to myself. What could they do anyway apart from tell me to rest my leg? Something quite impossible for me at that time.

I spend so much time in my thoughts. Not just when alone, but even when in company back home. The truth is that few people interest me enough to give them my full undivided attention. I could be half listening to someone while thinking of something entirely different. Take Bill Petch for instance. While Bill was telling me about his divorce, I was trying to think of suicide statistics. It struck me that they must be much lower than expected. I mean, given that most people's lives are abominable, is it just cowardice that stops a pandemic of suicides? But Bill interrupted my train of thought.

'You're not listening to me.'

'No, I am,' I lied.

'My life is falling apart. What were you thinking about?'

'Suicide.'

'You're not right, you know that? You're not right.'

I thought that if considering one of the most important subjects, one of the few that separates us from animals, is not right, then I was indeed not right. Bill moved soon after to Basel, Switzerland, where a year later he found some minor success with a philosophical work on the work of Jeanne Hersch called *Is Freedom Possible?* I never read it. I was too busy with my own thoughts. I am constantly aware of my small place in the cosmos. I am aware of my irrelevance. Like most people, I regret my life. It is the truth that most push their own situation out of their minds daily. Knowing everyone's inevitable end makes the whole idea of striving for better something of a futile task. Unless it is striving for some kind of temporary comfort. As for the big things in life, like love? Pah! I have long ago left them behind. As did Bill Petch when he fled to Switzerland.

The many padlocks attached to bridges that I passed signified lovers locked in a relationship. How many now wished they were lockpickers? I have never understood an outward and ostentatious sign of a personal relationship. It smacks not only of desperation, but of doubt, and not a little vulgarity. From the Middle Ages until the 1930s, in Eastern Europe, people often padlocked the dead in their coffins, lest they escape and seek retribution, chaos, and blood. Would Bram Stoker have been aware of this?

A drip from the bus shelter roof plopped and plashed on the back of my hand. At some point since I arrived the rain had become more natural and more beautiful. Or was that just what I was thinking at that moment? Before, it seemed to fall on the city like a disease. Everything about it was ugly. But then, even the ugly becomes beautiful with familiarity. The spilling sewers and piled up garbage had become acknowledged as part of the landscape, and not alien to it. Much the same might be said of the distant cries, the occasional whipcrack shots, and angry gatherings of police and protesters. As for the DIY bombs that exploded occasionally, I felt that I could come to terms with it all and rest easy. It really is wonderful how a stranger can quickly become a part of a community: the unusual, or questionable at least, becomes the everyday. I was part of the city tapestry.

I felt it. And in a strange way I also felt that I was being brought in and accepted. Certainly more than those that lived in the outskirts of the city who had been told that unless it was unavoidable, do not travel.

The city fathers, and mothers, had been troubled by the rumour of illness in certain satellite towns in my own country. It seemed to be something that might be contagious, but no one here seemed at all bothered by the dealings of another country. Their hands might it seemed been filled now with some other unrest. Just before I left home, illness was appearing in the local news. People were sick and it seemed to have been spread from domestic pets according to a medical academic on the local television channel. The message seemed to be that if you felt poorly then self-isolate yourself until the symptoms disappeared. What happened though was unexpected. Many people decided to slaughter their pets. They did this with a vigour and energy that put paid to the idea of a nation of animal lovers. The cries, screams, howls, barks, meows, wails, yowls, snivelling, and whimpering pierced many an evening's serenity. The cat and dog homes were blood-running sewers. It seemed the perfect time to leave the country and complete my task. You see? I have an abundance of excuses!

The sky had no clouds; it was a watercolour brown brushstroke across the heavens. The light sapped colour from everything I set my eyes on. The streets had a sepia tint about them, as though photographed perhaps in the late 1800s. But it wasn't just the streets, people also had a lifeless, bloodless quality, a pallor. Of course, the sun hadn't been out for quite a while. Or it had been out but could not penetrate the sky. This was much like home. I'm not sure if this had something to do with me and how I was viewing it. Maybe I was just remembering those days a particular way. Home seemed to have been drained of vibrancy.

Sometimes, when things get bad, and your world appears

to fold in on you; when you can see only darkness, and a breath offers an incomplete satisfaction, the morning sun and air comes and breathes into you that new life. The great fear is that tomorrow will be just like today. On and on. It seemed like the sun had been missing for so long. You would have to record the weather over a whole year to get an accurate picture of course, and who would do that? Well, obviously a meteorologist. Certainly not the general public. We can't remember from one month to the next. Someone will say, *Oh, we had a few good days in March*. And you'll turn to them and say, *Did we?* We know full well we cannot hold onto weather, so we let it go and it becomes lost in our memories. The past. The long summers.

Of course, it's not just with the weather that our recollection are poor. There has been a slow erosion that can be reflected in the drop of book sales and in the structure of books themselves. Putting aside the fact that most novels are detestable. It seems what the public yearn for are books that are short and contain chapters that are no more than four, five, or six pages — don't get me started on the stupidity of chapters. It appears that is as much that our tiny brains can cope with. Six pages tops. We might gather from this that the Victorians had much sharper memories. The big Victorian novels are testament to good memories. I am constantly surprised today that people can even remember how to dress themselves. There are no new ideas, just new ways of talking about old ideas. What is needed are novels without characters. That might get to the nitty gritty. And we all want the nitty gritty. Enough. I will say that I am done with art of any stripe, whether the literary or the visual. Fuck art, I say. All of it. I am done with the lot of them. All of my time needs me and me only.

Outside *Bump's Bookshop* I said as much to Bill Petch before he left. I told him that we seem to have forgotten about ourselves. This was tied into my thoughts of suicide and the human condition. It was just after he had been trying to tell me about his divorce. Approaching him with the full intention of apologising I ended up upsetting him even more. He assumed that I was making excuses for my behaviour and citing the fact he was talking about himself. To be honest, Bill was basically right. I couldn't truly apologise without putting my case in context. And why shouldn't I? The fact was that Bill was something of a liar. I've no doubt this was tied up in divorce accusations. His wife, Dandy or Danni, or Dag, accused him of abusing her verbally and physically over the fifteen years of their marriage. I never picked him up on this and regret that now. There's nothing a liar hates more being lied to. I wish I had lied to him more. He threw such verbal abuse at me I was surprised someone didn't call the police. Merrie Bump tossed a smile our way as she left the shop. For a split-second Bill paused the onslaught and smiled at her (the old dog), before resuming in quick fashion. If a man learns nothing from praise, I have learned much from condemnation. I didn't see Bill again, but heard about him through the usual small-town gossip, in which I have also indulged. I really wanted to talk to him though. I wanted to tell him about me and how I was. But then I would have been accused of doing the very thing he had done: sharing a problem. I was interested in the fact his book was doing well. I would never read it, of course.

The truth is, I'm on the edge. I have been on the edge as far as I can remember. The problem seems to be I don't know exactly what it is I'm on the edge of. Life? Death? Madness? Normality? In this, I feel I am much like my mother. Everything about her was jangled. Although you might think sitting by a window for most of your life is the calmest of behaviours, her thoughts were usually storms. It was reflected in her poetry. Anyone passing might have looked in through the window and thought she was just enjoying the blossom. I knew her mind was usually elsewhere. Calm had no place in her life. She had obviously gone over a precipice a long time ago. As a result, I felt she wanted to destroy everything in her path. Including me. I was just the collateral damage. That does not mean I didn't love her. It is possible to love those who cause you the most damage.

'The town has always been a place of gossip. When people have no real lives and nothing to do, when their souls are empty, their tongues lead. The fish dies by the mouth. My poetry saved me from that small town hell. But, of course, what if sometimes words aren't enough?'

Some believe that you never become a fully responsible adult until your parents die. I think it might be a long time before that. It's when you realise that they are wrong. From that moment your childhood reliance on those figures collapses and you understand that you are alone. I had been fighting my beloved mother since I was twelve years of age and my youthful idealism gave way to disillusionment pretty quickly, then a sense of abject pointlessness. Although I never said so, I think my mother had reached that stage a long time before me. Of course, the realisation that parents are wrong does not wipe out the fact that no one truly recovers from a parent's death. It haunts our minds, a constant memory of our own time ticking away. Yes...

As I sat staring at my feet, I felt that I was no longer real. Was I ever? The cold was always outside me. The rain; the people; the buildings. If everything should have melted before my eyes, I shouldn't be at all surprised. Or care. What is that Shakespeare line? *Melt, thaw, and resolve itself into a dew.*

I closed my eyes and when I opened them the light was dying. Had I missed a bus? I couldn't tell. I was dreaming that I was awake.

There were sounds ebbing softly from my mind on no doubt someone else's distant shore. A murmur of an engine perhaps. The more I think something is possible then it becomes a reality. The cinema back and to my right looked less closed than abandoned. There is a world of difference. The lights around the marquee only gave it a spookier sense of space.

I breathed in hoping for clean, fresh air, but there was the smell of something rotting. Yes, there were the bags of rubbish in the streets that had been torn open by dogs, or rats, or birds, but there was something else. It was the smell of sulphur, and an acrid smell of either bombs or burning rubber. Will a generation tell their grandchildren of the smell of fresh air? How will they describe it?

A bus! It was upon me before I knew it. Thoughts interrupted. Again. Luckily the driver must have seen me. I boarded and realised I had no ticket. I took a five euro note from my pocket and offered it to him. He waved me on without accepting and the bus moved off. There was one other passenger, sitting on one of the only seats that faced each other near the back of the bus. I sat opposite. He was a man of about fifty years old. He was dressed smartly and clutched a briefcase to him as it rested on his lap. I thought that he might be an Algerian, but I have never met an Algerian so could not be sure. When our eyes caught, I smiled and gave a quiet nod. He smiled in return and then looked away. I assumed him to be a businessman of some sort and wondered why he was travelling by bus. He could have driven into the city. But then a car was hardly safe in these times. He opened his briefcase and removed a few A4 sheets held together by a paper clip. One of the pages fell to the floor. As it was nearer my feet I reached down and picked it up. A quick look and I saw the heading *I. U. T* and underneath *Instituts Universitaires de Technologie*. A lecturer no doubt. But all educational institutions were closed by order of the *prefecture* the month before. How did I know this? There had been an Australian man on the plane over that I did not see but heard for much of the journey. He was decrying the strikes and the closures. I couldn't tell if he was a student or lecturer, or indeed any of those, but he was loudly complaining that the colleges were closed, although there was little reason to do this, apparently, as no one was turning up for classes anyway. As for the man sitting opposite me, I thought it curious that he appeared to be coming back from work when the work was closed. He nodded and smiled again as he took the sheet that I offered him. I smiled in return and looked out of the window.

The bus took me along the boulevard that I had walked up earlier in the day. My stop, closest to the hotel, was just past the gardens. As we approached, I pressed the stop button. It rang out, but the vehicle continued at a fair clip.

'Monsieur! Monsieur!' I cried to the driver but was ignored. I was on my feet and at the exit door pressing furiously, to no avail. I turned back to the gentleman in appeal. He smiled and put a finger to his lips in a motion of *hush*. I returned to my seat and watched as we crossed the river. We passed the docked riverboat that I had used on the night of my arrival, and then the bus wound its way up narrow streets. I tried to hold on to my sense of direction but was soon lost. The only positive thought I had was that if I walked downhill I would eventually get to the river. From there I could navigate my way back to familiar surroundings. Still the bus continued its climb. I assumed that once at the top of the hill passengers would be allowed to alight from the bus. I was wrong. The journey continued.

'Bonjour. Parlez-vous anglais?' I had leaned forward in the hope of some friendly communication.

The man pushed his spine into the back of the seat and pulled his briefcase closer to his chest. It seemed a smile was enough communication for the day. Maybe if I had not leaned forward the question might have been less threatening. Nevertheless, he did answer.

'A little. Some.' He smiled.

'Why did the driver not stop?'

'Trop dangereux.'

'Dangerous?'

'Yes. It was too dangerous. That area.'

'But that area is quiet. The shops, the gardens.'

'There was fighting there. An English woman was killed.'

'What English woman?'

'Tourist. English.'

I remembered the three English girls. Could it have been one of them? After I left? Was it another tourist?

'What happened?'

'A…' He thought as though to gather his thoughts in a translation. And then using a free hand he tilted it and twisted his face.

'A horse. A horse fall on her.'

Could the horse that crashed into the tables have fallen on her? Could I have not noticed such a thing? But when I left the women had gone. Would two of them have left their friend under such circumstances? Possibly.

'Oh, that's terrible.' I said, but I couldn't really care less. I was thinking more about myself and my possible connection with two deaths since my arrival. If the gentleman had known, and if the bus would let him, he would no doubt have got off before it crashed.

My words seemed to reassure him that I was not a mugger. His body relaxed and he smiled again. It seemed like an appropriate moment to invite a friendship.

'It's terrible what's happening all over. Are you going to work?' Perhaps this was too forward. He looked at me as though to say *What do you want?*, then relaxed.

'I am going into work to work.'

'I heard that people have to work at home if they can.'

'My home is too troublesome. Too much noise.'

'You have children?'

'Children? Non.' He looked out the window.

'Oh, I thought…' I assumed that the noise he referred to

was perhaps children but for some reason did not want to finish the enquiry. Instead, I told him of myself.

'I am a tourist.

'A tourist? Not a good time for a tourist.'

'No. But some places are still functioning as normal.'

The bus slowed and hissed to a stop and the doors were opened. The man stood up and walked to the exit. He looked back at me.

'You come off.'

'I will. I'm a bit lost.'

As he stepped off the bus I think I heard him say, *No one is lost.*

We stood in the street and watched as the doors closed and the bus left. We were at the top of a hill. It was one of the several the bus had climbed from where I started. I looked around and saw no shops or cafés.

'If you wait an hour on the other side of the street a bus will take you back down to town. Of course you could walk by that time.'

'Your English is very good.'

He laughed loudly.

'My wife is from the United Kingdom. She is from Wales.'

'I've never met anyone from Wales.'

'You still haven't. Why don't you come back with me to our flat? You can chat to my wife.' His English picked up at a clip.

'I wouldn't dream of imposing.'

'A coffee will do you the world of good.'

I couldn't argue with that, so I said:

'I can't argue with that.'

'Good. Come!'

'I thought you were going to work?'

'No. We were sent home to work from there. I have not explained myself well.'

'Not at all,' I lied. 'But coffee would be most kind.'

'Good!' And he was off briskly, with me at his coat tails. As

I followed it struck me that he seemed unconcerned by my dishevelled appearance.

His flat was at the other side of the building we had stopped at. It was part of a complex of perhaps eight blocks. The grass outside had recently been cut and the whole area gave the impression of suburbia. We climbed the stairs to his apartment and entered. There was no one at home, but the place certainly looked as though the woman's touch was responsible for the décor. There were also photos of the gentleman and a dark-haired woman. It seemed to me that they liked the outdoor life: hill climbing, cycling etc. She was an attractive woman, much the same age as the gentleman.

'You will sit down and I'll make the coffee.'

'Thank-you. This is very kind of you.'

He left the room as I sat on the small couch. There were some magazines on the table, but they were all in French. I heard sounds of dishes from the kitchen, and then cupboard doors being opened and closed. He appeared at the door.

'My wife is shopping just now. We have run out of coffee. I won't be a minute. I'll run upstairs and borrow some from Manon.'

I made to stand up.

'Please, don't go to that trouble.'

'It's no trouble. Manon borrows from us all the time.'

And on that he was gone.

I sat on the edge of the couch. It was a strange feeling being in a flat after what had been ages outside. How many people, holidaying alone have felt the same? To be a stranger and walk amongst crowds. Does it give you a sense of power? Or fear? Perhaps those you brush against know you do not belong. I felt that I didn't belong, not just here, but indoors. How quickly the streets can become your natural habitat. Was this a memory, something in the DNA, of the primitive man, the hunter, forever walking, tracking, killing? I stood up and crossed the room to the pictures on the wall and put my face up close. The rush to get back to the wide-open spaces, the hills and mountains, the rough tracks, the wild forests, the winding rivers. And then to capture the image and stick it on the walls of your cosy home to remember where you've come from. My father was very much like that. He was an outdoor man trapped indoors for most of his life. Once a year he would go canoeing in some river or other. And he would return two weeks later, red faced and smelling of the wild. He would go with a friend called Michael Norr. For a long time I only ever saw Michael Norr as he dropped my father off after the break. He wouldn't get out of the car and I rarely approached it. I can't remember my mother greeting them either as they arrived. She didn't go out much. She maybe would go to the shops in town only occasionally and seemed to have no friends or enemies. If she wasn't doing household chores, she would be reading or writing poetry. She had a pamphlet of her poems published by a small publishing office in the big city. It was called *Root and Branch*. One I remember from memory. It was called *Lover*:

Is your lover called Doreen?
Is your lover called Marie?
Is your lover sailing the seven seas
Longing to be free?

Is your lover a clever lady?
Is she dumb as a farmer's ox?
Is she holding on to a lover's flame,
Or locked it in a box?

Is your lover a sweet memory?
Is she poison on your tongue?
Is your lover your reason for living,
Or a sweet song badly sung?

I was young when I first read that poem and didn't question that the lover was female. But that was written before she married. Marriage didn't stop her though. She wrote for many years. All of her life. As far as I'm aware she didn't send her work to magazines or publishers. I asked her about it once. I was deeply embedded in college student life at the time and thought the world should hear my thoughts, so why not hers?. Her reply I accepted and never asked her again.

'There is a greed, a vulgarity, and a lack of intellectual critique today. I wouldn't soil my poetry by sending to these upstarts. Writing is enough for me.'

When she died, I went through her many notebooks and was shocked. They were beautiful. There was anger and frustration in her lines certainly, but there was a clear beauty. Titles alone reflected a questioning of where we are: *Where Does The Happiness Go? 'Twas Last Night, Alone, My Summer Ends, Night Blossom Turns My Mind.* Recently I decided to sift through and organise her writing. I am still in the process. She might be discovered yet. Too late for her, but not for the world.

My father had no apparent creative outlet. Maybe he saw the yearly fishing trips as art? He would work out with weights throughout his life and watch sports. It seemed enough for him. So, I got my love of the arts through mother, and in my mid-thirties finally wrote a novel. Well, I started in my late thirties, and finished in my early forties. I considered calling it *Mea Culpa.* It was actually my second attempt. Like mother, I did not send to publishers. It was not that I was afraid of rejection: I found something distasteful about being judged by someone in all likelihood was unfit to lick my now established academic and critical boots. I have been accused in the past of a literary snobbery. By whom? Ha!

With a smile to my lips, I moved closer to one of the photographs. It caught my eye, for it seemed different, and it was. Certainly it was the gentleman's wife, but this time she was posing with a different man. This man had long hair tied back. He wore a colourful woollen hat, had a few days growth of beard, and was a most handsome smiling chap. She looked happier with him than she did in the pictures with her husband. She also looked younger. Perhaps it was an old beau. There is nothing to say that a woman cannot have a series of beaux before settling down. Perhaps the picture was taken in her wild days back in Wales. There were mountains in the background, perhaps her homeland, but it could have been many other places. I lifted it from the wall and turned it over. A sliver of typewritten paper was stuck to the back. It said *Crannie and Tom*. I have never seen a person so happy. The words *Where does the happiness go* drifted across my mind. I replaced the photo and crossed to the window.

Below, a few people crossed the courtyard. I watched each, until they disappeared around a corner, or through a door. Skinny trees blew in a gentle wind. Fragments of my life scattered through my mind with them in those same moments, the thoughts of so many years compressed, fleeting, refusing to be pinned to the wall. Our greatest fear appears to be ourselves. I am alone. I know that. I feel that. I have always been alone. I have thought about my situation many times and many times it has sat heavily on my chest and in my throat. This *aloneness* is not something that just happened, it didn't just arrive at my doorstep. I could live with it because I have always lived with it. But it no longer made sense to me. Maybe the question I should be asking is, did I want to be alone? And that was one too difficult to contemplate. When it arrives I push it away and hastily drag in another question I find difficult answering: did I cultivate this aloneness? It is another question to be pushed away. Our greatest fear is ourselves. Like contemplating death, but strangely worse. Mother made death quite the thing.

'It's just like a window closing,' she would say. 'You can

return and look through at me any time you want. In that way memory always makes me available to you. Always.'

Always. In that you were right, ma. I just go over to that window and there you are. But I never really got to know you. Your poetry showed me that. There was so much more to you than a mother. A son couldn't see that. A son wasn't allowed in. Did you have a hand in my sense of being alone? Who knows anyone? And memory? As I remember it, so it is. I'm going to get that put on my gravestone. Or not.

A bang on a door somewhere close by pulled me from these thoughts. I felt tired. Thoughts can weary you. I thought of myself lying down; of a weight on me, pressing. I needed to lie down. Where was the gentleman and the coffee? The borrowed coffee from Manon? I was so tired. If I lay down surely he wouldn't be annoyed. He'd invited a stranger to his flat for coffee then disappeared. Look, I can take manners or leave 'em, but that behaviour is lacking the very basics of decent behaviour. I had to gather myself. Surely he wouldn't object? The couch wasn't big enough to stretch out on, so I found the bedroom and lay down on the bed. I had forgotten the pleasure that simple things can give one. Perhaps the last hours of sleeping rough and roughly had prepared me to be more appreciative of a good mattress. All creatures love their comfort; I was no different. My eyes closed. My bones were aching. I slipped my shoes off. I couldn't have lain there for more than a few moments when a woman's voice shattered the peace.

'You must leave.'

I sat up and swung my legs around to put on my shoes.

'I'm terribly sorry. I was invited. I met him on a bus.'

'You were invited into my bed?'

'He went to get coffee.'

'Of course he didn't.'

'No, he did. I met him on a bus. He went upstairs to borrow coffee from Manon.'

'No, he didn't. He told you that, but that's not what he did. He is sick in the head. He is a lunatic. He's my soon to be ex-husband. He can't cope with the fact that I no longer want to be with him. For some reason he thinks it's funny inviting strangers back to my flat. You're the third this week. I don't usually find them in my bed. I think he's having a breakdown. This is no bad thing. Maybe he will be reconstructed when he's put back together.'

I stood up to find she was a taller woman than I expected. Across the room, with the bed between us, she looked down at me.

'Couldn't you change your locks?'

'I've been trying to find the time. I'm a nurse. As you can imagine, I've been kept pretty busy. What happened to you? You look a mess.'

'I'm a tourist.' This answer struck me as ludicrous the moment I offered it.

'You look like a tramp. Would you like a shower?'

'I think under the circumstances that would be rather bold.'

'It's a matter of stench. Are you suggesting anything other?'

'Intimate gestures usually come from friends or colleagues.'

'You think a shower is intimate?'

'Getting naked in a stranger's flat I would consider intimate.'

'In a locked bathroom?'

'In a locked anything. Kitchen, bedroom, living room, bathroom.'

'I would hardly ask you to strip off in the kitchen. There is such a thing as social etiquette.'

'I feel this conversation is pushing those rules to the limit.'

'Are we adults?'

'We are strangers with a bed between us.'

'Much as I was with my husband. I thought you came here for coffee.'

'I did indeed. There was none. I was sleepy. I feel as though

I have been misinformed and somewhat played in the intimate games of a marriage breakup.'

'You should not have been used to get back at me. Are you married?'

'No.' Of course I would have been a rotten husband. My wife each night would have lain in my faithless arms and dreamt of romance and lovers.

'A coffee then you can be on your way.'

'Pardon me, but the lack of coffee seems to have put the kibosh on that.'

From her bag she pulled out a jar.

'Only instant.'

'I'm not fussed.'

'I can see that. I'll put on the kettle,' she said as she left me alone in the room. I followed her as far as the living room and let her continue to the kitchen. Once again, I gravitated to the pictures on the wall.

'You like climbing,' I shouted.

She arrived at the kitchen door.

'I like walking. I like the outdoors.'

'I see that one of the pictures is not your husband.'

'That one,' she said coming up behind me. 'That's a friend's brother. He died. Do you know what that mountain is in the background?'

I shook my head.

'That's Ben Nevis. In Scotland. What do you take in your coffee?'

My attention was on the picture of the smiling young man. Sometimes you can look at someone and feel that you know them though you have never met. A memory of something that never happened. A twinge of someone who never existed in your world. When I was feeling outside myself it was much like that. The world and reality was viewed as something distant, vague, translucent. The transmission of past light of memory to the present. It arrived indistinct, shimmering.

'Coffee.'

And the present arrived with a tinkle.

'Just one sugar, please.'

Her voice told me that she had moved back to the kitchen.

'I have sweeteners.'

'That's fine.'

'Why did you come here when the city is in such turmoil?' She asked from the doorframe.

I shrugged, 'The world seems to be in turmoil. What about you?'

'I've been here five years. It suits me well enough. You have to live somewhere.'

'You met your husband here?'

'I was on holiday. Like you. I met him on a bus. Like you. Where were you going on a bus? This isn't a tourist area.'

'The driver didn't stop beside the gardens on the boulevard. I had to just wait.'

'There was trouble there today. That's probably why he didn't stop.'

'I was there when it kicked off.'

'Are you an agitator?'

'I was sitting at a café.'

'Too many people want to get involved. I don't know where it will end. Where are you staying?'

'Near the gardens.'

'Near the gardens, is it? Look, I'm not going to visit you.'

She waited a moment expecting me to reveal my hotel. I felt the less people knew about my stay the better. I would like to think there were noble reasons behind this stance, that I was protecting her from a grilling from police investigating the assassination of an author. But that would not be the case. It would never be the case. I have never gone in for gestures of nobility.

Some minutes later we were sharing the couch while sipping the hot coffee. I confess that I felt slightly troubled by the seating arrangements. It is true that I had chosen to sit on the couch, and I could have opted for the easy chair opposite it. I had no reason for doing so except the fact that I must have found it to look more comfortable in its roominess. I expected her to come through with the cups and plant herself in the chair. Instead, she said *shift* and forced me to move up to the edge. I said nothing, but I believe my face displayed something of my annoyance. I have never been comfortable with the close proximity of strangers, or friends.

'We were married a few years, but the good times just seemed to grow further apart. We had parted before all of these troubles. But this seems to have exacerbated his mental problems. He phones me and is silent on the phone. I know it's him. Who else would it be? What is it with men and their treatment of women? What is it all about? Is it a brain malfunction? Is it an illness? Are they born with these problems with half of the human race? Or do they learn it?'

'Papers fell out of his bag. On the bus floor. I picked them up. I couldn't help but glance at them. He's a lecturer?'

'No, he's a bus driver.'

'But the papers in his bag.'

'It's his way in. It's an introduction into your life. He could have dropped bus schedules, but you would have been less trusting of him, That's true, isn't it? You thought, here was a professional, I can trust this man. But a bus driver you think to be less morally capable. You wouldn't have followed him to this flat if he had been a bus driver. You felt safe; less threatened because you thought this. Do you believe professional men commit less crimes?'

'Perhaps different kinds of crimes.'

'Where I grew up the poorer you were the more suspicion you drew. Do you think that people dying on the street is a crime?'

'Those without a home or shelter? Yes.'

I thought of Sam Blue our resident homeless person. Some

people found him a roof, but he didn't take to it. He always went back to pushing his trolley and asking for spare change. I didn't say this out loud to her. Sometimes we hold information back. Sometimes we don't say things that flit through our minds. If we said everything then conversations would be interminable. A few sentences of chat throw up many memories. To relate one is to throw up many more. It is never ending. I could have related my tale of Sam Blue, but then she would no doubt have asked me more about him and the conversation would then have taken a turn towards my childhood. Something I really couldn't be bothered relating to a stranger. I decided on a change of tack. I decided on a general conversation about what was happening in the city.

'When will this rain stop?'

There was a moment of surprise in this shift. It is often the case. There is a recognition that the person you are conversing with is bored or uncomfortable and throws into the mix a non sequitur. These are the rules of conversation. We either acquiesce or stop the shift dead in its tracks. To do this, though, is to strip away all pretence. It is to recognise the combative nature of dialogue. After that the gloves are off.

'Who knows? We're all drowning in our own little way. Why did you come here?'

'I told you. Your husband...'

'No. Here. To this city. Why here and not London, or New York, or Berlin?'

'Well...' I tried to smile and find some normality to what I was about to relate but my face seemed to have forgotten the correct procedure for a smile. Part of the problem was that I was only using the lips and they appeared to be learning a new skill.

'...It's quite a funny story, I suppose. I read a book.'

'A funny book?'

'I didn't find it so.'

'Was it set here?'

'No, it was set in Glasgow, in Scotland.'

'That's where my friend and her brother were from.'

'I didn't like the book.'

'What has it to do with this city?'

'The writer is giving a talk here. I wanted to see him.'

'To tell him you didn't like his book?'

'To…? In a manner of speaking.'

Again, a conversation went through my mind. The conversation involved assassination. This was something most certainly not to speak out loud.

'What was wrong with the book?'

'It was badly written. I felt insulted.'

'It seems like a helluva way to travel in order to offer a critique.'

'I love the city. I don't come from a great city. I come from a small town. That very fact shapes one's outlook, don't you think?'

'I come from a place called Mumbles. It's not a big place. But it is beautiful, in its way. It overlooks a bay. It might have got its name from the French, *les mamelles*.' She touched a locket that hung around her neck and rested on her chest.

'Where you come from shapes how you see the world for ever. Not that we all don't see things through a vision of our collected experiences. If you grow up in a jungle seeing a city for the first time must fill you with awe and fear. Much the same as we would be seeing a jungle for the first time.'

'How is your coffee?'

It was her turn to shift the conversation. I could have talked on about how we see the world, but her eyes would have glazed over and she would have found shelter in her own thoughts. The coffee was cheap and bitter.

'It's fine.' The small lies. Again.

'I might have to throw you out.'

'I'm a guest. You can ask me to leave at any time.'

'One man he recently invited back was violent. He was a

miner down from the Saar-Warndt coal mining basin. He arrived in the city to protest the government treatment of the coal mining districts. Some towns have been devastated by floods. There seems to have been no government action. When he arrived he was staying in the 18th arrondissement. With many others. They were about to march on the Minister of Interior when the Minister of the Interior committed suicide. Ironically, given the weather, he drowned himself. He took a header into the river. Well, I say drowned. It might be that the body colliding with a bâteau-mouche did for him. On the bus back to his hostel – the miner, not the Minister of the Interior – bumped into my husband, who took him back here. He must have told the man that I was some kind of prostitute for he kept trying to negotiate a price. I told him to return his change to his pocket and fuck off. His English was enough to read the situation and so he beat me with my husband's slipper.'

'That is shocking. Did you inform the police?'

'A couple of nights later I considered it, but I've been too busy. The hospital is fit to bursting what with the illness and the street violence.'

It occurred to me that nothing was normal. Not the streets, not the weather, not the people. It is as though the world has been turned upside down and emptied out of the many familiar rules that already seemed askew to me. I found it difficult getting my bearings and as a result had lost something of my confidence. I placed my empty coffee cup on the table and made to stand, but a rush of light headedness pushed me back on my seat. I must have appeared ill to the woman for she asked if I was unwell.

'The colour has drained from your face. Are you alright?'

I thought that much would have been obvious.

I felt for a moment like vomiting but managed to push it down. Her voice sounded distant as though she were talking to me through a dream,

'Are you alright?' she repeated and placed her hand on my forehead. 'You're sweating. Aren't you the boy?'

What sort of thing was that to say when in front of a man in my condition? Maybe she had not said that. I was often mishearing things people said, a result of my poor hearing in one ear. *Aren't you the boy?* But what could sound like that?

'I must go. Thank you for the coffee.' I managed to stand, if a little unsteadily.

'Look, I'm a nurse, and you don't look so great.'

'I have things to do. I must go.'

And so I left her and the flat. A gentle breeze on the balcony revived me somewhat, but I wished I had asked for a glass of water. From the balcony I looked down on a quadrant with a drinking fountain at its centre. Beside the fountain stood a tall young man wearing a tailcoat and breeches. The breeches were high-waisted, and the coat had long and tight sleeves, a wide collar, and the front flipped open showing a golden waistcoat. He had on a black silk top hat which he removed with a flourish and looked up. He flicked his dark curls from his forehead and smiled (at me?). With his hat in hand, he pulled the tail of the coat back and stuck out his backside in the most grotesque, exaggerated pose. I was stung with the embarrassment of having been caught looking down at him. Holding back the coat tail with one hand he brought his other hand to his face and smoothed his thin moustache. I carried on my descent. On the landing below a frail, elderly lady, leaned on the railings. She was breathing heavily with a mucus wheeze. She had a sheen of sweat on her brown face and it glistened in the wrinkles. I pushed her slightly on the narrow staircase.

'…Non…ça sent…le sapin…'

'Désolé,' I said, and rushed past her and down the stairs. The French came without a thought.

The quadrangle was empty. The gentleman in the strange attire was gone. For that I was grateful. Another vision, the residue of others' lives. There was no other sign of life either. An area empty of people in the heart of a city brings with it a sense of your own existence. There is a personal aspect to the emptiness. It is as though you have been deserted by those that have been close. The idea that those who normally inhabit this space have vacated it solely for your presence is, quite obviously, a nonsense. I felt a similar hollow some years ago when I was invited to the wedding of Jonas Mark and Jennifer Johns, of the science department and senior management, respectively. Most of the people I worked with suffered from the Dunning-Kruger Effect. Jonas Mark was in a class of his own in this respect. He once said to me *Jesus once said— and I can't disagree* ... How Mark managed to conduct an eight-month affair with a woman with a toe in the water of wealth and a future mayorship is a matter for others. How he managed to dodge at every turn new policy workload was a matter of speculation amongst the staff, until the wedding announcement. It was clear to me that the only reason I received an invite was because I was a member of the faculty. Nothing else. I held no illusions as to my collegial status with either of them. When Johns spoke to me it was always about curriculum matters framed around a barely disguised reprimand. I felt our relationship was more stony than thorny. There is an intimacy implied by *a thorny relationship* that was absent in our interactions. I accept now that perhaps that was partly my fault. I developed at a young age the ability to see people as they were and not always as they wanted to be seen. Maybe it was their tone, the subjects of conversations, or maybe how they looked at you, the eyes darting to the side, down, anywhere but into your eyes. That takes a certain strength of character, I know. There's an element of *Look at me, I'm in control of my life. I can look you in the eye and feign interest.* But hardly anyone had that as far as I could see, so I'd tell them. I'd say, *You're full of shit.* Or go Holden Caulfield on them and tell them they were *phonies*. I don't blame anyone now for all that hate towards me. I threw the truth of their lives at them. Like spitting in their faces. It just isn't done.

As for Mark, he was his own man. At all costs he was his own man, to the detriment of others. He was one of those people you tired of easily. The bullshit brigade. I just stopped listening to anyone who claimed to have all the answers. Most of the time they're just running their mouth off to construct a perception of power. Mark was like that. The work he managed to avoid was inevitably shared out amongst his departmental colleagues. If this bothered him it certainly never showed and the prat had little regard for what his colleagues thought of him. Johns and Mark had clandestine meetings in her office, the notorious *Room 876*. She had demanded the room was furnished with heavy blackout curtains to preserve their intimate tête-à-tête. It was not unusual to hear cries of passion when passing. Students giggled while staff members coughed loudly. Occasionally I would tap softly on the door and walk on.

It should be understood in a town as small as ours — although larger than the one I grew up in — a large wedding dictated that work associates were invited solely for numbers. The numbers, I assume, were meant to reflect popularity of the couple. No doubt she felt this would help her mayoral ambitions. As for Mark, his future bride was a steppingstone to greater things, and a softer bed, as his strategy paid off. Jennifer Johns is now the town mayoress and has fought off opponents for nigh on ten years. Jonas Mark is occasionally seen at his wife's side. His work, or his lack of it, was completely abandoned immediately after her first win. These days he is in the city a lot, making land deals and money.

As for the actual wedding reception, I was placed at the back of the hall with Clara Pett and some others of the non-teaching staff. When I arrived, they were obviously talking behind my back. After a silence Clara laughed and told the group that she once had a 'sparky youthful face', which I

116

couldn't picture as it had clearly given way to a pinched, middle-aged manner that exuded superiority and judgement. Later, everything changed. There was less banter. They were obviously talking behind my back. The funny thing was that they truly thought that I was unaware of the silence when I returned from the toilet, or the ripple of uncomfortableness around the table when I sat down. After a while I began to enjoy their uneasiness, settled into their guilt. I spoke to Clara for a long time about her husband's fingers and how they would tighten now and again as though he was receiving an electric shock, as if I genuinely cared. When there was a call to guests to move to the large hall for the dancing, I did not follow the crowd, as I have always found dancing to be something of a pointless exhibition. So, I was left alone at the table and indeed the buffet room. To be alone after so much chatter of tongues and clatter of cutlery exaggerated both silence and isolation. No one asked me to join them, not even Clara Pett. It was perhaps this fact that left me feeling quite sick and dare I say insulted? Something akin to a social betrayal. Perhaps it was all of this that caused me to drink more and more quickly and leave without saying goodbye.

All great men have light in their eyes and fire in their actions. My eyes at the best of times are dead things, and any spark was extinguished by decades of dealing with the ordinary. Not everyone has the potential for greatness, but I always thought I had it and lost it. It is this profound sense of loss that haunted me and often drove me to *Molly Malone's* or *The Dirty Cactus*. (It was not unusual to witness me slamming a bottle down on a table in one of these establishments and shout *To hell with everything!*) And the loneliness. Another social faux pas I was to learn that Monday at work when I was asked what had happened to me that night. *Well, I was fucking left alone*, as if it was their fault.

I have recently begun again to question this reaction. Was it indeed a choice that I made or was it thrust upon me by people walking away? Some years ago I could have answered confidently that I chose social isolation, but more recently I have felt that perhaps that it was a defence mechanism and that in all truthfulness I was a social outcast. Once these thoughts creep into your head they are difficult to release. Why had I been cast out of our small-town society? My lack of dancing skills were not reason enough to be shunned, so I looked at my personal habits more forensically. I liked reading, which is certainly a solitary activity. I also liked to listen to classical music, again a solitary activity, but in academia these are considered life skills. I understand that concert going is a social activity, but the only concerts in the town were by local performers. These were invariably excruciating. One girl who had 'excelled' at violin and gone to the city to join a large orchestra returned to put on a show. It was murder. Although heaped with praise from our lovely mayoress, the performance was little more than a fiddle scraping out Bach's *Partita No.2, Chaconne*. At one point I laughed, thinking the child had gone to the city to be first banana in a comedy show. The resolution in the piece had all the art and craft of a pugilist attempting the delicate construction of an origami swan. I vowed *never again*. And so most social events were, and still are, closed to me. But I really don't think one gets used to it. Of course, being an enthusiastic imbiber there is also the matter that drunks are invariably boors. Maybe I left the wedding because I recognised the fact I was boring them, but laid the blame on them. Another common practice with the drunk. I momentarily thought of our college geologist and part time volcanologist, Paul, who died as a result of a pyroclastic flow in India. Paul was a drunk who shouted at staff and students daily. He was on a short sabbatical when the tragedy struck. I remember thinking that I hoped he was drunk. To be sober and experience such a disaster would be the real tragedy.

My head dipped at the quadrangle well and I drank. I

immediately felt better. Straightening, I looked up at the balconies. From their railings hung plants weighted down with the constant rain. My first thought was that they were quite a pretty green, but I quickly realised they were in an awful state of neglect. Some hung like seaweed down to the balcony below. The effect was one of decay. Of course, no one could be expected to care for plants in such a climate. Nothing could be expected in such a climate. A glance at the windows of the flats showed that people seemed to have given up on cleaning them as well. There was a sheen of greenish-brown mould across much of the glass. The rain seemed to have seeped into the very structure of the building. Damp patches marked the concrete outer facing walls. God knows how much water had collected on the flat roofs. A rushing sound from the fountain brought my attention back to where I stood. My hand was still leaning down on the ornate cast iron handle. The water now coming out was brown and there was a powerful smell of rust. The odour was quite sickening. I let go of the handle but the water continued to gush forth. The heavy bowl was overflowing, cascading onto the water below, which had risen above my ankles. I fell. I should probably say *dropped*, as my legs gave way below me. My body splashed to the ground, and it was all I could do to keep my head above the water level. I spoke aloud *Where am I?* but there was no comforting answer. If the young woman from the flat had looked out of her kitchen window, she might perhaps have seen me. What was her name? She had not introduced herself, but I had seen the name on the back of the picture. It was Tom and…What was her name? Did that matter? Was that actually her name on the back of the picture? None of it mattered. If she had looked and seen me she could have come down and helped me to my feet. And what of others? There were dozens of windows overlooking this spot. Pressure exploded the whole fountain structure from the ground and the main pipe was forcing forth a water

119

canon of filth. Surely someone heard a sound and would be curious enough to pull back their curtains and satisfy that curiosity? In a panic I called out. I did not call out the usual exclamation of *help* or *m'aider*, but more a sound *Aaaaeeergh! Aaaaeeergh!* It was an animal cry, and with it came a break in the voice as though I was weeping. I have little doubt that someone must have heard such a noise, but no figure appeared at any window as far as I could see. How distanced the human race felt to me at that moment. I once again thought of the wedding reception of Jonas Mark and Jennifer Johns. Jean de la Bruyère spoke of *This great misfortune of not being able to be alone*. I felt alone now but didn't feel fortunate. Lapping water filled my mouth and nose and I spluttered another sound as a sour metallic taste of body odour touched my tongue. My eyes stung with the filth. Through my blurred vision I saw figures in the distance, then perhaps ten shadowed images rushing through the flood, which seemed to come up to their knees. They shimmered in my eyes until they were upon me and I saw that they were the children from earlier. *Help me*, I croaked, but they had not arrived to offer assistance. I felt small hands burrow into my clothes, my pockets. As some rifled my meagre change and few notes another small bony and cold hand picked at my watch strap. I protested, helpless and exhausted, but to no avail. The little bastards could have it all. The little bastards had it all. And they were gone.

And the gun in my pocket? It had been tucked handily under my left buttock, a chance fall and they had missed it. Such luck.

The water had now risen so high that my head floated on its surface. And still it poured out. Still it rose. And still not a curtain twitched. My mind fell and I was overcome with a sleepiness that I did not want to fight. I closed my eyes and my ears filled with sound. An engine of sorts and a sharp, regular, clanking noise. It receded as I drifted into blackness.

The Flaneur

When you are not working you have time to think. You have time to consider what has passed. You have time to take stock on how you have arrived at the point that you are at. I had been doing that a lot recently. This is not a fruitless exercise, although it can be a painful one, and a wake-up call. I understood my social standing in the town. It wasn't until I hit my teens that I realised my parents were looked upon as something of an oddball pair. The fact that they rarely socialised meant they rarely heard about events in the town. I might add that this was very much of their choosing. When my father did go out it was usually fishing or hunting and, apart canoeing once a year with Michael Norr, those were solitary pursuits. But even the hunting and fishing became rarer and it seemed he was always home lifting weights or punching a bag. He would work up some sweat doing these things.

'Work out hard and then shower. Don't ever be a stinkpot.' That's an image I have of my father, working out and then disappearing into the shower for a long time. Whenever I use the word *stinkpot,* I think of him. Words have connections.

Mother was always there too. She would sit by the window in her favourite chair. She would have a notebook and pen in her hand and woe betide me if I interrupted her. Maybe that's why none of my classmates ever knocked on my door to ask me out for adventures. I would sometimes wander down to the river and have a swim on a warm day. (Sometimes alkies would go down and swim in the ferruginous water as they believed it was a cure for alcoholism.) Mostly, though, I'd stay about the house too, reading, and it nurtured in me a fondness for being on my own. I think it was in my early teens I started being considered as slightly odd, as well as my family. Not that people said so directly, but they would give me a wide berth in social circles. Now and again someone would spit my name at me, as though it was poison on their tongue. It seemed the name itself was the greatest of insults. I just ignored them. I finished school with the best grades in the area and was easily accepted for university at the ripe old age of seventeen.

I remember well as I set off. My parents came down to the bus station with me. My bags were in the back seat of the car beside my mother; I rode in front with father. We spoke little. I always wanted to know what they were thinking during that drive. It's too late to ask them now, of course. No doubt if they were still here I still wouldn't ask. My father had what I can only describe as a stoic look on his face as he watched the road ahead. Of course, maybe that's all wrong and he was just thinking about his barbels or punch bag. Who knows what people are really thinking if they don't tell you? He told me nothing really. It was mother who taught me to tell the time and tie my shoelaces; it was Mrs Jackson next door who taught me how to ride a bike; it was Mr Buchanan in sports that taught me how to swim. I never knew what was in my father's head at any time. And so he drove me to the bus station in silence. One thing I do remember about that short journey is that my mother leaned forward and put a hand on my shoulder. It was just for a moment, but that gesture has stayed with me a lot of years.

There was an awkwardness at the bus station. We stood beside the bus, me with two bags at my feet. Mother ran through her mental list of things that should be in my bags and then another of things I had to do when I arrived at the university halls of residence. I knew it all. Hadn't I been up all night excited at the thought of leaving home, becoming another person, about being a person with many friends? The waiting was interminable and I said *I'll just…* and motioned towards the bags and the bus. My father made no move to help me carry the bags. I got them onboard and settled into my seat, which by chance was by the window exactly where they were standing. If there was an awkwardness moments before, nothing compared to this. I was embarrassed to look at them and laughed and shrugged my shoulders. And then the bus doors closed, and the engine started up.

It was at this point something happened that I could not have imagined. My mother's eyes opened wide in what I can only describe as a distraught look. She was wearing a blue headscarf and it caught in the wind. It was coming undone under her chin. She pulled it off letting her red hair fall down. A breeze was blowing her hair. She swept it from her face with both hands and took rapid steps forward as the bus moved off. Did she mouth the name *Babe*? I saw my father's hand grip her wrist. She raised her other hand and threw a goodbye kiss as she always did. She was running her fingers slowly through the air as though she were typing out a message. It was almost a gesture of surrender, of defeat. I softened and waved back. Nothing would ever be the same again. It crossed my mind that maybe I should have asked them how I should behave. Maybe how I should live, because I honestly think I don't know the whys and wherefores of the world. Truth is, I don't think they prepared me for life. They just sort of let me be, which is probably worse than a beating, if you think about it.

Yes, to have time to think and learn. Or not.

My eyelids lifted slowly to view the sky. The quadrangle. The fountain. The windows of flats all around. I knew where I was and made to get myself to my feet. It took some moments before this was accomplished. I needed to get out of this complex. The water had stopped gushing but had levelled in the quadrangle and was at shin height. I waded towards the exit. Within two minutes I was at the bus stop where I had alighted from the bus.

I started to follow the bus stops back to the city centre. My shoes and clothes were soaking. There was no way of drying them, and so I decided to buy a whole new outfit. I would go to the first clothes store I came across on my way back. No sooner had these thoughts gone through my mind when I chanced upon a small shop that served that very purpose. I pulled open the heavy glass door and made to step inside when I was set upon by a young girl with a floor brush.

'Sortez! Sortez!'

She swept me from the premises and back onto the street. I can only assume my appearance frightened her. I confess a quick look at my reflection confirmed her opinion. I was as much like a hobo as any writer's description of a hobo. This thought, rather than disgusting me, made me feel a certain pride. A gentleman of the street. A tramp. I had inadvertently recreated myself, much as I had tried to do when I left home for university as a young man. I took a particular pleasure knowing that my appearance was of the ragged edge of society. This was a man who would never be invited to any social gatherings, an outsider, as I had always been, without cause. Now at least there was a reason for my rejection. I was in control of my destiny. As I walked off the young girl was noisily locking the shop door. I smiled. What power in rejection! To be ejected from a shop in this age is a sign of empowerment. I thoroughly recommend it.

I looked down the street and saw in the distance the river. This was my destination. The city centre had an abundance of clothes chain stores. You could walk in and not be accosted every moment with the words, *Can I help you?* I would walk in, go to the *Gents* section, choose the correct size of clothing, go into the changing area, and dump my torn, muddied and soaking attire. The labels could be removed and brought to the till for scanning and payment. This was my plan, and it filled me with a new vigour.

The rain had come on heavier since I had left the apartment complex. It was now lashing and blowing against me as I travelled downhill. The novel that had brought me on my journey did not, as far as I could remember, mention rain. This thought troubled me. Not that there might be no mention of rain, but that I had forgotten. I reached in my coat pocket and stood dead still. The copy of the book was still there. The ragamuffins were obviously not readers. I pulled it out and searched through the sodden pages, some of which clumped and tore as I peeled them open from the back. Remarkably I found the line I was looking for. I read it aloud:

'Rain fell lightly on the coffin...' The scene returned to me. It was at the funeral of the young man who had committed suicide. How could I have forgotten such a woebegone character? I would say that he was one of the better drawn, and I recognised some of his characteristics in myself. I too had turned very much to alcohol as a student. It is perhaps not so uncommon for a young man to go slightly off the rails when he is, for the first time in his life, let off the parental leash. I do not recall the character's age, but these are the years when youth needs guidance and parameters more than any other, barring toddlerhood. It is the age when they are sent out to fend for themselves. The boy in the story seems, however, to have been brought to his sorry state through the death of his first love and then the unrequited love of his second. My introduction to booze was more sudden. After the first week of classes, at the weekend, I bought a bottle of red wine — no mean feat — and took it back to my room in the student halls. There, I polished it off in front of a mirror. I remember watching as my eyes grew heavy. My intention was to get drunk, and I succeeded. What I had not anticipated was the emotional impact of inebriation. I had begun to think of my parents and how much I loved them, even though they never acted in a manner I saw on any cinema screen. There was a coldness in their way with me. I remember nothing of hugs, or particular tender words. Planted in my mind were reprimands. Like when I entered the garage to find my father lying on a bench, straining to push up a 600 pound weight. He placed it on the barbell rest and screamed at me to get out. His face was red and some saliva came spitting out of the corner of his mouth. I ran out and to my room, where I sat on the floor against the wall with my arms wrapped around my knees, trying to hold in tears. Come dinnertime it was all forgotten. I was maybe more silent than usual at the table, but I'm thinking now maybe I was always silent at the table. There was, however, some emotion in my heart for them, and this I mistook for love. With this in my drunken head, and miles between us, I decided to phone them and talk about everything. I could start out slow, perhaps a general conversation about classes and how I was getting on with the work, and then move the dialogue up a dial to why they lacked even the basic fucking empathy to share some love with their son. Later, when I analysed my plan, it was poorly thought out from the very start. As I had only left them at the bus station days before, the classes hadn't even started. All I had done was register for the classes I had put down for. As it was, we didn't even get that far. Luckily, though, my mother had answered.

'Hello.'

'Hello.'

'It's me.'

'Yes, I can tell. Are you alright?'

'Alright? Of course I'm fucking alright!' And then I started laughing. I hung up. My wisest decision of the night.

So, there was some identification with that character in the book, although I did not kill myself.

As I stood in the rain atop a Parisian hill, looking down at the sodden paperback, I was brought back to the moment and could not remember why I had stopped and taken out the book in the first place. As I returned it to my pocket, I thought that maybe I had wanted to read about that character again? It's often the case you settle for any answer, even one you know not to be true. If you didn't then you would certainly be in the madhouse.

I have often asked myself what art is. Not asking if this or that is beautiful, or clever, or good or bad. What is the thing we look at, we read, we watch? What is art? What is the thing? How, out of all the different available components does the artist create this? Nothing comes fully formed; the clutter of ideas, the mess and hotch-potch create this or that. But why is it? What shape and shifts are needed for a work to be complete? And what makes the artist? What is this thing called artist? Was my mother an artist? Did she consider herself such? And does any of it matter? Do we need art? Is it our evidence of something?

A few steps forward and I remembered I had taken the book from my pocket to see if the author had mentioned rain. I now remembered several instances. Well, what do you know...

8

Walking downhill puts pressure on the knees, and I felt it more so on the knee that I hurt while hurtling off the park gates. The twisted ankle was also jabbing at every footfall on the same leg. As I limped on downwards, my tongue played with some grit that had entered my mouth, no doubt at the fountain. Being on a slope had its blessings though: there was no flood to plash through. My socks were still soaked through. Each step squeezed water around my shoe with a squeaking sound. When the foot was lifted the wool of the sock acted as a sponge and sucked the water back in. And so I went on, a reluctant, squelching engine. I passed piled bags of rubbish beside overflowing bins. Of course, I wanted some stopping point, but didn't know what that point was. Did I have in mind some ideal stop of heaped trash? This was a nonsense, as each hill of trash looked much like another. And so I walked three blocks, limping, squidging from the feet, and sucking from my gritty mouth.

The three blocks on, I balanced myself with a hand leaning against a corner wall. I removed my left shoe and then struggled with the sock. When it eventually gave, it sprung back, slapping the masonry. I put my foot down again and squeezed the water from the material. I thought again about the rain in the book. A buried thought successfully remembered gives one a rather satisfied feeling, a rounding off of an action interrupted, a finishing of a job started. There is certainly a quick rush of achievement. Rather than replace my sock and shoe I left them on the pavement.

The right shoe presented a problem: I could not raise my leg enough to get a hand on it. I was breathless and both my knee and ankle stabbed with pain. A sound emanated from me that started like a deflation of air, then became a grunt at my injuries. I realised that I would have to sit down to complete the task. The bin area at the kerb had its usual pyramid of rubbish bags. Sitting down on it was much like sinking into a beanbag. This agreeable site made more difficult the removal of the shoe. From my sitting position I pulled at my shin in order to get a hand on my foot. At each failed attempt I would roll back slightly off-kilter. Success eventually, but the greater problem was the sock. There was no possible way I could tug it off. Instead, I kneeled and reached behind me, slowly peeling it away from my cold, wrinkled, foot. I squeezed and twisted the hose until every drop that could have been squeezed and twisted out was squeezed and twisted out. After a few attempts at dressing again I gave up, and consoled myself that footwear was in fact hampering my journey. I stood up, placed the socks in the shoes, and the shoes in my coat pockets, with the gun and the book. I marvelled again that the young robbers had not rolled me over and made off with the gun. Had they discovered it would they have shot me?

The concrete under my feet was cool on my chafed feet. The buildings around offered a shade from the sunlight, which was peeking through a sheet of brown sky, and when crossing roads between buildings the wind would slice at me.

The pain from my ankle was easing in the face of fresh discomforts, and I felt after a few moments that I was walking more naturally. The bus that had dropped me off hours before now passed again, climbing the hill. I saw that it was the same driver. His bus was empty but he stopped a little further up the street at a designated stop. No doubt the bus company decided that protests, civil disorder, and boycotts, could not dictate their schedule any longer. Nor indeed intrude on their profits. If there were no customers there was no business. If the activity continued the company would have no alternative but to lay people off, or at the very least furlough them. The matter did not concern me as I was

R D McGregor

heading downhill, and had no ticket, but the consideration helped pass the time it took to pass several doorways on my journey.

A way of passing time quickly is to consider the nature of time and its speed. Some activities appear to move time on faster than others, and some appear to slow it down. A watched kettle most certainly will boil, but it appears to take a longer time than it actually does. I know this because I have conducted it as an experiment alone in my kitchen. Doing nothing but standing watching a kettle does not freeze the minutes passing but requires you to consider every second. This in itself gives the impression of a minute containing more than sixty seconds. On one occasion time did indeed stand still, as I had forgotten to switch the kettle on at the mains.

My reverie was interrupted by my present mind noting that I had passed several shops selling wigs. I stopped and looked back and saw that there was indeed a preponderance of *perruquiers* in the street. All of them seemed aimed at women, and given the appearance of the mannequins, specifically women of colour. For another block I pondered the reason for this cluster. If I could dismiss the idea that this demographic was more prone to hair loss, there had to be another reason. Perhaps I was considering more than one question and unnecessarily confusing the issue. Firstly, the cosmetology heads were perhaps of colour because that was the target audience in this particular area. Secondly, there was no reason to suggest that wigs bought or on sale were intended for those with hair loss. The bright colours and furniture in the window displays pointed more towards times of celebrations, parties, etc. Many women wear wigs and extensions as part of a night out paraphernalia. Thirdly, women were more likely to purchase a wig for such occasions than men. Those three points dealt with the generalities of the hair shops but did not deal with the reason for so many in such a small area — I had passed at least ten in quick succession. This question my mind could not answer, but the whole wig conversation consumed three blocks of walking, so all was not in vain. And I was an expert on wigs by the time I had moved on. It never ceases to amaze me that the more you think of a subject the more you believe yourself to be qualified on that subject.

I felt a shiver throughout my body when I stopped going over things in my mind. We should not rely on too much warmth and protection from thoughts. Cold and discomfort can be kept at bay only for a short while. Let us accept and settle on that. Two blocks further and I remembered not only was I no expert on wigs, but I was no expert on women either. That much has been clear throughout my life.

My teeth were grinding with the cold, granules of dirt, breaking between molars. I pulled my coat tightly around my body more out of habit, as it was as much the cause of discomfort as the rain and wind. But discomfort had been mine for such a long time. I had not felt at one with the world. I was an empty kernel; a disappointment to myself. I made a fool of my early gifts. I mocked a talent that I most certainly held and very occasionally displayed. My early reading and study pointed towards a life in academia or perhaps authorship of heavyweight books that would not sell but would be referenced and studied in future years. If my life were an Attic tragedy the Gods would have been rolling the dice atop Olympus and laughing. On many a particularly lonely night I have heard their laughter ring down the mountainside. But more fool me. I lacked the push that others nurture. My mother told me that it is the work and only the work that is important. Not fame or thirty pieces of silver. And it might be that disregard for acclaim and comfort that in the end ruined any chance of success. I published a few papers in some critical magazines that she sniffed at. I wrote stories that she told me on every occasion I could improve upon. An easy position in an undistinguished department in an undistinguished college in a small town much like a hundred other small towns was to be my lot. And was it enough? No, of course not. Who would choose such a thing? But I did indeed choose it. Or was it that I accepted it? It was the easy thing to do. It did not cause ripples. Ambition can be a storm that destroys everything it comes into contact with. I suppressed mine. Is that what she had done? Is that why she sat in her chair by the window writing her poetry? No one ever knowing what she wrote or asking why she wrote. It was safe. It was quiet. It was the calm choice. For truly what did any of it really matter in the end? But I do remember her once saying to me:

'After a while you have to be doing something. Otherwise, you're just sitting around waiting to die.'

A wind came blowing up the street as fresh as had been smelled in days. I breathed it in. It filled my nostrils and lungs. The sharpness of that clean air was the same as that you discover as a child. Where had it come from? Did it carry with it a hope of an end to this filth? But no sooner was it there than it was gone. Once again, the repugnant stench of refuse rushed in. No, this was it, you have to cut your life cloth appropriately. These were the times. How easy it was back then. If we had only realised. It's not so much appreciating the moments but understanding that they are fleeting and cannot ever be recaptured. Well, who does that?

Aaaaah, in the near distance, the Seine. A bus passed me and stopped at the lights just ahead. Reaching it, I looked inside and clearly saw the man that had taken me to the flat. Beside him was the woman who made me the coffee. Perhaps the stories both told me were untrue, for there they were, together, travelling. I believed him at the time, I believed her at the time, and now I believe what I see. Can all of it be true? She smiled and waved to me. I offered no recognition but walked on. I was filled with a new energy now that I had seen the river. *Blow winds blow.*

9

The river area was awash. Partly surplus Siene and partly rainwater, but I splashed through and took a bench seat. The bouquinistes stalls were out, but no one was around. Even on a day like this I would have spent some time rummaging amongst the second-hand books, postcards, and posters. I have always liked the smell of old books. They invariably toss up a memory or two. The sweet smell of the past often wafts through my mind, although the memories themselves are not always sweet. Most old books are reminiscent of chocolate and childhood. Looking through them is like clutching at the past. Many do it because they can't let go. The casual browser carries the weight of yesterdays.

It might as well have been the height of a bright summer's day for me. I sat for some moments with my arms hung over the back of the bench and my legs straight out in front of me. And to top it all I had a smile on my face. There was no reason for this behaviour, but I went with what my body seemed to want. It did not, of course, last long. I removed my shoes and socks from my coat pockets. I put them on easily. Although cold and wet they offered an element of comfort to my by now freezing bare feet. My next stop was to find a large clothing store. This could not be difficult, and I headed with a renewed purpose towards one of the city's largest avenues.

A sense of purpose in life creates its own body energy. I strode across the bridge like a man possessed. I cared not a jot about a chance encounter with the policeman. What could he do to me? I was a tourist. I had broken no laws (well, not intentionally). This new found confidence was a great thing. But how had I chanced upon it? I put it down to the fact that I had removed my shoes and socks for a while. If one can walk through one of the great cities shoeless and sockless one can do anything. But how swiftly this confidence crumbled. Was that as a result of donning my footwear again? My gait slowed to more of a shuffle as I remembered I had been robbed. I felt through my pockets again but the young rogues had pilfered everything while I lay in the quadrangle incapacitated. How was I to survive without card or cash? It seemed that life had decided to throw every obstacle in my way to stop me completing my task. I took this as a challenge, but I was exhausted. How a moment's realisation can change everything.

Sitting down and contemplating my next move seemed like the best thing. A wet ground could do little worse to my clothing. I saw, from the far end of the bridge, a woman approach. As she got closer I could see she was eating a shawarma sandwich. Approaching me she bent and placed a ten euro note in my hand, and the rest of her sandwich. She walked on. I pushed the note deep into my coat pocket and tossed the sandwich into the river.

Getting to my feet I calculated the money would buy me two coffees. This fact spurred me on at a clip. Every positive in this misery of a life should be grasped with both hands and one should act accordingly. I was going to a clothing store, and nothing would hinder me. My walking rhythm allowed me to consider how I might pay for the change of clothing. And the answer was clearly that I would not. Much of what I had planned earlier I could carry out, but the ending would be different. I would walk with a determined gait into the store, choose the clothes, go to the changing area, and remove the price tags. I would then leave my sodden clothes and just as determinedly march out of the store, congratulating myself on a job well done.

It's interesting how easily I have slipped into illegality in my mid-life, for I certainly had no criminal tendencies as a youth. The more recent thefts and planting clues to point the guilt towards another, was not lifelong behaviour. And I can offer no explanation as to why this started. There has certainly been no decline in my circumstances. I have been overlooked when the sniff of promotion was in the air, but that's of no matter as I have shown little interest in advancing my career. I always felt that promotion leads one away from the area of one's real interest. Of course, the fact that I had no desire for it does not mean that I did not want to be considered. For me, not to be mentioned in dispatches reveals something of the poor opinion held of me. I was not at any time deemed worthy of advancement. Perhaps this insult lay festering in my mind without my knowledge. Could that be? And why would I turn those feelings into petty theft? And the setting up of others? There comes a point when you have to give up and realise that too much self-analysis is a dangerous task. I might land on a theory, and it might be correct. But all for what? *All for what?* I repeated the line aloud and smiled. It might as well be my epitaph. I started my academic career with the motto *Work as if you live in the early days of a better nation*, but was quickly brought to heel by a tradition of hopelessness. I found alcohol a decent escape route. My thefts offered some spice to life's pot.

And then Mary Orr, the weather "girl" (Mary was easily nudging fifty) on the local TV station came to mind. There was no reason for her to pop up, but up she did indeed pop. Mary wore a variety of wigs while battling with alopecia. My recent ruminations while walking down the street of wig shops must have manifested her. It never ceases to amaze me how often thoughts from a past internal discussion will intrude in a moment without urging or notice. I acknowledged this aloud with a *Yes*. This kind of externalization was not a result of the creeping years, but something that had been with me since youth. If I was particularly engrossed in a book and a particular passage took my fancy I would often utter *Yes*. I knew of no one else who did this, but for Sam Blue, who my mother diagnosed as being *away with the fairies*. I thought nothing of it until one day while sitting on the campus grass in my second year of university, reading *The Iliad,* a fellow student, a pretty dark-haired girl called Emily, told me I was weird. She had been sitting under a tree nearby and heard me say *Yes.* I told her that I often got caught up in a great story, and this was indeed true, but I did not mention that I could easily get just as lost in a comic book.

We passed the afternoon talking about our dreams of the future. I thought mine was somewhat boring compared to hers. She said that she would like to document the streets of cities by recording the sounds of traffic and snatched conversations of passers-by. This, she told me, would not be appreciated at the time but in fifty years it would then be an historical document and would carry with it more weight.

'That's a long time to wait.'

'Well, I don't mind. I'm not going anywhere. If I don't pursue my artistic dream then my life will be mapped out for me. I'll marry a man who will bore me to death. I'll be tied down for twenty years with kids I love but unsure I really wanted. I'll crawl into my own head to survive. And there, I suppose, I'll stay. So, I'll record people. I'll document my time with the chatter of the streets. Everybody is looking for something else. I don't want to be like that everybody.'

Emily replaced my mother as the most interesting person I had met. There was an innocence in her ambition, and how she spoke about her future. There was an honesty and an openness to her that I don't believe I have found in anyone since, while I felt that there was a burden on me, a weight of the need to succeed, to make a difference. I told her this, and she asked me who I wanted to make a difference to. But I didn't really know. Society at large was meaningless to me. Maybe I simply wanted to make a difference to me. Or to stand in front of my parents and say *Look at me. Look what I've done.* But my mother wasn't a woman who got impressed, and my father wouldn't have cared. When I was eighteen it felt special because being eighteen was supposed to be special. But my dad just said *so you get to be eighteen. That's it. That's all. Next year you'll be nineteen. It's nothing much.* The truth is it was a lot to me. But I couldn't say why. Emily seemed to look at things another way. A better way.

I suppose my parents hurt me a lot. I kind of felt let down by them. The word betrayed came to my mind, but I'm not sure why I felt betrayed. Maybe we're led to expect things of them, beyond food, shelter and protection. I felt that they weren't there, although they always were. Emily became always there. On quiet nights I would dwell on her and the promise in a face.

And as for Mary Orr, though? Nothing. Part of the thought-clutter.

The energy that I had felt when striding across the bridge had pretty much left me by the time I arrived at the other side of the river. Moods can turn in a moment. I slowed but eventually arrived at a clothing store which was open, in defiance of the disruption, albeit with very few customers.

The store was on one level. It was as big as an aircraft hangar, (I assume, never having actually seen one outside films or photographs.) To enter I had to take an escalator to the floor below street level. I glanced around and spotted the *vêtements pour hommes* section. Urgency without drawing attention to myself was necessary. I made a beeline to the rails and grabbed what came first to hand in my size, moving quickly on to the underwear and sock section.. The same manoeuvre and then to the shoes. All of this was easier than I thought.

The changing room was awkward for a man of my size. I am tall and *angular*. Before putting anything on I tore off the tags that held the barcodes. The last thing I needed was the shop alarm screeching out as I tried to leave. While undressing and dressing I managed to knock and bruise

138

knees, elbows and my head several times. My cut knee, I saw, was now suppurating. I removed the beret from my coat pocket and put it on. Once dressed, I folded the damp filthy clothes I had removed and left them on the seat. I am a clean and ordered man. Something to do with my upbringing. My house was always immaculate. My mother rarely did housework, but my father was obsessive about a tidy house. In addition to his weights, I remember him many times with a vacuum cleaner in his hand, or a duster. For all of his faults he was not a man constrained by traditional gender roles.

I pushed the pistol firmly down the back of my fresh slacks. With the back of the jacket hanging over it couldn't be seen but could be easily reached. I exited the changing area. To leave the store I would have to walk between racks of clothing. At the far end, near the escalator, there were two assistants chatting. Passing a rack of men's winter coats I grabbed one and approached them. I handed it to the young man (the other was a young girl) and said, rather loudly, while smiling:

'Too grand. Le pel…le pelage…est trop grand…'

I stepped onto the escalator and was taken again to the street. Theft is an activity that requires a brazen effort to be successful.

The rain had died down to a spit. Although I had a new suit, I still felt dirty. Several days of rough living had taken its toll on my grooming. The ten euro note would afford me a sit down in a café. Once there, I could use their washroom facilities and make myself presentable. As with pilfering, the number one tip to gain illicit access to the author's reading is not to bring attention to yourself.

A shop I was passing, much like the one I had purchased the beret from, caught my eye. Baskets outside held the usual tourist junk, and many trinkets hung down at the entrance. Inside, the flooding had taken its toll. A shallow puddle covered the floor. An Asian man rushed out from behind the counter with a brush and started sweeping the water out. On a shelf I saw what I was looking for: a comb. It was only two euros, leaving me enough, I thought, for two coffees. The shopkeeper came rushing back around the counter and smiled at me. We said nothing as I paid. I wondered what his life was like as he dug my change out from a drawer. What was his family like? How long had he a shop here? Did he suffer from the rise in racism in politics and on the street? What was it like being that man? Maybe he was thinking many similar questions about me. Today's problems are the result of blindness to others' humanity, I thought. But I honestly could not care less. I smiled, nodded, and left. Across the street was a charming café. I crossed, found a table, and sat.

While I waited on a waiter, I considered my position. It is wise now and again to take stock of where you are and, indeed, who you are. Everything brings us back to who. It is the one motivating search in great literary and common lives. I am a man pushed on by circumstance. And, I believe, reason. I am open to change, as I understand the man who is fixed is a fool. In the great novel *Don Quixote* the knight may appear foolish but is no fool. There is a goal in all of our lives, a destination point, that we might not know, but move ever towards it, regardless. It is the force that Dylan Thomas struggled with in his poetry; it is what drives me ever forwards now. We are connected, I know this. I understand it. But something is rotten at the root. Those who leave, or opt out are trying in their own way to survive. They recognise the lies and betrayals, the hypocrisies and cruelties at the radicle. A new way has to grow a new connectivity. Is this what the artist has been searching out for millennia? A new connectivity. A new way to live. The coffee was ordered. The coffee was delivered.

I stood and made my way through the café, past the long marble counter, towards the washroom at the back of the spacious interior which you had to descend a flight of stairs to reach both kitchen and washroom. This seems to be common in restaurants around the world. Perhaps it is a matter of space, or plumbing, but I have never found it anything other than disgusting. Orders from the kitchen were sent up via a dumb waiter that I spotted behind the counter. At least the waiting staff didn't have to manoeuvre along the narrow corridor that led to the kitchen, washroom and what looked like a storage cupboard.

The door to the gents was wedged open with a block of wood. I removed it quickly and jammed it closed. Standing at the washbasin I stripped off completely and started squirting hand gel onto my body. I rubbed this in and then rinsed off. Next, I washed my face and soaped my hair. I then stuck my head under the tap banging it several times as I rinsed. I dried everything with bundles of paper towels and dressed in double quick time. I combed my dark hair back off my forehead with my new comb. I was a handsome chap, though my eyes displayed a tiredness and were slightly, dare I say, rheumy? The unshaven appearance would be assumed a fashionable growth. It crossed my mind that the reason I was not successful with the opposite sex was wholly my behaviour and not my appearance. A woman will not accept eccentricities unless she herself is odd. I should have married Emily. I should have asked her to marry me the day I met her under a tree on the campus. Of course, I would have learned her surname first and married in haste. Maybe we too would have divorced the more we discovered about each other, like many other couples with many years' engagement before marriage. One day or one year made little difference. Why not jump in at the deep end after a few hours? Why not clutch that excitement? But I did not. I seized nothing but my copy of *The Iliad*, said goodbye, and walked on. Where is she now? Is she an artist? Has she fulfilled dreams, or have they been crushed? What an old head on young shoulders she had. If she was ever real.

I removed the wedge from under the door and started to leave. Looking back, I saw that the gun was lying beneath the basin on the floor. How unused I was to be carrying a weapon like keys or a wallet. I retrieved it swiftly and left.

My coffee was still sitting on the table. Beside it was the bill. It was €5.80. There would be no second coffee. Sipping, I realised that I did not have cigarettes. A coffee without a cigarette is pointless. I added another lump of sugar to join the two I had already dropped in. I have never ceased to be fascinated by a sugar lump dropped into coffee. The air bubbles pushing up to the surface, through the clouds, each time different, and each time the swilling of time into new shapes. In those shapes I fell into more memories, more considerations.

Like many, I spent my childhood running. I ran to shops, I ran to school, I ran to the local cinema, I ran to my mother, I ran to my father. At what age do you start running *from*? This little nugget of a question popped up while the sugar lump melted away. I was always pulled towards my parents in times of crisis, yet their reaction was rarely normal. A cut leg would be followed by instructions as to where to find the medical kit. (on the floor underneath the bathroom cabinet). Perhaps it was during my university years that I realised I was no longer part of them. I was aware that everyone was in a rush to get home once a term ended, but I did not have that eagerness to return to the family bosom. Possibly because there was never such a thing for me. I was very much alone at home much of the time, although my parents were only feet away from me at any given time. I was not encouraged to search them out, and they most certainly did not search me out. I became comfortable with my own company at an early age, and so my arrival at the university presented no homesickness.

Unlike the many who sought out parties and immediate friendships out of loneliness I took my time. There was one fellow, though, that was something of a disappointment to me — not that many aren't. He was in the room next to me in my first year in the halls of residence. For some reason I admired him. He went to many parties, fucked many women, and carried throughout much of his university career the spirit of rebelliousness that was attractive to a small-town boy. When, though, he got an average degree, and secured a position selling insurance, the rebelliousness was shown to be nothing more than a cloak to hide his traditional values. It was either that or the spirit was crushed out of him at twenty-one years old. I understood then that I had been always myself from a young age. I truly did not need anyone else.

I put the spoon in the cup and stirred. For the moment I was back in the café. How we slip in and out of remembered moments and time. How easy it becomes. Some moments, though, recur often in the memory. Like my mother stepping forward and my father holding her wrist as my bus left the station the day I left home for the first time. She had never displayed emotion like that in my years with her up until that time, so why then? Was it the pull of some invisible umbilical cord? In some fashion I liked to think so, but as I never asked her, I cannot be certain. Even then would I have got the truth from her? Life is full of niggles of what we have not done or said. Just moments, brief though they are, can consume much of your thoughts in future years. A few words thrown at you in insult in youth can prey on your mind for the rest of your life. I believe the great characters of literature are made of such memories. My father mocking the length of my hair and my slight pigeon-toed walk has stayed with me and if I'm honest, still stings. Of course, I seem to have the memories to make a character but little of the talent. It has been a frustration in my life that I could not express myself adequately in the novel form. Or maybe I could have but was just too afraid to face the slings and arrows.

I made an early first attempt though. In my twenties I wrote a bad novel. I did not destroy it, as I often thought of doing. And so it sat in a dark drawer like a dormant ghost. Occasional nights I thought of taking it out and rewriting it, or throwing it on the fire. I am not brave enough for either. No one has read it, nor will they. There is something vulgar and arrogant in thinking others might be interested in your ramblings. My pointless thoughts on fictitious people. Maybe that was at the back of my mind while I spent the years writing. There was a narrator but no character. How much better if the author I had come to confront had had similar misgivings. The sheer bloody arrogance of the man putting out such trash for quick titillation. My pistol twitched in my belt. I would certainly put a stop to his arrogance. I looked down to find my hand shaking. Not the moment to pick up the cup.

There was something else that got to me. The author places little value on time or place. I always like to know where I am when I'm reading. I need some kind of an anchor. After that I can wander freely with the characters and their situations. The time and place gives the imagination of the reader freedom to roam. In his novel, the scenes in the Orkney Islands allow us something of that, but are mere crumbs in the story. I certainly pecked at them but found them unsatisfying as a main meal. I am someone who wanders greatly while reading. I can finish a sentence and be transported in my imagination to a completely different tale. So great has this dreaming been I create characters and incidents so vividly outwith the narrative at hand that they become entwined with the author's world. An instance is the scene in the glass houses with the two girls. I imagined that the female protagonist had pulled out a gun and shot her flatmate. This did not happen, of course, but so strong were my imaginings that I actually related the incident to someone in the staff room. I really don't know if anyone else has experienced this level of interactivity. The relationship between writer and reader becomes personal, and the reader becomes an active participant in the creative act. The giants of literature, from Homer to Cervantes to Tolstoy, give a reader room to stretch their own imagination, but those struggling through poorly written books must find other means of escape. Of course, if it all becomes too much hard work chucking the said book on the trash is always a viable option. A good book is the excitement of turning a new page; a great book makes you think every page turned. You think of your own life, you're the own experiences. And then what do you do? You try to shoehorn them into the characters on the page. You write the book as you read.

'George!'

Your name called when you're deep in thought is an unpleasant jolt to the system. A ghost touching your shoulder. I knew it was of course Clara Pett calling out, for apart from recognising the screech, only she calls me George. I had no intention of correcting her at the book shop earlier, and I had no intention of doing so at the café.

'George!' she repeated.

As she approached my table I was struck by her figure hugging flower print dress. Her look smacked of a wealthy and glamourous tourist. She wasn't wealthy; she was a librarian.

'George!' she screamed again, as though an incantation to be repeated three times that I might appear. I stood up.

'Clara,' I said.

'You bastard, you didn't call. How did you know to come here?'

'I didn't. Maybe it's the gods.'

She let herself fall into the wicker chair.

'I need a drink. Get me a drink. Get me a Savennières. Large.'

The waiter who had rushed over as Clara approached, nodded. He obviously saw someone who does not wait around to be served. She continued:

'You're having a drink. What'll you have?'

'I...' My hesitancy was a result of my cash flow problem.

'Jesus, George, turn on the engine. I'm dying here.'

'A whisky and ice.'

'Bien, or whatever.' The waiter nodded to Clara and disappeared.

Clara rifled through the bag that she had placed on the table and pulled out a packet of cigarettes and a lighter. I also helped myself to a cigarette.

'What's wrong with your face, George? You look like a goo-goo.'

'A...' I had no idea what a *goo-goo* was. But I assumed it was not good. 'I was mugged, Clara. All my money and cards.'

'Oh, my dear god! Are you all right? The damn bandits! Have you been to the police?'

'I think they're a bit busy just now with the collapse of social order.'

'The embassy is closed. Otherwise it would be the next stop. Do you need cash?' She suddenly pulled her bag onto her lap and went rifling again. With her cigarette hanging from her mouth she continued. 'I have plenty of cash. I can get more. How much do you need to tide you over?'

What does one answer?

'Here's three hundred euros. I'll get you more.'

And she shoved three hundred euros into my hand, which I immediately pocketed. A librarian's savings. She asked if I had been hurt.

'My pride, Clara.'

'Pride schmide! You have a bruise on your forehead.'

'I was knocked to the ground.'

'The bastards! Did you get a good look?'

'They were young.' This was no lie.

'The old don't mug, George. They become a burden. The effect is the same.'

God only knows what she thought of her comatose husband. She wanted to know all the details, but I could not deliver all the details. The bus journey? The man who took me back to the flat? The Welsh girl? Or the man in strange garb sticking out his backside? My collapse? The flooding? The children descending on me like Fagin's band? People wanted too much information, too many details. I often found that when filling out forms. Forms for banks, forms for credit, forms for renting a flat, forms for applications to clubs and societies, forms for promotion, forms for ordering goods, forms for travelling. Your blood type, your gender, your marital status, your dates, your years, your minutes on this earth, documented and filed away for future use.

There was something of relish in the voice of Clara as she probed the crime. *Was it in the street? How many? What age? Did they speak? Have you got a description? Are we safe here? Are we safe anywhere?* Clara was someone only interested in her own line of questioning, not the line of the answers. I had met many like that. I had met most like that.

'I saw nothing, Clara. They must have come up behind me. I saw nothing. I heard nothing.'

'How did you know they were young?'

Fuck me sideways, was this an interrogation?

'When I was on the ground, while they were going through my pockets, I caught a glimpse.'

'Did they push you down or was it a blunt instrument?'

'It's upsetting to go over. I just want to forget about it.'

'That's what rape victims often say. Move on. Forget the horror. I'd cut their damn nads off! Good God, you weren't…?'

'Raped? No. No, I wasn't.'

The waiter had appeared with the drinks and set them down on the table. He then gave us each a large menu. She held onto hers as she leaned forward with a non sequitur.

'What is it you want from life?'

'I only ever wanted to startle.'

Maybe that answer was too simple, or too direct, or too difficult, but Clara picked up her glass as she dismissed me with an audible sigh and disappeared behind the menu. People often ask questions but don't really want answers. My mind runs with this. Life is nothing. It starts with nothing; it ends with nothing. Ten thousand years arriving at…nothing. We fooled ourselves. A long time coming. Realisation. I wanted to tell her what was going through my mind, but she wouldn't begin to understand. They never do.

She took a slurp of her wine. I laid my menu on the table and stared at it. It was in English and French. I understood none of it. A voice from over the table said *I'll order*. I replied, *Yes*, as though it was understood from the start. I drank my whisky which sanded my mouth and throat. Her hand and arm appeared from over her menu and shot straight up. It must have been a new way of signalling the waiter, and it worked. He appeared, pencil and order book in hand. She ordered and he disappeared. The one whisky seemed to work on my senses immediately, for I felt, if not drunk, then certainly a little tipsy. Time moved in the blink of an eye and I noticed the clouds above shift and darken as the sun fell and twilight was upon us.

When the dishes arrived I realised that Clara had been talking and I had been staring at her blankly. Would it have mattered if I had been there or not? I felt it wouldn't. The waiter arrived with a chartuterie platter. Dishes of brie and chicken liver mouse, pickles and pears clattered with the tray of crackers, prosciutto and sweet walnuts. I was salivating at the sight. Food is not generally high on my priorities on a daily basis, but when presented with this gastronomic heaven I could not resist. She had ordered a bottle of white that hit the palate with a crisp explosion of honeysuckle and pear. I had four crackers and half a glass before she broke the silence. There had been no room for my whisky glass and I had offered it to the waiter, but he looked at me as if to say, *Can't you see I'm busy?* I had slipped the glass on the ground by my chair. When leaving he pushed the by now empty trolley around the glass, stopped, and picked it up. He looked at me as though a schoolmaster reprimanding a naughty pupil.

Before the food had arrived I couldn't remember what Clara had been saying, but how she started her next conversation told me it was related.

'Look, George, I'm not given to hand holding or bedside comfort. My husband has been in a coma or more a catatonic state for years and no one can tell me what's wrong with him. Every doctor enters with enthusiasm and the usual bag of medical tricks. They all leave scratching their heads. And so I live with it. Daily.'

It is something of a lonely exercise entering a discussion that is in full flow. The first words you utter you wish to be relevant and will not mark you out as an intruder. You want the first words to be diamonds dropped on the sludge. You want everyone to stop and recognise your genius in staying silent, waiting a chance to consider before speaking. Unfortunately, most of us drop in with heavy boots. My next words were such an example.

'Does he shit?'

'What?'

'I mean, do his bowels function?'

'Everything can function, George. Everything can function. It just isn't doing so. That's the tragedy. There is no damage to anything. It seems the motor neurones are just sleeping. I think he is aware of everything around him, but there are no signs, no signals, no eyelids blinking, no twitch of a finger. That's for the movies. Real life? Nothing.'

On the word *nothing*, she sliced a butter knife through the air between us.

'The first year I hoped he would spring out of it as easily as he fell into it. It wasn't to be. The second year I grew to hate

149

him. And then, eventually, that hate turned to something else, something in some way worse. I had no feelings for him. He became as relevant as a coat hanger, but of less use.'

I interjected with a stupid, *I've been through it all*, comment.

'True love.'

My comment irked her and she sprang back with, 'Who are you to judge?'

I had been well and truly slapped down.

'I am no one to judge.'

That comment seemed to put a spoke in her particular wheel, though. She fell silent and picked the last walnut from a small dish. Eating it slowly she eventually finished and licked the tips of three fingers.

'I heard that you were stealing things and pointing the blame at students?' She raised an arm and snapped her fingers.

'Garcon!' she shouted, 'This course has finished!'

10

Between courses there was little chance to answer or to argue with Clara. I fell into silence and let her voice drone on. It has been my habit for some time to stop listening to people. Particularly when they go on a rant or an interminable diatribe. It struck me that most people do not want conversation; they want a listener, or at the least to hear the sound of their own voice. Most of what we hear is forgotten, particularly the older one gets. I have little time for the opinions of others. Unless it is a doctor fielding his opinions in facts and data. How many people do such a thing in their daily business? It's all gossip and tales. And who needs gossip and tales? Most people know less than they think. You let them prattle on. On another day you might engage. I occasionally engaged. Frank Steeghs, an ambulance chasing lawyer that I would see in *The Dirty Cactus,* would often repeat that we're given a window in the darkness, and that window is life, and we have to grab it. Eventually I'd had enough, for Frank repeated his thought many times. I suggested to Frank that how does he know there's only one window? What if there are many windows to grab, to pull open, to live a life? That's all I said. And what did Frank do? He just repeated what he'd just said. Another man not listening, hearing only his own voice. *If there were lots of windows in the darkness, I would rush to them all, to get things…to get things right at last. You know, Frank? You know? Right?* But Frank had long gone, and now there was only Clara's voice. Across a table. Another place. Another country.

I was going to explain about stealing things and blaming students. It was not true exactly. I was perfectly happy − in fact happier − to plant evidence of my criminality on those with an equally precarious position: i.e., the other staff. I once stole a box of sanitary products from the Spanish teacher's bag and planted them in the Dean's top desk drawer. I thought a note might have been sent around asking about the owner, but it was not to be. Did he regard them as a practical joke? There are so many unanswered questions in life. Not only the big ones of life and death and our place in the cosmos, but the minutiae encountered in the daily business of living. Like what happened to those sanitary products? I would never find out. And what of the Spanish teacher? Did she think them stolen? She left soon after, for her hometown of Sanlúcar de Barrameda, north of Cadiz. Were her leaving and the missing sanitary products connected? I did not enquire.

'Well?' Clara asked.

I was caught drifting, of not giving my full attention to her. 'What?' I said.

'Stealing things and putting the blame on students?'

Had she been talking all this time? Or had I imagined spectral chat?

'I deny that. It wasn't just students.' Would I tell her about the teacher of Spanish? I would not. 'It was anyone. I dropped a book into the bag of a gentleman in *Bump's Bookstore*. The alarm sounded as he tried to leave. Merrie asked him if he would open his bag. A fight ensued which resulted in Merrie and Mackenzie sitting on him. I stood at the Self Help section, giggling throughout.'

I regretted divulging the last piece of information.

'I don't know where Bump's Bookstore is. I don't know anyone called Merrie. I don't know anyone called Mackenzie.'

'My hometown bookshop. Merrie and Mackenzie are — '

'But why do you do these things?'

'It's fun?'

She sat back in her chair as the waiter approached. Her look. I had seen it a hundred times before. It was telling me she did not approve. It was the same she gave me once when I turned up with turned down pages of a Sébastien Japrisot novel.

'This is dog-eared.'

'It's how it was when I checked it out.'

'The Principal is looking at the library budget.'

'It's how it was when I checked it out,' I repeated. I find repetition the best position when being disbelieved.

And then the look. I felt like a grape drying in the sun. She changed the subject.

'I never order the main course when contemplating the first course. My body will tell me during that starter what it needs. It seems to have done so.' Why did everything she say have to be in the tone of an army order?

The waiter flipped his order book and his pencil was at the ready.

'Blanquette de Veau, and none of that shoulder shit. I want veal tenderloin. You understand?'

She was taking it out on the waiter, her frustration with me. Unfair as that was, I did not speak up. There would no doubt be many more verbal attacks throughout his waiting journey.

In perfect English he smiled and said, 'I spent four years in London, Madame. I understand perfectly.'

I surveyed the menu quickly and ordered:

'Sheet pan steak with Boulanger potatoes.'

'An excellent choice, Monsieur.'

Clara shot a look at him to show she was impressed.

'A waiter with more class than our restaurateurs.'

He disappeared.

She picked up the wine menu, scanned it in double quick time, and lifted it in the air.

The waiter reappeared.

'Wine, of course, Madame.'

'1980, Rigal Bovila Malbec.'

'Perfect,' he said. It struck me that a compliment would follow every choice. These were the building blocks of a tip. It was also discreet of him not to raise an eyebrow about how fast the first bottle was demolished.

'Damn right, François!'

He left and returned quickly with the wine and poured. It tasted good.

Clara started on about her husband and wine. I wasn't interested and started to drift again. I was thinking about the section in the novel that brought me here. I understood what he was trying to do. I had gone over it so often in my head. Everything was the opposite of how it should be. When you think left, he goes right. The reporter or detective, Barstowe, is old and rather grotesque. We find him, to our surprise, in bed with a twenty-two-year-old. The unlikelihood of this leads us to only one possible conclusion: the author wants to surprise and shock his reader. This in itself is dubious in intent. But let us accept it regardless. Compared to the other vagaries and vulgarities contained within the story it is of no matter. But let us consider how the author achieves that shock. He creeps up to the punch. He mentions the headrest, he mentions the phone, the cigarette, the ashtray. And then he describes what is on the television. It's the fall of the Berlin Wall. The reader is assaulted by these images; they are separate to what he intends to tell us. We consider those flashing images that we all remember. We are pulled in and remember our own lives when the wall was pulled down. He has involved us personally. But then he intrudes in our thoughts. He seals his literary deal with the line: *But Holly was too deep in sleep to rise to the bait.* It is nothing more than cheap manipulation. The end of a paragraph; the end of a chapter. The shocking image; the element of surprise. I mean, if anyone was going to fuck Holly it would be Gladbody, surely? Or even Calvert? But Barstowe? Quite impossible.

When I drift from a conversation into my own thoughts, I am not entirely deaf to the speaker: I am just removed. I was so removed the waiter putting out the food passed me by. Often, I return my attention without any comment being made on my abstention. Such was this moment. Clara had obviously gone off on a deeply personal journey, of the kind I find not only uncomfortable, but tasteless and often obscene.

'It isn't easy for me. I find it difficult. A woman – a human being – has needs. Some general communication between people. Even that was lost when he didn't wake up. After a while I started to analyse our relationship and I was shocked by what I recovered. The wooing process was nothing more than a precursor to rape. The rapist arrived with a box of chocolates and a bunch of lilies. Lilies! The damn funeral flower!'

She leaned forward with a forkful of veal in her hand and pressed down on my arm.

'You know he smelt of petunia? Isn't that odd for a man? A sickening smell. It was a wonder I didn't throw up when he eventually came over my Calvin Klein-like faux leather pencil skirt. We women have to put up with a lot. I truly believe that we're all suffering from a form of Stockholm Syndrome. The truth is I put up with him. I put up with his heaving on top of me like a damn bull. A damn bull I tell you. Pushing me up towards the headboard of the bed. My head banging off it. I put up with it all. I thought about leaving. I thought about it every day. Just packing my bags and skedaddling. But, of course, I couldn't. I didn't have enough money. Where would I have gone in a village that hears a sneeze?'

I was drifting. The small village she lived in is just outside the university town where my flat is. Far too small for her and all her words. It was very much like the place I grew up in. How many boys like me did she come across on her trips to and from the village store? Did she notice them? She talked on.

'The truth of the matter is that I was afraid to leave him, to be alone. So, I guessed I would just have a few good years in

155

old age. I actually believed that. The man dies before the woman. That would give me a few years. I was looking forward to that. That was my plan. Bided my time while the clock ticked and the calendar shifted, and the years rolled in and out. Not much of a plan, I'll grant you. But it's the same one many women have. Waiting for the husbands to croak and then become respectable widows. But fate threw a different course. Sure, he was taken from me, but his heart was still beating. He just lay there. My purgatory.'

I shifted again, watching the waiters glide between the tables, and I imagined it like a dance where the tables and customers become nothing more than scenery and props for their choreographed movements. To transform everyone into the inanimate was to contemplate life as a fiction. I was entirely focussed on this fantasy when Clara's words entered stage left.

'Are you listening to me?'

'The waiters seem to be gliding.'

'What the hell are you on about? I'm spilling my guts here.'

'I'm listening. I'm also watching the waiters.'

She took a slurp of wine.

'You're losing it. You have to hang in there. Reality, George. Don't let it slide out of view.'

This was an interesting analysis. The fact was that reality was always in view and my daydreams projected an alternative concurrent existence. That alternative was providing a more attractive world to me of late. I mean, if anyone was given the choice of focussing on Clara's marriage or dancing waiters which would they plump for? I rest my case.

'I have to go.' I hadn't intended speaking at all. But out it came.

'We've only started the meal.'

'I can't eat it.'

Before I knew it I was on my feet, confused. I backed away from the table still aware that my actions would be piquing the interest of other bored diners.

'Nothing I've done…you see…' I was struggling to say something that could explain what I was going through. It was the book I'd read; it was my mother sitting by the window, my father on his back, pushing weights; it was the staff, the people in the town, the people everywhere. 'Nothing is what I wanted it to be. Do you understand…? Always the inevitable disappointment…'

The waiter glided over and stood behind Clara. She softened.

'Come back, George. Come back. There are people that want you back. Back home. You've been lost. What you think is not…It's all right. It can all be sorted out. Come back now. It can be worked out. Trust me.'

'What do you mean, *worked out*? I don't know what you're talking about. You don't know me. In your library. Stuck among the books.'

She stood up, rather unsteadily, I thought. The waiter reached a hand out to her.

'What are you talking about? I know you.'

'My name is mine alone.'

I had fallen. I knew I had fallen. From what I was and from what I could have been. I could have broken away and led the pack, discovered new lands of thought. There had been potential in my life, but it disappeared. My wings had been clipped before I could soar. There would be no gliding above the ordinary. When did I accept the common coin of reality over the wealth of dreams? When did I sell myself out? My life could have been different if I had taken a step back. I understood something at the heart of Sam Blue as he pushed that trolley all his days: he did not surrender; he would not resign himself to the pack. Get thee behind me, Clara. I refuse you.

'There's been tragedy. We know that. You've suffered. Come back, Georgie. We want you back.'

Her voice was back over my shoulder before she had finished the last sentence. I needed none of it. I walked quickly down the street. I had to get a distance between myself and those eyes. I had to get the distance between me and the town. I only returned to look after my mother, now and again. It was not running away, it was self-preservation. Christ, the town knew all about that now. Half of it was swept away when the river burst its banks. The post office and Frank Steegh's lawyer's office were gone in minutes. Martha Sweet was found, bloated, wrapped around a tree trunk. And Mrs Gosse and her twin babies, only one was found, twisted up in its cot. Everyone had known that the south side was at risk. People just don't listen. Well, I read the signs. And the signs told me that I should shift. I knew that there would be no happy returns; I knew I was never going back. Sometimes going back is not possible. Sometimes you make sure that it's not possible. I had burned my bridges; drowned my past.

What brings us to the moment? I cannot tell what really brought me here. I am feeling that it is less and less the assassination plan. My past, different as it was, is it enough to make me the oddball that I am now? Is it enough to have borne me to this here, this now? This street?

My Christ! The rain had stopped!

SUN

11

I realise that I was a fool. Not returning to my hotel room for fear of bumping into a policeman might have seemed like logic at the time, but I see it now as part of a pattern of odd behaviour that I had displayed for some years. It is still with me, even though I recognise and face it.

There was nothing to stop me booking into another room, though. I had money. Clara had given me cash before I fled the restaurant and her. What must she have thought? Another crazy action to be added to a hundred others? What does it matter what she thought? Why should others' opinions matter a jot? But they do. They always have. What the other kids in town thought of my mother and father and me. We were outsiders. Not romantic or intriguing, but true outsiders as in *viewed with suspicion*.

When mother went into town for essentials – this was when I was very young – they would be polite. They would speak in short sentences. There was never that small town chat like they would engage in with locals: no engagement. Maybe mother felt self-conscious and that's why she stopped going in. No, I can't believe this. She wouldn't have cared. Anyway, when I was old enough, I'd do the shopping. What did any of it matter to her? But it must have mattered to me, even though I didn't want it to. When we live in a society there is an unspoken etiquette, rules if you like. You might not want to play by those rules, but that doesn't mean they don't affect you. As I grew up I was affected by everything around me. So now, strangely, it mattered what Clara thought.

Still, if I needed more money, I could always walk into a bank waving my gun about. No, that was me contemplating the fanciful again. I am more than capable of minor thefts, but to rob a bank takes more courage than I could surely muster. And yet I had planned for the next evening the assassination of a writer, in full view of witnesses, in a public space. We are full of contradictions. Is that why I left my home country? No. I was running out of people to meet, to talk to. People who weren't afraid of me or bored with me. Had it ever been otherwise? Maybe I had always been the oddball, a dreamer. Where I come from dreams are everything, but mine were always of leaving.

I was lying on top of a hotel bed, below a five-blade ceiling fan that whirred and clicked above me. I saw it coming away from the metal brace that connected the motor housing to the mounting hardware, and decapitating me. A sweet and swift death. A chance to sidestep the lingering and painful end that most of us are fated for. Even with the fan, the room was airless. There was a mustiness to the bedding. Perhaps the sweat and dead skin of a thousand residents. A girl running away? No, a girl would not book into such a place. A woman escaping a bullying husband. A woman who'd had high expectations. Married young. A church wedding. A white wedding. Both families were there. Everyone got along famously. There was laughter, and dancing, and wine, and advice, and speeches. And then there was that point where she was alone. Her new husband had popped out for cigarettes. She had waited for him. But her thoughts were not of a joyous future. They were of loss. Akin to grieving. What had she lost? But, of course, she had lost herself. These thoughts were put away in a drawer. And then, after raising a family and watching as lines appeared on her skin, and grey hair appeared, she was still alone. And she reached out and opened that drawer that had been shut for so many years. And she cried. And she packed a bag and left her marriage, left her family home, and came upon this hotel. And she was tired and needed rest. At the desk downstairs where she had booked in, she tried to give an air of control. She half smiled to the girl behind the desk:

'Just for a few days.'

But the girl knew. And the woman knew that there was no way to hide that kind of ache. So, she climbed the stairs, and lay down on the bed and left dead skin and sweat. I would do the same. It was a hotel that people chanced upon.

Some hours before I had fled Clara and run, confused, along some avenues, streets, and boulevards. I found myself in an area that I did not recognise in the stopped rain and puddle-glazed fallen sunshine. I leaned against a wall to catch my breath and saw that I was recovering outside a small hotel. Without much consideration I entered and signed the book. I explained to the receptionist that I could only pay in cash as I had lost my wallet earlier that day. She appeared sympathetic to my plight and accepted some of what Clara had given me and looked behind me. Was that a slightly confused look on her face? It struck me that the only people who pay hotel bills with cash are men with prostitutes. Was I once again reading too much into a normal transaction? I thanked her and entered the small lift. It rattled and shook as it ascended to the second floor.

In the room I stripped, showered, dried and lay naked on the bed, contemplating the useless fan. My eyes closed but sleep did not arrive easily. The night was hot, and quite airless. The gutters had stopped running; the rain had ceased slapping the streets, their absence accentuating the silence.

I can never fall into sleep easily, always thoughts pressing against my imagination to deny any rest. Our imagination contains worlds within worlds forever. There are no endings. We throw a bucket of thought into an infinity ocean. For no reason whatsoever my childhood teacher enters my mind: India Nose, who would teach me to write. *With the t curl around at the bottom. It's the handle of an umbrella. Straight up, so high, boys and girls, so straight. But you need the covering, and that goes straight*

162

*across. Your book shows you how far to go up. Stop at the line. Now drop down slightly before making your cover. That's it. And that's t. That's t for tree. Or t for two. One, two. Two boys, two girls, two sweets, two blue balloons…*Where are you now, India Nose? Where did you go? I saw two boys, two girls, and two blue balloons flying high up to the blue summer sky. Oh, where did you go? With your ruby red lips, and your black hair piled high; the tweed suit and the elastic bands about your wrists. Oh, where did you go? But of course, I am not looking for India Nose, I am looking for the boy that was me. Where do we go? What is lost forever? I am a wretch. I am nothing now but thoughts.

All the words said that must have cut. Words said that tore at people. And with some I bring my imaginary lips to an ear and whisper softly, words brushing quietly 'I love you…'

I drifted to the novel that had brought me so far from my own hearth. I would soon be leaving behind the story which had held captive many of my thoughts since I last read it. It wasn't so much the story, as how the author filled the space. As with all novels, one thing led to another, but it was the pace that interested me. The author forces the reader to take his tale at a clip. There are no moments of rest, it moves towards what I now consider an inevitable conclusion at a rate of knots. The main character transforms from an awkward boy to a young man who is completely comfortable in his own skin. This *comfortableness,* I would suggest, is more suggestive of a man in his middle years. The author in effect takes over the character to fit the plot rather than letting him develop in a more natural fashion. This jarred with me from the beginning. We move through time, or are pushed through time, without the chance to stop and consider events or character arcs. It is quite clear to me that he does not want the reader to question his narrative. Speed is his endgame, and we, the reader, are therefore not in charge of what we are rattling through. The author is in control, but he has failed because he has underestimated the power of the reader. This cannot be allowed to stand. The reader must approach the author as adversary.

Obviously, there can be no dawdling with this whippersnapper; he is not an honest broker. We are not characters to be manipulated by his vulgar hand. And I would suggest also, his clumsy hand. One character is described on each entrance as having a different hair colour. I considered the options. The author:

1: forgot the previous description each time the character appeared

2: deliberately had the character change hair colour every few days for effect

Option 1 is unforgiveable as it points to the slackest attention to continuity. It suggests that there was possibly only one draft of the manuscript, or that there was more than one draft but it was poorly edited. If it was the latter I am inclined to the conclusion that the author edited his own work. If that was indeed the case we might surmise the author is short of funds or friends. Or, he might have friends, but they might not be up to the task of editing a work of fiction. Not impossible, as reading has become a minority pursuit, much like kayaking. Going in to edit a three-hundred-page novel with no previous experience in editing, or reading, would be akin to climbing Everest in flip-flops.

On the second option I can't give the scribbler the benefit of the doubt. The constantly changing hair colour might be more than a literary quirky contrivance; we might, as readers, glean some insight to the inconstancy of the character and her personality. But, surely the constant application of chemicals in her locks would have rendered her bald before the climax. Unforgivable.

The clock on the bedside table was silent. I prefer a ticking clock. I like to hear time being measured. At home I listened to the tik-tok whenever I fell into a deep slumber. It seemed to nudge me from consciousness, to sleep, to dream. I could not drop off in this room, that much was obvious. It was too silent, and the street still had sound. Who could sleep in such circumstances?

There were voices outside. There was laughter. Natural human curiosity woke me entirely, Like most of us would, I arose from the bed and went over to the window, which was open slightly to allow a modicum of breeze to enter. I stood naked and looked down the street. There were tables outside a café bar and groups of people, mostly young, stood and sat and discussed whatever they might discuss. I cannot but think I shall not relive my days of interacting in such a fashion. Some experiences are bitter in the mouth but sweet in the belly. My experience of people has, all in all, been bitter, without sweetness.

I wondered who the bearded fellow was, the girl with the long brown hair, clutching a glass of what appeared to be white wine. Who were they all with their talk and laughter? The thin fellow with the long coat sucking at a cigarette. Why was he wearing a coat on such a warm night? The other fellow with light coloured trousers and a cord jacket; he had just joined them with a beer. He had not newly arrived at the bar but had newly arrived in their company. I deduced this from the half-drunk glass and his hesitation just outside the perimeter of the group. He would no doubt join them in moments with a witty remark. There is an etiquette of joining such groups. And there is also an etiquette of keeping people out by some imperceptible reshaping of distance. I would, for instance, hang around in such a position but not be allowed to enter. I would be ignored, not physically pushed out, but the barrier would be there, the drawbridge would be drawn up.

And then there's the silence that might greet your opening words. The awkwardness crackles until someone starts a new discussion and they all lean forward and give that someone their full attention. I would retreat and watch as their shape reformed. Who are those people down there with their laughter and their words and their bodies moving? Why are they there? Why are they ever there; ever there congregating on the street on a balmy evening, across the world? But not me.

A shout broke through, rose up to my window and carried down the street: REVOLUTION! All but one of the group I had been studying raised their glasses, repeated the call and the other tables followed suit. REVOLUTION! The young man with the cord jacket and the light trousers did not raise his glass and did not call out. Instead, he threw his glass to the ground. It smashed, and splashed the shoes of those around with beer and shards. They looked at him. Who was this oddball? Who was this outsider that brought awkwardness to company? He walked quickly away. A girl with blonde hair and a long flower print dress picked up an ashtray and flung it down the street after him.

'Salaud!' She shouted, but he had disappeared into the dark. I wanted to know his story. I always want to know the story of those on the outside. Where did he go? I didn't imagine him returning to an empty room. I imagined him returning to a family, a well-presented house, a mother and father, a dog, and a coal fire. He does not want revolution. He cannot contemplate why anyone would. Only those with friends and laughter want revolution. Those on the fringes only want friends and laughter.

I returned to the bed and sat on the edge. The wound on my knee was still suppurating. I thought that I could quite easily take the gun from my pocket, point it to my face, and fire. I laughed long and hard. I had to leave the room. I had to leave the walls and the bed and the non-ticking clock. I had to leave some thoughts in this room. I realised that the few days that I had spent on the streets had seeped into my bones. Out there now seemed more my natural habitat than a comfortable room. To wander street to street without destination was a kind of freedom I had not experienced for a long time, in fact, ever. The open town seemed to me now a release, before returning to the pillows, the TV, the furniture, the trappings of the gaol. I belonged in the open air, without a goal of returning to wallpapered walls. There is an achievement to open spaces, a feeling that you have arrived and are not still journeying. We can grow accustomed to inclement weather, to sleeping rough. Once it is accepted the mind relaxes and the urban exterior becomes a more fitting environment, healthier in some ways than the family home.

My whole life and everything in it seemed at some point to go (as *Alice* said trying to walk up the hill) *the other way*. All my rights were lefts, all my certainties were shaken. I looked into mirrors and wondered *what if?* My life had been a clutter of things to obscure the four walls. The books, the records, the CDs, the tables and desks, the cupboards to hold even more, the chairs, furniture of every stripe, TV, boxes, cables, clutter of every sort. It was pushing me out of my own home. There was no room to move. I was bumping into things at every turn. The computer, lamps with shades, footstool, every fucking turn. I left to escape all of that as much as anything.

It is not acceptable anymore. It was not acceptable the night I booked my flight. Everything was crowding my mind; people, things, thoughts: yes, it was dreams of leaving. Everyone wants to but who has the nerve? To leave everything. Who really has the cold nerve? Or the cowardice? Is that really it? Is the leaving a way to avoid the sifting and the sorting of the objects that have formed new walls around you, that might collapse on top of you like Jenga blocks. Is it fear that makes people leave? Are they afraid of the normality of life? From, or to? Was I running away from the town because I could no longer function in it, or was I searching out a new kind of life? A new kind of life? What, as an international assassin? What an idiot! These are the things that were going through my head as I dressed. I was sweating before I had left the room.

The streets were drying in the airless night. The gutters running still, but slowly and silently. The smell of garbage was resurging after the rains. It was food, certainly, disposed of by the many cafes and restaurants. It stank and caught in the throat. The *revolutionaries* were just ahead, still drinking at the tables. I made a decision to walk through their scattered throng. I could have easily headed in the opposite direction and avoided all contact with them, but I was an individual in this alien society. I would show my individuality by walking, disrupting their solidarity. There was a determination in my steps which was in itself abnormal. As I got closer, I started thinking that I should have taken the opposite route. This thought sapped the energy from my pace and as I reached them, I slowed to a stop. Unlike the young man earlier, I did not have a drink in my hand. As expected, the voices and chatter quietened until the group was silent. Its eyes looked first from the corners, then, as I continued to stand, I became the focus of all their gazes. I was going to speak, to say something of significance, but thought better of it. I walked on. The laughter behind me was tentative at first, then kindled. It crackled in the swelling night air, until it was loud and challenging and asserted their inviolable unity. I wanted to look back, for I wanted to show them that their laughter didn't bother me. But looking back would prove that their laughter did indeed bother me. As I walked on the sound receded. Why do we care what others think? Why do we care about anything?

I arrived at the wide boulevard to the sound of a can stuttering on tarmac in the distance. In normal times this place would have been alive with people and traffic and noise. But these were not normal times. Most locals it seemed were not going out at night for fear of being caught up in some act of social unrest such as I had witnessed earlier. Here, in the more respectable quarter some cafes were certainly open, but empty. Their lights shone cold like a morgue, and the waiters who stood at the entrances looked like funeral directors. The night heat was suffocating and the shirt under my jacket clung again to my damp newly showered skin. I passed a waiter who was mopping his brow with a napkin that might normally be laid neatly over his wrist. I wanted no more restaurants, no more the distractions from my task.

I recognised the boulevard, as I had walked along it several times since my arrival. I realised that, although I did not know the hotel or the street I had earlier found myself in, I had not travelled far. My bearings had become so confused that I now believed myself to be miles from where I had been this morning. But there it was, the fountain, the café, the metro sign with the stairs. Empty now. I also felt empty. I wanted the streets busy. I wanted people going into shops and cafés and restaurants. I wanted now to hear voices and laughter. I wanted to hear traffic and the sharp trumpet of car horns. I wanted to hear friendly shouts of person to person, and the clatter of dishes and the clack of cutlery. I wanted to smell the smells of cooking, of cigarette smoke. For a moment I thought of returning to the side street and joining the young people that I had passed, but there was a lack of joy in their gathering. The times had cast a sombre shadow even over their laughter.

In the distance I heard an approaching public announcement being blasted into the night. As the police van came into view the words bounced back and forth like tennis balls off the buildings that lined the boulevard. I stood watching from the shadow of a doorway as it passed. Suddenly, the girl that I had seen moments before with the blonde hair and long print dress, was standing in the middle of the road blocking the van's route. The vehicle slowed and stopped. The bull horn barked out what I could only assume to have been a warning to move. She did not flinch. It was a standoff she had no hope of winning. The back doors were flung open and three black clad special police jumped out, rushed towards her and without any words grabbed her. Her arms and legs were flailing to free herself from their grasp. She was hurled into the back of the van. The police leapt inside and pulled the doors closed. The van moved on at its snail's pace and the bull horn announcements started again. Somewhat shaken, I stepped out from the shadowed doorway and made my way up the boulevard.

Claustrophobia. What I felt then was not induced by the heat, or of the kind we often associate with enclosed spaces; it was the claustrophobia of the edges of life itself. The older I become I feel that I have become trapped, and it is a tomb of my own making. Life moves inexorably towards corralling you into a place without hope of change. The heart stops because there is no more room left to shift yourself into. I had to come here, that's the nub of it. I really had no choice, no space left. I had to keep my heart beating and my blood pumping through my veins. Maybe that's what happened to Clara's old man. Maybe he just ran out of room. Maybe that's the easy option for all of us. Just to stop. Stop moving, stop eating, stop talking. Stop the whole business of life. And in a million years a new species can examine what happened and how it came to pass that we just stopped. There was no disease that brought us to a standstill. No war that ended us. No natural disaster that annihilated our world. Will they comprehend that people just stopped? There was no anger. There was no passion. There was no nothing. The world ended not with a bang or a whimper. The world ended with a collective shrug of the shoulders. I wrapped my hand around the gun in my pocket. There was passion. There was anger. There was that girl being bundled into the police van.

The moon sat low in the sky, setting, or rising, I didn't

know. It had not been seen, it seemed, for weeks. People should have been congregating in the streets, celebrating the end of the rains. But they were still afraid. Only the protesters seemed unafraid. And the police. And the feral children. And tourists in their ignorance. Behind the blinds, sat the families. They awaited a return of ordered streets after police and protesters leave. They had long ago given up any belief or trust in the authorities. They were as wary of them as they were of the rebels. Perhaps more so. They blamed the government who allowed the situation to reach this state. The common denominator in every protest is bad government. They didn't just lose touch with the people; they lost the people. There was big talk of new highs and record lows. Equality. It had nothing to do with their lives. It never had anything to do with their lives. There was big talk of many things. None of the big talk meant anything. The disenfranchised remained, on the edges, peripheral. The words filled a silence about the real causes. Perhaps that was their sole intention.

Is my task really any different from those out in the street? Does it spring from the same root? I would hope not as I have never associated myself with the mob, or "the great unwashed" as my grandfather used to say. When I grew up he was the only man that I believed truly did not give a damn for anyone or anything. I loved that. Some might have called it self-centred and selfish, but I saw the rebelliousness in his actions, or lack thereof. Well, that was until I was about eleven when he told me that he had wasted his life. He was a jeweller by trade but felt he had sold out by becoming one. I asked him what he really wanted to do and he told me that he just wanted to hit the road and walk around the world. He wanted to take odd jobs when the money ran out and be accountable to no one. But he had become a jeweller and been unhappy his whole life. His daughter, my mother, sniffed at this. That was when I became aware that most people are unfulfilled in life. Grandfather was bitter, not a rebel. Through him I saw absolutely everyone I met like that, including myself. I didn't give a damn about lecturing or the students or my colleagues. At last I found my true vocation: to hit the road and walk around the world. The sorry fact is, that to live like that you generally need cash, and to get cash...well, you get the drift. Unless you become a Sam Blue. But his world was just one small town. Maybe it was even smaller than that.

So, grandfather was a kind of anti-role model. Maybe that's how I got to where I am and wandered away from those life borders, defined by mother's sniffs, a long time ago. While thinking that, at the very same moment, I seemed to have been thinking of my footsteps hitting the street. My grandfather and his troubles and my feet pounding the streets. My thoughts cross oceans in a moment. That power of thought, to shrink time and distance, might appear something to be celebrated, but it feels safer perhaps not to acknowledge or entertain.

And so increasingly I kept silent when my thoughts would drift beyond borders during conversations. It had become more prevalent just before the principal suggested I take a few weeks off, which prompted me to go to Rome. Even while he was speaking to me, I started to drift. I remember I was thinking about the bicycle helmet that I had stolen from Nancy Murski. There was a big fuss about that. Nancy had burst into a politics class and attacked *Spaghetti Legs* O'Dowd with a bicycle pump. She really set about her. The boys apparently couldn't stop laughing. The more serious side was that Nancy was thrown out of school to return to *Smalltown* and a job in the sugar factory. I heard that from some of the other students, but they might have been making it up. The thing was I really had nothing against Nancy; I had simply enjoyed the fun and excitement of taking the helmet. Anyway, I was thinking about all this when the principal was droning

172

on about my 'odd behaviour.' I wasn't so deep into my reverie that I couldn't follow what was being said.

'What do you mean by that?'

'There have been some reports of you drifting off in class.'

'In what way? Have these been official complaints? Shouldn't I have been informed if they were?'

'No, no, no. On the contrary. People are concerned about your health.'

'People? My health?'

'Look, the long and short of it is that we think that maybe you should take a little time off.'

'We?'

And the conversation went on like that. It was the first time I was consciously aware that I could respond while still thinking of something else. I thought that displayed a particular skill that shouldn't be dismissed easily. The trick is to separate the mind from the here and now. Why is that looked on less as a skill and more an illness? What if you can't control it? What if the mind just wanders because it can? Others can do it too. Sometimes you're talking to someone and they say *What?* as though they had just been shaken awake.

So, I embraced this ability and extended it to other modes of my being. Along that Parisian boulevard, while my feet moved and my heel hurt, my body propelled itself forward, upright, while thinking, that is my reflection in that store window. Six million years for this? I pulled my gaze away and looked ahead. We are not meant to see ourselves in such a way. On.

12

There is something about my thoughts taking me outside of the here and now. They provide a certain comfort; they pass time and they fill time. When my mother sat by the window writing her poetry, I think she had surrendered totally to this. When she spoke to me it was as though she was just visiting the present. When she walked her feet were always just that touch above the earth. She glided across floors.

'Horizon is the perfect word, don't you think? The sun rises, the sun sinks in the horizon. When you say it, you imagine the sun and its colour. You see the colour?'

'Yes.'

'Good boy.'

It is to her I owe my love of literature and learning. I can't say that she sharpened my critical faculties, but she certainly sold me the idea that perhaps, within books, lay better worlds than the one we inhabited. She told me that fulfilment in life could only be achieved by stepping outside of it. I don't know that she had said this to anyone outside the house, but certainly she had something of a reputation in town. Some of the guys around called her my 'crazy' mother. I didn't like that. It hurt me. I wanted her to maybe be like all the other mothers. As I got older, though, and I wanted everyone to be like her, because she was interesting, and seemed more at peace with herself than the crazy bastards that walked around where I grew up.

People begin to die when their memories become untethered. When order is lost, and they blow around like September leaves.' She read that to me from one of her notebooks, and then said, 'I'm going to write a poem about this now.'

With such a mother it could have gone either way: I would write; or I would never attempt anything creative. My first attempt at a work of fiction was just after I had left university and just before I secured my first position in a minor college a few miles outside of the town. It was a novel called *The Everlasting Maybe Not*. When I write, I thought, it will be the sound of the hammer hitting the anvil. Again. Again. Again. The words striking against the page. Again. Again. Again. I was about a third of the way through when I realised that I had absolutely nothing to say to anyone about anything, unsure what was original thought and what was *deja entendu*. (I am still of that mind now, but that has not stopped me saying it.) The manuscript petered out and was then slipped into a drawer. Every chapter a stinking flower. My second bash at it was ten years later when I was firmly ensconced in my current position. Its working title for some months was *Mea Culpa*, but it became *Pseudepigrapha of the Mushroom*. The story took the reader through one year of an ancient magician's life. Once completed it joined the other in the same drawer. I took the greatest perverse pleasure in doing this. No one read one word of it. I deemed it a great success. I intended afterwards to write a crime story without a crime, or a love story without love. A novel without a novelist where the reader would insert their own story within a story, their own fiction. I was ahead of my time. Or not. My words on the page constantly questioned, signifying others' words, others' thoughts, others' ideas. The words would be shaped into a hoped for new form, but my voice always intruding, indicating nothing. The drawer like a coffin for a dead thing.

My story is no longer far behind me. All before is the passing of time. Each footstep a cascade of thought. I was park bound.

I stopped to remove my jacket. I thought at first that I might be ill, but that was not the case. The night had grown warmer. It felt like the sun was out. I was tired. I wanted to lie down again. I could of course have returned to the hotel room, but I had to be outside in the open. I knew my destination was the park I had left earlier. I wanted to return to the same bench and lay down. But what did it matter which park or which bench? We get these ideas in our heads and become so focussed on them that there can be no change. Some things are how they must be. Sam Blue and his trolley would stop every night at the same bench in town. Did he see that bench as home? His constant wandering up and down the Main Street, looking in bins, in gutters, filling out his days until he could lay down that great lion's head of his on that bench. And his trolley containing all of his garbage possessions by his side. In all the years I never saw Sam add to or take away from its contents. I never saw him look through them even. If there were any changes of clothing I don't know where or when those items were changed. He always seemed to me to be wearing the same stuff. Apart from his footwear. In summer he had sandals on his feet, in winter a well-worn pair of brown boots.

Maybe Sam found out a long time ago what I am realising now. He rejected a roof over his head. He rejected the clutter of society. But that would be as far as that comparison goes, for Sam was close to being insane. He would shout at people and stand at corners dribbling and making animal sounds. However attractive the idea of shouting at strangers, I have always resisted. Resisted? Too much of a damn coward, that's me. I would not or could not shout at strangers. Instead, I caused them mischief, some upset to their lives, leaving my mark in some way. They are all my *Chanticleer* story, every day the thirty second of March. Me, trying to outfox the world.

It appears that more thought goes into my japes than actually does. The truth is it comes more naturally and is more often than not a spur of the moment thing. An opportunity might present itself for a minor theft and so I go with it. Those who have never stolen even a sweet or trinket in childhood cannot understand the rush of joy doing so brings. For those that have not pilfered since childhood might I suggest they experience the naughty pleasure in adulthood?

The Flaneur

The punishment on being caught is obviously greater than that a child would receive, but for that the gratification increases. If it is a minor theft — and for our purposes it really is all that's needed — a term of incarceration is unlikely. A small fine or a rap on the knuckles by law enforcement will suffice. Of course, if the crime should gain traction within the community, then you might risk ostracization (often a bonus). Or some do-gooders might decide to take up your case and vow to set you back on the straight and narrow. Might I suggest with the latter that you welcome them into your life. Give them a hard luck story; have them believe that you need to be diverted from the stony path of immorality. At the first chance take a small amount from their wallet. It might not be enough to be noticed, and if noticed it might be swept aside as their own carelessness that it has gone missing. At the second chance take a library card perhaps, or a bank card. If the latter, might I suggest that you don't use it? Chuck it on the fire. While they are toiling through the weeks to rehabilitate you, target items of their clothing: gloves or a scarf or hat. Eventually you will be suspected and accused. Be outraged and angry. Demand they apologise and then dismiss them. A nice fantasy but I must confess that no-one ever offered to lead me back on the path to a decent and constructive life. But if they had, this would have been my strategy. Those thoughts propelled me another half block faster than the snapping jaws of the Dracula ant.

It is the filling in of time that I have always found curious, and pointless. Its dilation is of some interest. Boring activities pass more slowly than interesting ones, but, obviously, that cannot be. I have played around with that concept often when going from point A to point B. Walking, in itself, takes a fixed period of time between the two points, if you move on each occasion at a consistent rate. But that time may appear to pass more quickly if you distract yourself with another activity. I have often sung songs or read poetry to myself in order to make a journey appear shorter. The distance has not changed but the experience of covering it has. You in effect lie to your mind about it. I tried this out as I saw the park about half a block from where I was. Several minutes had passed and I had not recited one poem or sung one song. As so often in life I became distracted by thoughts, other than those intended. I have been considering the element of chance in our actions. If I had taken one road rather than another would I have ended up in the predicament I found myself in? The question itself cannot be answered with any degree of certainty, but I have difficulty with the question in the first place. Once the action is taken, it seems there was only one possible road to take. Once the road has been stepped upon, and walked, the others are no longer choices; in fact, it becomes apparent that they did not ever exist as choices. In this there is a certainty to our actions. We could not have done other than what we have done because everything ever has brought us to this point. Now, we may look back and say I chose this road because it offered possibility of a better outcome than any of the others. Even if the outcome is less fruitful than what you hoped, the rest is irrelevant. Perhaps the road you thought was the worst might have offered surprising benefits. No matter, as it's not the option you chose. Thoughts of this nature pass time certainly, but a broken mirror does not piece itself together. I was now measuring distance covered in shards of temporal asymmetry and the ebb and flow of the nagging pain from my heel rubbing against my shoe. Much can be overcome by thoughts of a philosophical nature, or the promise of an ice cream.

There was some commotion up ahead. Figures were moving about restlessly at the park railings. As I got closer my mind sharpened to the moment. Should they rush me or attack I would have little chance of outrunning them or fighting them off. Of course, I could have crossed the road and disappeared down a side street to return later, but I had

had enough of skulking and continued to approach them. There were five males on their feet kicking and punching one who was curled on the ground. I considered calmly walking past and finding the entrance to the park, but it was not a choice. I immediately cried out *Ho!* and continued towards the assault. They stopped and looked towards me. And then they walked away in the opposite direction.

I can't say my presence in any way intimidated them. At first I thought they might believe me to be a figure of authority, but then I saw that the figure on the ground was uniformed. Perhaps they had recognised him as an officer that had laid into them with a baton some hours or days before. Perhaps his uniform was a symbol to them of violence perpetrated by the state. As I got closer the officer rolled over and I saw that he was badly beaten. The mask of blood could not hide his identity, though: it was the young cop who had accosted me on my first night and set me on this road of turmoil. I kneeled down and looked into his eyes, one of which was partly hanging out of the socket. There was a temptation, brought about by the desire to help, to gently push it back in. Thinking this might cause worse damage, I refrained. His radio hissed from his jacket breast and crackled loudly and a voice spoke. I couldn't make out what it said but I leaned towards it, and said *Hello? Hello? Ambulance. Apporte une ambulance!* The young man was staring at me as his hand reached up and grabbed my throat. He began choking me. I grabbed his radio and hit his hand until his grip loosened, then dropped it and stood up. For a second I thought of kicking him, but looking at the blood drenched uniform I saw he might be ready for death. The white symbols on his stab vest were now a darkening pink. He tried to say something but his front teeth had been smashed in. I turned and walked away.

Under any other circumstances I would have stayed with him until help arrived, but the situation made such a humane action quite impossible. I would have been questioned. They would have wanted details. They would have demanded my passport. Why are you in the country? Why are you travelling in such a time of global danger? What could I say? That I came to see the most beautiful city in the world? That I came to see it fall? That I came to bring horror and violence and betray that beauty? And then I would have had to justify every thought and intention. Is that what I am afraid of? Are my actions just one step further down the road from pilfering small objects and shifting blame? I would not entertain such thoughts and tried to move on. Is that what I have always done?

Three years ago I got a call from my mother.

I have bad news.

She told me that there had been an accident and my father was dead. She told me that she was terribly sorry to break such news in a telephone call but that she needed me to return home immediately.

'Was it something to do with his weights? He spent so much time with them. Was it that? The equipment looked like instruments from a torture chamber. I mean all those hours he spent. What was that for? What was he really pushing against?'

She interrupted me before I went on another ramble. Sometimes I had trouble keeping my interior dialogue where it belonged. In medieval times the ruling body of the church understood this inner voice and tried to suppress it. That voice could spur revolutions. That voice could inspire insurrection. That voice in the head could question their power. And so they called the voice the devil and warned people to be afraid of it. They told people this voice was evil and whispered to capture their souls. And they demanded that people tell them of the plotting in their heads. In confession they could unburden and free themselves of the devil. They did as they were told, and many insurrections uttered only in thought were nipped in the bud. But for many the thoughts would continue unrelieved, then unconfessed, and these people, would walk through their lives dragging the burden of guilt.

'Listen to me, listen to me, it wasn't the weights. Your father took his own life.'

I have heard those words every day since.

13

I didn't belong in this city, in this country. I knew this. I understood that I was an outsider, a visitor. I walked these streets and they were new and exciting to me, and in every step I took a new adventure unfolded. Such is the power of the strange: it creates stories. Behind me a young police officer lay in his own blood. What had he said to his assailants to provoke such a brutal reaction? Or was he just a symbol of something else, a bigger problem? I could have returned and asked him, before he died, what happened. Had he stopped them, or had they stopped him? Did he imagine that his uniform was a shield against violent blows? What made him want to become an officer of the law? Did he want to protect the vulnerable and weak in society, or did he want power to exploit them? Or did he just wake up one morning and think that he had to do something to put bread on the table every day? One story leads to another. One question opens others. It's maybe enough that I put one foot in front of another. Every day.

More time passed. I arrived at the park gate on the south side of the park. It was closed, of course. It would have been locked many hours before, perhaps by the park-keeper who had locked it the night I had slept on the bench. I looked down at the gravelled ground, and memories of sharp pain crossed my knee. With more consideration, I realised the climbing manoeuvre would have been easier if I had stayed close to the concrete column by the gate hinges. There was a space at the top before the first gold painted speared railing. I climbed easily at first and tossed my jacket over. It landed on the other side with a huge bang. I had forgotten the gun in the pocket. I stopped my climbing and listened in the amplified post-shot silence. Nothing. *Idiot*, I said through clenched teeth as I continued my ascent. I did not jump from the top this time but swung my leg over and rested my foot on the mane of a cast iron lion's head that made up the gates ornate design. From there it was an easy drop down.

On the ground, inside, I examined the jacket for any burns or a bullet hole. It was intact. The gun must have fallen out before hitting the path. It lay a few feet from the jacket. I retrieved it, replaced it in the pocket, and put the jacket on. While doing so, my mind, for a moment, tossed up the image of the blonde police officer who was thrown from her horse. It occurred to me that she might have been killed, and there was I robbing the dead of a gun. A momentary twinge can easily drag you down even further.

A trickle of sweat ran down my back. From the distance a loud wailing of sirens. Looking back, I could see through the railings flashing lights of police cars and an ambulance. They flew past the gates and up the boulevard. As I pressed against railings, I saw them come to a stop. The young officer owed me a debt of gratitude rather than his hand around my throat. I headed for the pond.

I could have been resting in a comfortable, though musty, hotel room. Who would swap a comfortable bed for a park bench? Well, some do. And there it was: my bench. It was to the side of the pond at the bottom of the hill I was on. I felt much like one does returning home after being away for some time. A sweet pleasure. Someone, children probably, had discarded a pram they had been playing with. I thought of those who had robbed me, imagining them as the children pushing the pram, my mind too tired to create new faces. Was this the contraption that I had seen upon waking on my first morning in the park?

The pram lay on its side by the grass verge. I could have walked past it, but there was something that demanded I set right the object and leave it somewhere easily noticed, to be collected by the park attendants perhaps. As I righted it, and pushed it along a few yards, I noticed a figure walking around the pond. A fellow traveller, one perhaps without the option of a room. I stood holding on to the pram's handle — lest it rolled and came crashing into a different journey — and stared at the figure. No doubt he had his story, very different from my own. No doubt. Everyone has their story. Some of them overlap. Quiet coincidences, things shared together and apart. Most are of no interest to me whatsoever. It's enough sorting out your own without having to listen to others'. Autobiographies insult library shelves. The art of storytelling has suffered greatly in modern times. To be perfectly honest it took something of a dip after Homer. My mother often said that with a smile playing on her lips.

When I was young, I thought she must be writing stories while sitting at the window. When she told me it was poems, I was a bit confused. Were poems not just stories too; but shorter? Not until I read her poetry many years later did I realise that those hours had been spent considering philosophical ideas. Her writing told no tales of family gatherings, no paeans to motherhoods, gave no personal insights into day-to-day survival. Instead, in her many notebooks, she contemplated morality and reason, the irrational in human decisions. The struggles within her poetry that reflected a mind owing more to the analytical than the emotional. When I finally read her words I realised that I didn't really know her. I mean, these thoughts took up the best part of her day as she sat by the window. I wondered why she hadn't engaged more with others, discussed the philosophical problems of the day with like-minded people. There were certainly enough reading groups in town. Did she believe herself to be better? There I go, pushing a theory that my mother was some kind of snob. When she was alive I never thought any such thing. How strange that time and distance can make us consider the most unlikely traits in others. I will have to bow to my younger self who certainly knew my mother better than I ever could. She was a tender, softly spoken woman, who, although not a natural mother, gave me a great deal of her time. No, I realise now, my future behaviour cannot be put down to an unloving past.

Then what can it be put down to? To whom do I owe my current state of mind? Why have I dealt with problems in such an extreme manner? Can I not be like others and simply move on with life? I sometimes wonder if the questions I ask myself were considered by my mother as she sat by the window. Her poetry suggests she did. Certainly the philosophical questioning within her poetry pointed towards someone who understood something of the behaviour of others. She might have told me the journey is less important than the destination. The fact is I know full well how I got here. Some thoughts, though, are unacceptable and so are pushed away. How can we go on with the unacceptable? My mind is as my mind is; determining why will not change the here and now or the there and then.

Detective Jay Plangman investigated my father's demise. I was happy to prove that I had been miles away at the time of his actions, for the detective had the look of a man who saw foul play in everything. He was trying to find the exact time of death. I told him I didn't know as I wasn't in town. My mother had called me and told me to come home because my father was dead. She had then apparently returned to her window rather than phoning the police. When I arrived the next morning my father was still hanging there, his buff body horribly incongruous with all that comes with death by hanging. I asked Detective Plangman if he was suggesting my mother or I strangled him and then strung him up. I told him the very idea was ludicrous.

'You seem angry,' he said.

'If you're insinuating that I killed my father then you're right; I'm angry.'

'You weren't close?'

185

'That's a crime now? Better arrest half the country.'

His suspicions seemed to rest on my mother who could offer no explanation as to why he might want to end his life. He spoke to her in the living room, and, based on the tone of the chat with me, I hung around. He was surprised when she told him that she hadn't been in the garage *for some years*.

'You never visited your own garage?'

'Well, why would I? The car sits in the driveway and I don't pump iron.'

'But this day you went?'

'Yes.'

'Why?'

'I wanted to show him a poem.'

'Were you in the habit of showing him poetry?'

'I never showed him my poetry.'

'Then why this time?'

'I really don't know. Curious, isn't it?'

'What is it you do exactly?'

'Exactly? I'm not sure about the exactitude, but I suppose others might say that I contemplate life.'

'From that window?'

'Mainly. It's a pleasant outlook. The blossom trees are particularly lovely at this time of the year. They bring a sense of calm to the contemplative mind.'

'Your husband didn't seem particularly depressed?'

'No more or less than everyone else. I'm sure your job must result in some depression.'

'Rarely enough to prompt tying a rope around my neck.'

'Maybe there's a point we reach where we feel it really is too much of a bother to continue. Sometimes people don't know they're hanging by a thread until it's too late.'

The detective went over to the window and looked out for a few seconds before sighing. He nodded towards me.

'Your son told me that you spend your days writing. Isn't that a bit unusual?'

I was sitting in a chair staring at a frayed bit of carpet. Hearing my words in his mouth made it a betrayal. She must have felt that too. Her reply seemed to blow across a frozen landscape some miles away.

'Writing? Unusual? Would it suit your turn of mind if I stitched perhaps, Detective? Or maybe crocheted?'

It was not, I imagine, the usual reaction to a husband's suicide, and may have added to his suspicions. But what the detective was dealing with was a woman who was not *usual*. Maybe I inherited that from her. And if I did, then so what? What did any of it matter? There were other more important things to consider at that moment in time. And my father? We all know that the dead do not reawaken. They feel nothing, like a stone at the bottom of a cold pool, feeling nowt or nothing, breath shut like a coffin lid, closed forever; an eternity of silence. The worm or flame strips us to the same fate. Those with gods must have an easier time. I've no idea if father found God or eternal silence at the end of his rope.

My hands loosened their grip on the pram handle, and it rolled some yards downhill before toppling over much as I had found it. I couldn't see whoever was walking around the pond but decided to walk down anyway. If he was anywhere near the bench I was making towards I could scare him off by waving the gun. There were enough crazy angry people around that it would not be considered out of the ordinary. Strange days indeed when someone waving a weapon around in a locked park in the dead of night might not feel entirely unexpected. But then many things we consider outrageous can be accepted as the norm given the passage of time and fresh circumstances.

As I walked down the hill my thoughts were with the novel that brought me there. I feel that it should be in my mind constantly for it was my reason for planning the taking of a life. Whatever the situation that shouldn't be considered an

Everest of a decision. For that very reason should it not then occupy my every thought? But it was not so. I had grown accustomed to my task and so familiar with the trigger for that task that I could quite easily shove it to the side for most of the day. At that moment though it popped up and demanded some academic consideration again.

It struck me that most novels set in a university are not very good. There are obviously a few exceptions to this, but in general I do not rush to the *university novel* for any kind of enlightenment on the struggles of humankind. And how wise the writer was in recognising this and having the university play a minor role in the telling of his story. The campus is nothing more than a backdrop; it could have easily been set around a bank, or a parks department. Certainly, the dreaming spires may have pulled in some readers who believe themselves to be a cut above the mob. (Grandfather?) That, of course, has nothing to do with the author. As with families, the writer doesn't choose his or her reader. Likely those who write *university novels* have never truly grown up. They probably had their best days there and ache to return. Imagine treating any reader like that? Selfish egotism.

Those were some of the thoughts that propelled me to the bench. Down the hill and around the pond other ramblings tumbled out, but I will not relate them. I will erase them. If this scene was on film you would see me stutter in a series of jump cuts from the hill to the bench, rather than softly fade out and in. There would be a disarming quality to it because I am allowed to play with my thoughts. I am allowed to arrange my thoughts as I please. I am allowed to wipe them. That is how it is. But, of course, nothing has been that planned. The uncomfortable fact was that I didn't know how I got there. Distance was obviously travelled but I could not recall what thoughts filled that time. Even seconds before. I struggled to remember. This is definitely a new behaviour, and one I do not feel entirely comfortable with.

The Flaneur

Whoever I saw from atop the hill had gone. Their disappearance left something, though. Perhaps a resonance of having been. Not in my memory specifically, but in the actual park. I have often thought that people leave something of their presence when they leave a place. As though they are occupying that space still. My wanderings over those days are somehow still echoing in the cafés, the flat, the shop, the rooms, the boulevards, the bateaux. All still tell something of me, as though I could turn to them again in a moment, as though flicking back through the pages of a book. I have blown through my life like a piece of paper caught in the wind. There has been no real sense of order, no sense of anything. One thing has not so much led to another as fallen into it. I have lived on the ragged edge of being, without purpose, to arrive at the moment in time for no particular reason. I might as easily have been somewhere else. I might as well have been someone else.

As I sat in the hard and damp seat I leaned forward with my head in my hands. It is an archetypal position at times of great stress. The hands hold the head as though keeping the thoughts in place as they rush forward, pouring down towards the frontal lobe. The eyes are closed to project them behind the eyelids. You are never closer to yourself than at those times. It triggers an emotional response, perhaps because you are gently stroking the primordial self, the root of your being. It is, of course, a dangerous territory to explore. It is the subject of all great art.

The truth is I am unmoored from reality. Unlike those who have suffered mental collapse, my unravelling of those ropes was a deliberate attempt to survive in a world that was sinking under the weight of its own stupidity. I was prepared to go down with the ship. The problem for others is that they do not see what is clear to me. In fact they deny the obvious. When I tried to speak of the floods in town they refused to engage.

'Parts of the town are being swept away.'

'There's always heavy rains at this time of year.'

'But the lives that are being lost.'

'There's been some accidents. Look, how about we go for a beer?'

How can catastrophe be happening but not be recognised?

I constantly place myself not just outside of others but apart from myself. This is, I know, akin to a mental illness, but let's be honest, who stares into a mirror and knows who the fuck they are? Go on, do it. Stare deep into your eyes. Try to tell me you know anything that's going on behind them. The fact is you try to fool yourself. You make up absurd stories to justify yourself to others. Your ridiculous fictions become more real, closer to truth that the daily junk you are fed by others; the grotesque spectacle you are asked to swallow daily. We escape by running towards cracked theories and absurd anecdotes. Society casually averts its attention from the flickers of reality. No one sips from the clear glass of truth. I refused to roll the weighted dice.

The moon hung, fragmented, behind a row of chestnut trees. From where I sat I could have been looking at an Indian *Tholu Bommalaata*, the trees a shadow pinned to a screen. How wonderful the moon looked during the performance. Full and fat, like an electrical current giving the moon its *mooness*. In another state of mind I could have enjoyed the show. My mother would have enjoyed it. She liked to sit in the dark and look out at its rise. She appreciated its otherworldliness. This is no mere fantasy woven to endow her existence with poetry.

'I am the moon,' she told me once.

'But you're here.'

'No, that's just what you see with your eyes. I can leave here in an instant. The imagination is greater than anything.'

'But I see you.'

'You only think you see me.'

But I do see you. I see you now, mother. Thinking yourself

a Virginia Woolf; thinking yourself different, above others; thinking yourself taking a stroll down by the river.

I shrugged off unpleasant memories as I lay down on the bench. I swept away yesterdays. For those who dwell in memories become drenched in sobs, a weeping past, a chthonic nightmare. But I could consider the future. I could stay here. Get a flat. Become a *boulevardier*. I could write stories and tell tall tales. The rich and the rogues would slap me on the back and call me a wonderful fellow. I would run up bills in restaurants and bars. When money was demanded I would laugh and saunter away like a man of means, always waiting on a cheque coming through. And always tomorrow.

My position was such that the moon was at the back of my head. I could deal with that. I could deal with not seeing. I could deal with not engaging. I no longer needed a world of people. Did I ever? People with their stories. All their foolish interactions, their love affairs, their tears, their jealousies, their griefs, their boasts, their insults, their laughter — Stop! Close. Your. Eyes.

I had been taking a stack of books from the library when I dropped the lot on the floor. Clara looked over immediately and rushed over to help me, or save the books. Some students laughed. At some books falling? No, it wasn't that: it was me. It was me dropping the books that produced the snickers. Clara gave them a look and they stopped. If I had done so the hilarity would have increased.

Later, I went over the incident in my mind, and thought that I must have looked a comical figure trying to catch the falling volumes. Like an inept juggler. Maybe the laughter was warranted. Maybe the laughter was spontaneous. Maybe I think too hard about trivial things. Maybe I think too hard. I wondered what Sam Blue thought of. What images went through old Sam's head as he wandered up and down the town? What griefs did he harbour? His mind couldn't have been a blank canvas. Had he succeeded in blocking everything out? Did he care nothing for the giggles, the insults, the looks? Is that what you must become? A derelict pushing a trolley up and down the street all day, thinking only of food and drink and shelter? Perhaps he had become the animal, free of societies constraints, that we all dream of. No. He was a sad figure who had lost everything that he had to lose, until eventually he lost his mind. He was no one to envy. Pity was the natural reaction. And when you run out of pity, there's always anger.

My eyes reopened. My head hurt leaning back against the wood and cast iron. I removed my jacket, folded it, and put it behind my head. I felt the gun safe in the pocket, but it was not uncomfortable enough for me to remove. Of course, where else would I place it while I slept? On the path under the bench? And if a policeman should wander up? I imagined sleeping on municipal property would be considered a misdemeanour. Sleeping over a loaded police revolver might be considered more. And what of when they questioned where I obtained such a weapon? I stole it from an officer who was brought down by violent protesters. That answer would guarantee a kicking. No, all in all, the gun was safer under my head.

From where I lay, to the left, I could see the pond. The water lay still, reflecting the sky. A breath of cloud passed over the water and figures formed. They walked, singly, in pairs, in small groups. Children, men, and women. It is as though the park had come alive, as it would on a sunny holiday afternoon, long ago. I don't know why there must be this historical aspect to the strange visions that come upon me. Some form of macular degeneration is melding perhaps remembrances of gentler times. Or do I resort to a time I cannot possibly identify with; something so outside of my understanding, that I cannot find fault in it; a time that cannot know me and cannot expect anything of me? Did my mother have these imaginings and pass them on to me? Is that why she spent her days by the window? Did she have visions of past lives? Young ladies with their summer dresses, light colours, the jut of the bustle, corsets, bonnets, with the parasols to protect them from the sun, the faces pale, diaphanous, eyes down to reflect the modernity of innocence, naivety, and flirtatiousness; all from books read, from movies seen. They cannot harm me. The gentler times that produced wars and slavery. The great lies, each generation telling itself how well it's doing. I can no more conjure up the reality of times past than I can fly to the moon. I manifest warped renderings of things seen or told to me, that are themselves copies of others' past. I have only the here and the now. I have only the moment.

My eyes opened. There were no figures, only the moonlit park, empty of all but me. I turned again, lying on my back, looking up. Through slight clouds the dark sky showed some faint stars. I defy anyone not to feel something of their own mortality at such times. The significance or insignificance of being. I questioned my very existence. There is no choice in the things I do; they were done and that was it. I could say that I did this rather than that, but then when I considered what was actually done I asked if it could have been done any other way. Did I truly have the last word on it, or was it chosen for me? If this was the case then my very existence is pointless.

And it struck me that I had this conversation with myself before. Many times. No, but more recently. Before I found the policeman lying in a bloody heap. Thoughts recurring. Does that give them more significance and the world more shape? Maybe the town I grew up in never existed and the people, my mother and father, constructions to colour a story that never happened. (No – I saw her daily by the window.) Am I predicting the past as my story unfolds? My father in the garage pushing against weights, Clara lying night after night with a man half dead or half alive? And what about the places in the towns, or even the towns themself? The bookstore? The bars? The college? My colleagues? And the things done, like the petty thefts? Created? The extreme weather? The child's building blocks have been built high, but some have fallen. The reality structure is under attack.

I pushed these thoughts from my mind as I have done in the recent past. There is nothing to be gained from this line of enquiry. If anything, it had brought me to some sorry state. I reminded myself that I was lying on a park bench, in a foreign country, after midnight, with a gun in my pocket and an assassin's plan in my head. This cannot be deemed *la dolce vita*. What did the neanderthal think while lying on his back in a cave? Food and fucking certainly. These are dreams that we share with all the animals. But beyond those basic needs the primitive mind must have drifted to problem solving. How to kill an animal more efficiently than wrestling it to the ground and laying into it with fists and feet and teeth? A technique perhaps that would allow distance and therefore an element of safety. Throwing stones only angered your prey. To cause damage to the creature would take a stone too large to throw accurately. A long stick, heavy enough to give momentum, but light enough to feel comfortable in your hand. But that again would just be like a stone and inflict little damage. A higher level of thought would be engaged. Only sharp objects break skin. A sharp stone, a broken branch. The end of your stick might be fashioned into a point. How would that be done? Well, if a sharp stone can pierce flesh it can pierce wood. Hitting the wood with the stone would take some of the wood off the top, leaving a point. The group would watch the creature fashion his weapon and throw his weapon. At that point there would have been a realisation, an interest in this stick with the sharp fashioned end. An animal couldn't contemplate such things. To consider something that exists, but in another form, is human.

As I lay on the bench, I forced myself to be as wise as the neanderthal and create something new from what existed. Something that could advance our species. We must have crossed into a thought space more sophisticated than anything that had gone before on this planet. I am in awe of the neanderthal. I fell into a pre-historic dream that carried me across oceans and time and millennia. I was pulled from this dream just before I was snapped in the jaws of a sabre-toothed tiger. I came up with nothing to propel human evolution.

The sun was rising. The colour of that tiger. Above the horizon. Another location, I could have watched it shine through the Eifel Tower or the Arc de Triomphe. Instead, it came through the glistening trees. A murmuration of starlings swirled, bent and twisted in the sky. I watched in sleepy fascination.

14

That tiger scratches at my soul after waking. Proust's metempsychosis. The morning dew sparkles on the grass and I remember why everything hurts. I put my jacket on and stand. In the distance birds and the jangle of a key in a lock as though I am hearing the sounds for the first time. I am in the here and now. The moment. When I awoke it was from the memories of the last days. If I don't shift the park-keeper will enter and remember me as the madman who was perched on his gates. The one who took a death-defying leap and tore the leg of his trouser and the knee of his leg. He would have to report me, as it must be part of his job. Trespassers. I am a trespasser now. That must be added to my crimes committed on this earth, and others about to be committed. I am no better than the immoral protagonist in the novel. But he is better than me for he embraces his actions. I run from who I am. He is at peace with who he is. My mind is a storm of denials and excuses, a broken thing. My father's mind must have been broken, but he was dumb to tell it to anyone. And my mother? What sort of person sits by a window for their life? But then what sort of person is anyone? Everyone seeming crazy to everyone else. The passionate and dispassionate eventually amount to the same thing. Those who march in the street are little different from those that sit at home. Those who believe are no different from those who do not. Those who do are ultimately no different from those who do nothing. Things my mother said that might have helped me understand her, just opened up other possibilities, other questions.

'Son, you just live long enough for the old battles to not really matter anymore. You've fought them and won some and lost some and none of it seems important anymore. What is important? Maybe the act of breathing. And thinking.'

The Flaneur

My thoughts will be the death of me. They rattle around like stones in a tin can, constantly shifting. I have gone over this before. Describing it differently. If someone could read my thoughts or hear my thoughts, would they know me any better than a passing stranger? Would they know me as I know myself? Well, that's not much. Everything is about history and memory. Without it there is no civilisation. My thoughts…my thoughts…But I cannot be the man who digs too deep. What motivates me must lie just under the plough.

I have a day to kill. Hours of wandering this city. It will be my last day here, perhaps ever. I should start afresh. I should wander like the tourist I am. No, I am not a tourist here to experience a city; I am here to track my prey. I have come prepared to the land of Proust and Hugo, Camus, Sartre and Beauvoir, the land of Matisse and Renoir. The land of everything I love. I have come with a gun. I have come to use it. I have come to murder. I have murder in my eyes. I have murder on my mind. Assassin. The coward with a gun.

I must leave here. I must walk out of the park for the last time. I must fill my day, spend time. I feel clearer in my head than ever. Something has gone from me but I can't grasp what. A burden has been lifted. Is it that I am nearing the end of my journey? Is it that I have made a decision? It has forced me to confront at last myself and my place in the world at this precise moment in time. All my life I have had a feeling that I was doing nothing more than passing through. Each experience leading unresisted to the next but without real purpose. Was everything I have done for the sole reason of just doing? Is that the weight and worth of actions? Should I have sat more with friends, laughing, talking, and drinking wine? Would that have made everything richer and more fulfilling? Perhaps I should have joined in more and become the life and soul of life's party. They could have called me Georgie and slapped my back and laughed with me. I could have been more giving of my time, my experience, my knowledge. I could have been a better person than I am. I could have married and attended reunions, gone off for weekends with the boys. returned with tales of innocence and lies. We could have had children, made people to carry on the old genes. I could have been a respected member of the community and joined boards and clubs that maintained the towns values. I could have been a million other people. But I was made to be outside of these things. I was different.

'You're a special boy,' mother said, 'and will do wonders in this life.'

I walked through life believing her words. Different indeed, but nothing special. What gave her the right to damn me? What gave her the right to separate me from others? I am not disengaged; I am just engaged in another way. I couldn't follow the given way of the world. Should I be condemned for that? Should I care?

These thoughts of alienation brought me back to the novel. Why do so many characters have absent parents? Gladbody's mother has died, Morris's too, and Calvert's parents are mentioned but never seen. Holly has been ruined by hers. There's a lack of children too, as if everyone exists in a single tier of humankind. Barstowe is childless. Doesn't Barstowe's wife mention this? I reach into my jacket pocket but the book is gone. I am certain that it was dropped in the park, but my certainties these days are pretty worthless. I could return and try to find it, but what does it matter now? If I believe Barstowe's wife mentions being childless then that's how it is. Why would the author have her mention it unless it was in some way significant to the story and the characterisation? I try to remember the wife's name and it comes to mind in an instant, like a cog turning and clicking into place. Her name is Barbara. She is the only person who comes out of the whole sordid mess of a story with any moral authority, and yet her mind has come loose from its moorings. I am considering whether Barbara is meant to be viewed as an actual character

198

in the story or is she a symbol of…of what? What is a reader to understand from this? That the only way to survive morally in this world is not to engage with it? That is a preposterous idea and one that shifts the novel into the genre of miserabilism. And yet, regardless of the rampant immorality of pretty much all of the characters, the story is presented with a spring in its step.

A bicycle swishes past me and brakes suddenly. The cyclist takes off his helmet and shakes out his long hair, and amongst his rant I hear the word *mort*. I'm too tired for French so I reply,

'I'm sorry, I was distracted.'

'Do you know how fast I was going?' he asks in English.

'No.'

'No? Well, neither do I but it was pretty damn fast.'

He seemed to take in my appearance and his annoyance shifts to concern. He walks towards me, guiding his cycle with one hand on the handlebar.

'Are you all right? You look pretty shaken.'

'I was just thinking of something else.'

'These are busy roads, man.'

'Yes.'

'You're not from here either? A fellow traveller.'

'No.'

'It's a busy city.'

'It is.'

'You look in shock, man.'

'I always look like this.'

'Come on, I'll get you some bread and coffee.'

'There's really no need.'

'I know there's no need, but it'll be my good deed for the day. Look, that's a good place.'

He indicates a small café on our side of the road. There are two other establishments alongside it, but he seems to know the best. He parks his bicycle against wooden latticework and we sit at a table next to it. He waves a waiter over. It's clear they know each other as they talk fast and laugh easily. The waiter leaves with his order.

'This is some morning, man. The sun shining. It's been nothing but rain for weeks.'

Is that all? A climate emergency, the city flooded, rats in the streets, social unrest, shootings. I feel that, since he was buying me breakfast, I should agree.

'Everything is better when the sun shines.'

'Never a truer word, my friend. What brings you to my city?'

His city?

'I'm just visiting. Are you visiting?'

'Me? No way, man. This is my city now. I've been here eight years. I came to get out of a romantic entanglement and just stayed.'

Further evidence that most people who live abroad are running away from something, in a permanent state of escape.

'A romantic entrapment, perhaps, to make you leave for good.' I haven't meant to sound challenging and I'm in no mood for disagreement or argument. Sometimes my mouth vocalises my thoughts before I have a chance to weigh the pros and cons of speaking. It seems to chime, though, and the fellow continues to open up.

'I guess I did feel trapped. I felt trapped by everything in my life. I wasn't at peace in my soul, and you need that to go on each day. Otherwise, it's just existence and that's no way to live your life. I packed up as little stuff as I could and left behind family and friends. Things like cars and houses and the rest of the junk suffocates you. It's not needed, man. So, I should really thank the woman who made me realise my problems were bigger than romance. I'd built my life on sand, and I was sinking. Do you know what I mean?'

I nod. It's uncanny, like listening to myself. I had upped and offed when I was young. It's tumbling out of him as if he hasn't spoken to anyone in years. He goes on.

'Every day I'd awake with the possibility of a better way of living. I just didn't know what it was. I didn't really understand what it was I was in and how deep. That's the worst. It means you've been taken over. Your life is no longer yours; you're being manipulated by something you didn't have a say in. Sometimes you have to shake off everything, including your country. So, I spent a couple of years just moving around, at first in the states, but that only showed me that the net was wider than I'd imagined. Everywhere still felt the same. And then I just flew off one day, away from home, and the strangest thing happened. On the plane I knew that I was heading towards my destiny, my future. I knew I would get that peace that I'd been searching for. It was beautiful. I knew my life would never be the same again.'

As he spoke I was relating my own life. I know that I should have stepped away a long time ago. I should have left everything and started afresh. I envied his resolve. I also hated him for acting on that resolve.

The waiter puts down coffee and bread and walks away. The young man attacks it as though it's his last supper. He sees me watch him and maybe feels the need to explain.

'Coffee and bread are the greatest things on the planet. No one should miss out. Wire in.'

I dip a piece of torn bread in the coffee and let it soak the bitter and the sweet. It tastes sublime.

'I feel I belong here. Not to a person but to a city. I never felt that before. I was always a stranger in my home town but I hadn't grasped that before coming here.'

I notice that he doesn't name his home town, as if doing so will conjure that lost version of himself, and I don't ask.

'When the sun rises here, I feel reborn. Every day. In eight years I've never felt anything other. It's invigorating. I cycle around and I'm part of the city. The roads are veins, and me, like the blood, being pumped through.'

I smile a little at the thought of me in this city, like something being washed through the sewers.

'It took me a long time, though, to trust people, to involve myself in any kind of relationship like before. Slowly, I fell in love. I would meet her from work and we'd go to the movies or dancing. She liked to dance. Last year we moved in together and I can say without hesitation I was the happiest I had ever been. Buying our own place was virtually impossible. We were only earning enough to live not to save. I was working for a courier company, delivering business documents. Long hours, but short wages. Believe it or not, I'm a practical kind of guy. Emotion comes from the brain not the heart. I didn't want to give up something I liked. But then something happened that shook me.'

I know, of course, what's coming next. I would break his monologue.

'Pregnant?'

'Yep.' He pauses, exposed. 'Well, there are various ways that you can take such news. Me? I surprised myself by being over the moon. I was about to give the city I loved a new citizen. We had something to do that was important, apart from celebrate. We had to consider our futures and lay the foundations for a new life. I arranged to meet her after her work was finished, but like always I couldn't wait, so I went along to the café she worked in. I sat outside with coffee and bread because I like coffee and bread. When she served me, she smiled, and I could see she was happy I was there. There were only two other people at tables, a woman reading a magazine and a man looking like the weight of the world was on his shoulders. After they left her shift would be finished. Have you ever worked in a café, bar, or restaurant?'

I nodded, although I hadn't.

'That moment is a good moment. But that moment was corrupted.'

It's like watching a movie you saw decades ago. You think you know how it ends but you can't remember how it gets there.

'The man ordered another coffee, picked up a magazine from another table, flicked through it. Such an odd thing to do. Anyhow, he then left briskly, without paying. His bill would be deducted from her wages so she couldn't let this stand. We were in love, but we were struggling to make ends meet. She couldn't let him just walk away without paying. And so she ran across the road after him. There seems to be trouble and so I shout on her to return. *Marina, laisse-le!* And she's coming back across the road looking at me and smiling. She's crossed that road a thousand times before. She knows the traffic and how to move in between the cars and buses. But she's distracted by our happiness.'

He pauses, seeing it again in front of him.

'She stepped from between two waiting cars into the path of an oncoming bus. And all of our joy, and all of our love, at that moment. Nothing.'

At some point during his speech he had gripped my forearm, like a cop taking me down after sentencing, stopping me bringing my coffee to my lips. In the silence, I speak my next line.

'I'm so sorry.'

When all is done and dusted, when everything comes home to roost, at the close of that day and all things being equal, this is how the nitty gritty is gotten down to. Like a knife to the gut across a table. There is no escaping this one. Shivved by the truth. Death caused by my actions. No trigger pulled. I kill without trying. Two lives for the price of one. A goddamn professional. I open my mouth to explain how a lifetime of wrongs led to that appalling scene, but the young man squeezes my arm gently.

'There's no need for you to be sorry. I should be sorry for dumping my grief on you.'

By Christ, can it be? He doesn't recognise me from the café. The whole back story isn't just some preamble to him leaping onto me to perform a citizen's arrest and a severe beating? What a stroke of good fortune. Although something of a lanky chap he looked like he could swing a stiff Southpaw. To think myself as lucky at such a time surely reveals a morality. I am nothing more than a beast of the field. I have soiled my humanity. No matter. Am I about to remind him that I was in that café that night? That I picked up the magazine? That I left without paying? I am not. I'm skilled in the sport of pilfering objects and redirecting the blame to others, and there's some mileage in pushing my luck.

'Do you remember the man in the café?'

'What?' I was obviously pulling him from his own thoughts. I press on: 'Perhaps he lives near the café?'

'Oh, I don't know him. I wouldn't recognise him again. He was a tourist. They all look the same.'

'What makes you think he was a tourist? How he dressed?'

'Perhaps. I can't really remember. None of the witnesses can. There was something, though, that maybe was a giveaway.'

'Something he said?'

'No, he didn't − '

He stops as he remembers something. Was my goose about to be cooked?

'You remember something?'

'He had some trouble with the language, I think. Oh, I really can't remember. I have no bad feelings towards him. He might have forgotten to pay. Anyone can do that. I'm not someone looking to blame. It was a tragedy. Tragedy is part of life.'

By God, this boy is magnanimous. I feel like pushing it to the hilt. *Well, I am the man that left the café. I am the man who had your girlfriend chasing after me. If I had not been there she would be alive. You would be planning your future. A young family, a son or daughter. If I had not been there you would be growing old together. You would one day be grandparents. You would look back on a lifetime of memories. It was I who snatched these things from you. The damage that one person can inflict is really incalculable. How far would your spirit of forgiveness go in the harsh light of truth?*

'It is indeed.'

His next statement knocked me for six.

'Look, I was wondering if you might give me some support?'

I am a man who is partial to making surprising gestures, but this fellow beats me by a mile. Coffee is dripping from the bread on its way to my mouth.

'I've registered the death at the *Mairie*. There were no real suspicious circumstances. It was a road accident. The driver was not to blame. She rushed out in front of an oncoming bus. I was given an *acte de décès*, the death certificate, immediately. When you stepped in front of me, I was rushing to order a coffin.'

'What?'

'It's illegal to be buried without a coffin. Did you know this? I've never had to do this before. Have you ever purchased a coffin?'

'I...'

Sometimes we are dragged into dark corners we don't want to go to. A few words, anything, a smell, or an image, can send the mind into the maelstrom of memory. These times snatch our breaths and stuff them in a box. To be forced into memory is the curse of life. We keep on simply to leave behind. To leave behind the past and all its monstrous triggers. Returning to it is like visiting the dead, and visiting the dead, although long a wish of many, is not a healthy option for the living.

Bobby Ryan, the police officer who first investigated my

father's suicide had worked in the town his whole career. He knew the people and the people knew him. He had occasionally spoken to my father in a more getting to know you chat rather than in the line of duty. I saw him once walk up the driveway to the open garage door and say hello. He was just passing and making sure everything was good. It was more like a social visit to me as my dad and him started talking about sport and fitness. When he was leaving he waved to my mother through the window. I never heard him speak to my mother in those days. When I came home, he told me that he was worried about my mother as her reaction to my father's death was not normal. I wouldn't have expected anything other from her. He told me that people who don't display emotion after the death of a loved one concern him.

'I suppose my mother has her own way of dealing with things.'

That was something of an understatement. Her *own way* of dealing with things was to shut down entirely every normal emotional expression. My family was odd. Of that I am willing to confess. But aren't all families odd? The family home is one where outsiders can never really breach. There are intimacies in manners and behaviour that cannot be shared with others. There are experiences that bond families in ways that cannot be undone. An outsider who joins a family, perhaps through marriage, might be accepted, but they can never truly be a part of that unit. They have arrived too late. Sure, they might build years of different experiences, but the years when they were absent cannot be made up. Within families, though, there are also differences. And mine was indeed different. I felt that I was not really wanted, that I had arrived like an uninvited guest. I was tolerated. I have no memory of intimacy with my father. Most of my memories of him were of lying on a bench pushing up weights, his face straining at every push. I have difficulty picturing that face, though. At this moment. This had no doubt something to do with time. Many people experience trouble in bringing to mind the face of a long dead parent. But even when he was alive, and I was at an age when a child relies on his parents, I had trouble in that respect. I would often confuse him with the school janitor. Other times I'd remember clearly.

I think Bobby Ryan recognised something in my reaction similar to my mother's. God knows what was going through his head. But whatever it was, he wasn't satisfied and that's when Detective Jay Plangman was called onto the scene. No doubt the good detective had seen some odd fish in his time and was used to dealing with the curious in our society. I would suggest my mother and myself might have scored high on the *bizarre* scale. I think that he believed there was foul play of some sort, but he couldn't work out how a five foot five, one-hundred-pound woman could lift a two-hundred-pound, six-foot two man into a noose. He ordered an autopsy and, I believe, a toxicology report, but found nothing. There were some questions asked back at my college, but my alibi held up. If he had read some of my mother's poetry his suspicions might have been raised further. Going through them, after her death, I found one that began *I killed my husband because he never held my hand.* The rest of the poem was a portrait of loneliness, from a philosophical position. To a policeman it might have sounded like a confession; a killer teasing the authorities.

We got my father's body back from the police eight days after his death. I went alone into town and ordered the second cheapest coffin. And then the priest, Father Berntsson, refused to conduct the ceremony because it was a suicide and he had never seen my father at his services. I turned to the Reverend Jason Bull. Good old Protestants: they'll bury anyone. The service was short and poorly attended. My mother kept playing with her watch. Michael Norr, his old hunting and fishing pal, wept throughout. Mother was not pleased and at one point drew him a look and said quite clearly *Oh, for Godsake.*

'I…Well, never abroad.'

How quickly a memory can flit through your mind. Days of experiences covered in a few blinks of the eye. And the person in front of me hasn't a clue where I had gone to or that the question he asked necessitated my trawl through terrible memories. His focus is on my hesitant response, not how it was reached. He gulps at his coffee and drags his forearm across his mouth. He's waiting for more words. If I speak on he will feel less alone. He wants me to give him something to help steer him through this time, as if the coffee and bread could buy advice and succour.

'Maybe you could come with me. Help me out.'

'Choosing a coffin?'

'All the details. I could translate. I could be there to help you.'

To help me? The grieving chancer. All of a sudden it's me who's lost my pregnant girlfriend. Disgusting, even without the irony of my involvement in her death. The Greeks had it right, the Gods are up there, conniving, laughing, manipulating events; waiting to see what the fools down here do with them.

'No.' I have perfected this abrupt *No* over some years now. I have learned that even in a moment's contemplation an inconvenient deal can be done, tied up and delivered, inconvenience and all, with one word. So there can be no hesitancy in a refusal; it must be swift and blunt. Of course, there's the danger that the recipient will be offended, as much by the speed as the refusal. The sharp *No* says *How fucking dare you ask? How fucking dare you put me in a position where declining makes me the one who feels bad?* There are various ways to react to the 'No'. They might follow it up with a desperate repetition, or rephrasing, or flattery of the request. They might take umbrage at the delivery of the answer and make wild accusations, turning a straightforward request and denial into a torrent of insult and abuse. They might cry. What they will rarely do is accept your decision with good grace. For them, you have to be at fault.

'If you could do me this favour, I'd be eternally grateful.'

The second try is wrapped in a cloth of guilt and fares no better. I find his use of the phrase *eternally grateful* quite ludicrous. I have little doubt that before Christmas he will have clean forgotten about me and will be using his grief as a chat up line in bars along the river.

'I thank you for the coffee, but I really have to say again, "No". I am a very busy man. I have things to do. I have appointments.'

'But you told me you were a tourist. Tourists aren't busy. Tourists don't have appointments.'

I am not surprised at this new aggression.

'I'm sorry,' I say, and wait for the inevitable insults and abuse and confirmation of the inherent selfishness and egocentricity of humankind.

'What sort of tourist are you? A fellow human being reaches out for the hand of help in troubling times and you slap it aside.'

Okay, he's grieving, but there's no excuse for the tone.

'I'm going now.' You have to deal with these situations straight.

'Who are you? Where are you from? Who asked you here? You don't belong here. Your kind are not welcome in this country.' Grief is the orphaned child seeking out a warm breast to lay its head on. Many wear their grief like a lead lined cloak. They are dragged down into silence and private reminiscence. Others shout their grief with attacks and abuse. Few, like me, take it on board and continue a steady course. My grief is the one looked upon with most suspicion.

I move away sharpish to create a distance between us.

People are now looking at me. They see the young man, upset, and assume that I am the cause. Which of course I am.

Looking back, I see the young man standing and shaking his fist in the air, an act I have only read of in the pages of the Victorian melodrama. The waiter is standing beside him looking towards me. He looks at the young man and, as though trying to curry favour, he too begins gesticulating and shouting after me. This seems to create a domino effect around the tables, as customers rise from their seats in a wave of indignation and join the harangue. With one angry person I could walk hurriedly on without too much public fuss. Two people shouting and waving their fists in the air attracted some attention. A café full of coffee fuelled customers forming an angry mob, particularly in this political climate, galvanises commuters already on edge. Some of them join the protest, shouting along the street at me. In terms of keeping a low pre-assassination profile, I am an abject failure.

The traffic that was quiet moments before is now a bustling rush of horns, beeps, brakings, and out-of-window calls. I limp swiftly between car, bus, and bicycle, all calm, lost. Embarrassment and fear fuel my flight until I am clipped on the left shoulder by a bus. I don't have time to note the number of the vehicle, but that it is a bus is irony enough.

The best behaviour should anyone find themselves in such a predicament, is to walk on at a normal pace, looking directly ahead and ignoring what is behind. The trick is to not catch anyone's gaze. Your disinterest will confirm to them that you are not the object of the public ire, and they will move their enquiring eye towards others, until some poor sap returns the look and is condemned. I learned this some years ago when I was on a trip to the big city for an educational conference. I remember the conference was called *Learning To Learn*. Some bright spark in the Marketing Department no doubt proud when this concept got the green light cracked open a bottle of champagne to celebrate their creative ingenuity. The fact that the title was meaningless was less important than its alliterative cleverness. I skipped most of the conference and failed to deliver my paper *Learning To Look, Looking To Learn*. My paper title came to me at a table in *The Dirty Cactus*. I had been standing at the bar and caught a glimpse of myself in the *guilty mirror* on the wall behind the bar. Not liking what I saw I shifted myself to a table by the window. I'd had many beers and several whiskies and remember giggling as I removed a pen from my handkerchief pocket and scribbled it down on a beer mat. Of late I have taken a step back from the dipsomanic fug, fearing I would fall forever.

Having decided not to attend much of the conference proceedings I opted to travel to a big store, visit basement to top floor, and buy nothing. This is in itself a wonderful and liberating way to spend a day. Of course, there was fun to be had with the customers. It was while in the toy department on the fourth floor that I picked up a colourful battery-operated furry object. I flicked the on switch and the toy whirred while the arms and legs moved rhythmically back and forward. Switching it off, I dropped it in an unattended open bag of a young lady who was dealing with her young brat. I positioned myself strategically to the left of the till while she paid for the bribe toy she chose to quell his tantrum. I had hoped for some high jinks at the exit when the unscanned item triggered the alarm, but, as luck would have it – my good, her bad – the toy reanimated in her bag at the checkout. Her genuine bafflement confused the cashier. She dipped in and tried to explain while the cashier gave her an accusing stare. I couldn't control my mirth. I laughed out loud from the corner.

They all looked round at me, so I coughed and apologised, and settled into the role of a concerned customer. A woman with a shopping trolley pointed directly at me.

'It was him. He dropped the toy in the bag. I saw him.'

The incident took on a whole new complexion at that

moment. Everyone looked to me. I was clearly guilty as hell. The child shouted at me.

'He's a stranger!'

I don't know what confusion the youngster had about the word *stranger*, but it was clearly someone not to be trusted in civilised society.

I had to leave, and pronto. And it was then that I developed the idea that walking at a normal pace and not catching anyone's eye was the best policy for such moments of public accountability. I escaped the scene, returned to the conference hall, and stayed all day awaiting a tap on my shoulder from the local law enforcement. I was both terrified and exhilarated. After years of such behaviour, though, the excitement of being almost caught has all but disappeared. I am happy with the action. I do not seek out near misses.

And so, as I flee the café, all I know is fear and pain. My left arm is not lying as it should. The dislocated limb looks as if it has been assembled backwards. Unless I fix this there will be little chance of me proceeding with the etiquette involved in an assassination. Holding and pointing a gun at a target with one arm popped from its shoulder socket is hardly ideal.

One damn thing after another.

15

When you grow up in a small town the city is a place of wonder. You might have seen pictures of cities, television programmes set in them, and big screen projections at vast sprawling environments. Nothing prepares you, though, for the reality. When I was about ten or eleven my parents took me to see a psychologist in the hope of finding a remedy for a severe blinking habit I had developed. I don't know why, but we had not taken the car, instead opting to travel by bus. As the vehicle entered the city everything I held as true and real in my very small world changed. It was crossing into a magical kingdom, but not one that filled me with joy and light. The closely packed tall buildings bore down on me inside the bus, and consumed much of the sky and sunlight. Shadows fell across streets like giants. My heart pounded and I gripped my mother's hand, blinking furiously.

It was the same feeling I would have later when visiting other great cities of the world. I understood something that was beyond what I saw in the concrete and stone and glass. The people who had built the structures had reached up to the heavens and surely came close to touching the hems of the Gods. One slab of stone perhaps weighing over a 100lb. One on top of another, on top of another, and on, side by side by side, rising. It might take half an hour climbing the steps to reach the top. I was in awe. But a sense of shame crept across my wonder. It was shame that I had lived in a place little better than a shanty town, where people believed themselves to be superior to those architects and workmen from centuries before. I saw my neighbours as a community of the ignorant, their lives lived in arrogance, denial, and lies. There was no grace to be found in the banging in of a few nails. It was, I found, in the expansion of intellect, the towering fonts of knowledge that had designed spectacular monuments to God and man and ideas. My favourite cities — Athens, Rome, Paris — had been built on the knowledge of those long gone. I had been taught that these people were ingenious but uncivilised, but how could they be less than us if they produced a sophisticated more?

I asked mother and she told me that people were frightened of the past because it showed how shabby the now was. It showed how petty we had become, chipping away at our ancestors, trying to gain an advantage over the dead. It was she who told me that I could only grow if I left. I would only be fulfilled if I turned my back on all I knew. She told me that the town had tried to destroy her, denying her the opportunity to soar. She had fought it not by shouting at the intellectual oppressors but by escaping into books and poetry.

'I decided to tell it to the bees.'

By the time she had realised the freedom that could have been hers, it was too late. She had a husband, a house, and me. The only space left for her to grow in was her imagination, so she packed her bags and left for her mind. After a time the window framed her world, where she could spread her wings and soar. I think that became enough.

Until that profound bus journey, the future had looked as bleak to me as the bleak winter leaves that were brushed up and left at the end of the yard. When we have nothing to wait and wish for then we have nothing. Every breath and heartbeat becomes a preposterous waste of time. I thought, I'd be done with this life, or I shall have this life.

It was that other bus journey, years later, that provided me with possibilities. I was leaving for college, standing on the shoreline of possibility, all wind and water, fresh as tomorrow, I could have changed then. I could have let the leaves blow away or become mulch for the fresh and new. Instead, I let the past extend its roots, and entwine my mind forever. Before we had all left for the station, that morning I asked my mother straight out about how she lived. This had

214

always been taboo, but I figured since I was leaving I was allowed to broach the subject.

'Why didn't you ever go?'

'After a while you become afraid. I don't want you ever to become afraid.'

She's been with me every step of my life. I consider the people of the past as flesh and blood who understood their time. I see history not as vague images in books and screens but a real time inhabited by people with real needs and feelings. If you consider them as exactly like you then you truly touch history. You breathe its horror, feel its fears, its moments of joy and laughter. Make the past real to you. As I stepped onto that bus to university and sat by the window, and I saw my mother strain towards me, I saw the pull of history, her heart in the present, the future, the past. She became real to me for the first time. Her love was unsaid, the stone reality of ancient buildings. I want to say *I love you*, to both of them, but they never taught me to say it. I want to say *Forgive me*. Every brutal moment they are not here by my side I am afraid. The overwhelming, suffocating shadow of remembrances offer nothing. I want to stop these thoughts, shut down my mind. I want to stand before the world: nothing.

16

I find myself in a tree lined leafy cul de sac. My intention is, no doubt, to escape all eyes. At the end of the narrow road there is a tree with a wooden bench under it. I can only guess that it was placed there by the residents whose houses backed onto it. If they step out their front door they are in a busy street, but exit through the back and it is like wandering into an idyllic country scene, not unlike those by a Dutch Golden Age painter. Perhaps a Dujardin, sans the animals. How the noise of a city can be muted by buildings placed next to each other.

I sit carefully on the bench as the slightest movement catches my breath. I have to take stock. I rise or fall by decisions made now. It is certainly a good spot for reflecting on my current circumstances. Am I doing all of this on my own or am being led to it? There are things that I know have contributed to my current situation. I do not *fit in* at home. Is this my fault? But, of course, I quite deliberately refuse to follow the daily etiquette of life as presented to me. I have tried, through the course of this trip, to understand my frame of mind, why I reject social norms and take my place outside the common herd. My failure could partly be the fact that I have viewed my personal past as history. I am reminded of an old college professor who told me that it never seems like history if you have lived through it, but I self-consciously transform every now into a then as the expectation of future reading. Perhaps history is further away than my experiences. I have read novels where porters have carried the bags of bright young things as they have run along the railway platform holding tightly to their cloche or bucket hats while being enveloped in a burst of steam from the engine. Such a thing is most certainly beyond me as I have never experienced it in real life. That old college professor might dismiss it as unworthy of study. But what if he had lived at such a time and had witnessed girls running along a railway platform holding on to their hats? Would he consider it history now? Perhaps I should reframe my past simply as personal experience rather than part of some grand narrative in which I play a part. Maybe then I will touch the root of me.

The pain in my shoulder is here and now. I am no aimless wanderer. I have purpose. I remind myself constantly of this. For filling time in miles walked can unsettle the mind and distract from an ultimate destination. It is refreshing to drop a goal into the musings. Sometimes focus is needed. Sometimes a steady thread is needed through the wavering eye of the needle.

The consciousness of shoulder pain inevitably revives that in my knee. What I thought was a bruised bone is obviously more serious. Something is going on under the kneecap; a constant tingling and a weakness when weight is put on it. My limp is obvious with every step.

My shoulder appears to be attached to an invisible string that pulls it inward towards my chest. It is difficult to give serious thought to your existential crises when pain is pulsing through your body. I have to deal with the shoulder problem immediately or my cause would be lost. I take a firm grip of the wrist of my injured side. I lift the arm straight out in front of me and try to guide the ball of my arm bone back into the shoulder socket. Dear God in Heaven if there is an eternity of Hell awaiting me surely this procedure will be one of my tortures. I am slowly pulling at my arm from the wrist and turning it this way and that with the hope it will pop back into its natural resting place. The child's game comes to mind; a handheld plastic contraption to be manipulated to roll tiny balls into small holes. My last move is the most dramatic. I pull hard at the wrist and the arm jerks: the ball slips into the cuplike socket and a wave of pain rushes over my whole being. For some time I am still, frozen in a strangely dislocated agony as though I have left my own body. This feeling eases and leaves me with a pain that is intense, but in the right post-procedure location. I knew this would ease off with time. My knee I was less certain of.

Someone had tied a balloon to the top of the bench. With difficulty I untie it and make a makeshift sling, with the flaccid rubber providing more comfort at my neck. I lean back and close my eyes. My thoughts are a continuation of those I had on first sitting.

The fact is that I've grown into someone who does not accept the world as it is given. This is less a stance and more a disinclination towards involvement. I have in the past contemplated the possibility that I am slightly crazed, but I lack the recklessness of madness, the chaos in the thought process. I am not of that sort. I have always had an enquiring mind and there is perhaps an unusual clarity and order in my thought process. Learning is like stepping on the proverbial stones to cross a river. One leads to another, then another and so on, until the opposite side is reached. My colleague, Jonas Mark, accused me several times of being irrational. I eventually told him that because I did not eat from the public trough did not necessarily make me irrational. I explained that his idea of 'irrational' was more a societal tic, but if I was wrong, I apologised, and was only too eager to discuss with him Schopenhauer, Charles Sanders Peirce, and *logic*. He told me to go fuck myself, while he went to room 576 to fuck department head and future wife and mayoress, Jennifer Johns. I expected better from a scientist, but he was a poor judge of people.

Jonas was not a stupid man, but, like many others, just not as clever as they believe themselves to be. I've always thought how comfortable it must be to be truly stupid. Perhaps that is not the correct term: ignorant perhaps. But what of those that are wilfully ignorant? What of those who quite deliberately shun knowledge and facts? Those who make a calculated decision to attack expertise and evidence? This cannot be simple ignorance of a particular subject; surely this must fall into the realm of the stupid? Now, some people thought my mother was stupid, but she was far from it. An eccentric perhaps, but those terms are not interchangeable.

'You know what you should do with your life? Sit by a window. I mean in the future. You have adventures to experience first.'

That was the advice she gave me when I was filling out my college application form. The campus was outside the town in a neighbourhood slightly larger than where we were. Even at a young age I realised my mother's words were not the soundest parental advice for a future academic, but there was still something Zen about it that sat well with my youthful rebellious spirit. At the time I thought I understood what she was saying: do not enter the rat race and conform to social norms; do not fall for the trappings of achievement and a swelling bank balance. Later, I think I understood her. More could be learned sitting by a window, contemplating life and lot. More could be gained writing down one's thoughts and considering them in relation to the world. Or maybe she had just flipped. Maybe those two things are not mutually exclusive: you can flip and stare out the window considering the options. It speaks volumes for society that a person would rather do this than engage with the outside world.

The journalist in the novel lives with his wife. We only ever see her at the window gazing out, as though she has spent a lifetime doing so. The parallel with my mother does not go unnoticed by me, but they are very different creatures. My mother chose how to spend her days. The journalist's wife appears to be ill. Obviously, this characterisation is not completely believable. We can assume such a person would rise and go to the toilet, or eat, or go to bed. But the author decides to omit the functions of living and only allows us limited glimpses of her in her home. Was he trying to tell us something deeper about the restricted lives of the characters, about the pointlessness of all the running around, the effort to survive or to achieve? Unlike mother, this character has no release from her situation. She has no recognisable talent or indeed interest in the outside world. She is lost in memory, fragmented though it seems to be, through illness. Alzheimer's perhaps, but we never find out. I am one for homing in on minor characters or incidents as the key to understanding a text. The wife mentions twice that she had visited Paris with her husband. Since I am in said city, I have been contemplating the reference. To mention a place once in a story has significance, to repeat that place name must mean something.

'What are you doing?'

The voice penetrates my thoughts and tugs me back to the moment. I feel as though I have been caught executing one of my japes. Slightly embarrassed, slightly shocked.

'Clara...' I feel inexplicably guilty.

She had walked along the lane and right up to me and I'd seen nothing. And I had no answer to her question. As a result I counter with a question of my own:

'How did you find me?'

'You sound like it's a game. This isn't a game. We're worried about you. We care about you.'

'I'm a grown man. I don't take kindly to being followed.'

'I saw you run from a table down the street. You ran past me. I saw you dart down here. Your shoulder...'

'It's sorted now.'

'What's wrong with you?'

'What?'

'What's wrong with you?'

'I...'

It was this *I* that brings me fully into consciousness. Clara is not in front of me. The lane is as deserted as when I had arrived. It is myself that I have to face, not Clara. I return to half-remembered conversations with colleagues. Maybe they saw something in me that I could not. Joseph Benn, on tenure, thought that protected him and he said whatever he damn well pleased. There are certain inalienable truths, not least of which is that no idiot knows he is an idiot. I had no respect for Benn, but on one occasion he might have hit the spot.

'I've never met a functioning alcoholic. Sure, they may hold down a job, but their social skills are usually broken. Loud or extravagant, or weirdly withdrawn.'

'Are you saying I'm an alcoholic, Joseph?'

'I just think you're…' and he thought about this as though he were some kind of psychologist. '…you're…off kilter.'

'Off kilter?'

Maybe that's what I've been: off kilter.

Now is maybe the time to say more about myself. I have been told that I am a handsome man. My mother was the first to describe my attractiveness, in her fashion. I am of course willing to concede that there might have been an element of bias in this appraisal of her son. But that's not quite it. She didn't say exactly that I was handsome. I was about fifteen years old and sitting at the dinner table and I asked her straight out if I was good looking. It is an age when a boy needs reassurance about such things. She was direct in her answer:

'Well, you have character. You have an interesting face.' She went on to comment on my high hairline, my large nose, my weak chin, and my face being too long to be considered handsome in the accepted sense. I was, though, interesting, and girls for that very reason might look twice at me. I cried that night, face down into the pillow, for I wanted to be handsome as other handsome young men were. I did not want to be interesting, but she was, of course, right.

By the time I arrived at college I had pretty much come to terms with my flaws. As I matured they became attractive.

College ironed out many of my anxieties, or perhaps it was being away from my mother and father and the town, being on my own and responsible for my own actions. And so to here, and free will. Thoughts too have their own freedom of course. I cannot accept some and so I push them away. I am now rowing slowly towards that shore to escape them. There was the chthonic hell of memories. A place too rotten to visit, but I have at regular intervals been dragged into the bowels.

As I stand, a pain throbbing in my shoulder. I wind towards the main road. As I walk images consume my mind. These I cannot push away. Back at the family home a year after my father's demise. I felt it a duty to visit every now and again, offer support, or just my presence. Mother had become forgetful, and although she sat clinging onto a notebook, she rarely wrote. Maybe it was her life raft. I had gone to town to pick up some groceries and when I returned, I called out that it was me. There was no reply, but that signalled nothing at all. In the living room a pillar of sunlight from the window toppled across the carpet. Dust particles caught in the beam danced like fireflies around the empty chair and cushions that bore the mark of mother's body. Walking along the hallway I saw that water was coming from underneath the bathroom door and could hear the gushing taps. It wasn't the first time that she had forgotten about a running bath and so I was still unconcerned. I shook my head and muttered *Mother*, as though a camera was on me. I pushed the door open, *Mother*. My call was cut short. She was fully dressed in the bath, submerged up to the neck with the running water. In her right hand she clutched my father's open razor. As I entered, she looked up at me with a smile that only a mother can give to a loved child and said goodbye as she always did; running her fingers slowly through the air as though she were typing out a message. The same gesture as when she said goodbye to me as I left on the bus to college. Her bloodied hands fell under the water, and a billow of crimson rose like a cloud to the surface. Oh, mother, in those moments my life toppled and fell. I rushed forward and plunged my arms under her, pulling at dead weight. Her moaning was the same as I would hear while she slept; a certain contentment, an acceptance of life slipping away. Even as I frantically wound towels around the gashed wrists I knew she was falling away. The cuts that she inflicted upon herself were not light slashes, but she knew to push the razor's edge deep into the flesh across the radial artery. It was not a cry for help, it was a longed for release. This fact, this certainty, cleared my mind. I held her to me, kissing her head gently.

I will phone an ambulance but first I will hold you. I will not leave you alone.

And so she died in my arms. Quietly. Softly. As it seemed she lived her life. Of course, I asked myself why things ended as they did. Greek tragedy shied away from double suicides, but the Japanese have the word *Shinjū*. That word, though, is only used when the loss of life is in a pact. I never really knew my parents. What kept them together for so long? Why did they have enough of life? What brought them to the end they chose? I cannot give answers to these questions and a hundred more, but everything I've read and have been told suggests that all things have a resolution. Loose ends are always tied up, questions are always answered, lives are edited neatly into chapters and sections and arcs. But it has never been this way. I am not a man at the end of a journey seeking denouement, I am unmoored in a sea of uncertainty. Life is ragged borders blowing wildly. How do you cope with the crater of loss? How do you speak? How do you walk? How do you breathe with this damage?

By the time I arrive at the busy street the memory of my mother and father is gone, buried again. I have found it the best way.

17

The heat is intolerable. I was hoping to be greeted by a slight breeze on the boulevard, but it is as airless and suffocating as everywhere. My shirt is damp and sticks to my body like a second skin. I could walk towards the bookshop. It is early, but being in the vicinity might strengthen my murderous intent. I have the feeling that I have a relationship with this area. I feel close to streets, the boulevards, the hidden lanes, and have a sense of arrival, of home. Is it my purpose that gives me this knowingness of the cityscape? A green uniformed éboueur with a broom, is sweeping muck from pavement to running gutter. A thankless job at the best of times, I suppose, but since the civil unrest street cleaning is a dangerous occupation. I smile at the gentleman. He sees me but immediately drops his gaze to his sweeping, as if he knows I'm up to no good. I look away almost as quickly, and the smile becomes a scowl. A stranger making me feel guilty. How dare he! He has done me a disservice. I stride past him. How fucking dare he. A few steps on I halt. I consider striking him but dismiss the idea just as quickly. Sometimes it pays not to get involved. I walk on. *Joy cometh in the morning.* Then again, I thought that just before I fell off that park gate.

The ground below my feet is hot, but not anywhere near as hot as those where I grew up. In the July sun the streets in our town were baked and children were told not to play barefoot in it. The younger ones did, of course, daring each other to run a block, past the bookstore, past the toy shop, past the bakers, and the – well, usually by then they surrendered in tears to the throb in the soles of their bare feet. The older ones became slow and tetchy in the heat, There was pretty much nothing to do but maybe dream of being old enough to move to the city. That rarely happened, of course, and most were married or half way there before their teens were passed. Then the town didn't seem so bad after all, and those dreams were locked away somewhere. Then they took on a new set of values and aspirations, of running their own business maybe, or raising a family, of being a solid citizen maybe. That dream didn't really pan out either. Sure, they got married, started a business and a family, but long before the kids had grown disappointment ate away at the solid citizens. They began to ask themselves what was the emptiness that carved its shape in their hearts? And after years they discovered the answer: their dreams had been stolen. That's something that couldn't be reported to the police, so they kept the theft to themselves. And I know these people. Every one of them with the slightly distant look in their eyes. But they're only recognisable to the few who left. It's a road I refused to walk. The road I took led me here.

Was I always different or was I made so? I've always thought the ways of the world are too many and too complicated. I try to think myself perfect, but I understand that I am a broken thing. I am a mass of contradictions. Father John Berntsson spoke to me before I left for college. He said I should consider religious orders. I was taken aback and told him I had trouble believing in God. And he told me *that will come*.

'He's a damn clown,' mother said when I told her. 'He doesn't want anyone leaving. He takes it personal. Part of his flock leaving the fold. It's a personal slight to him. Keep them here and fenced in. Put as much distance between him and yourself as possible.'

But that was so long ago. The older we get we start to give some credence to an afterlife. We let the thoughts enter and attempt to put roots down. *Maybe your dismissal of religion was extreme.* And then we say, *Well, maybe not a God and a heaven, but some other afterlife. Maybe a spiritual home where we will find peace and, more importantly, be aware of that peace.* As we head ever more rapidly towards that last door so we are gripped by the obvious truth that the force, spirit, soul, or whatever drives our lives, cannot just end when the body ceases to function. We push away all reasoning about the life force being nothing more than neurones in an active brain. When the heart stops the rest of the body quickly follows. The brain will not function, so those neurones are going nowhere. And yet…And yet…And yet…We will convince ourselves otherwise, defying all logic, all evidence to the contrary.

Father, I have been a sinner all my life and now at the close of my days I'd like to repent and get in the warmth of the bosom of the church. I've been a fool and denied God. I have spent a life turning my back on salvation.

Oh, that I could find salvation in a smile…

I've seen the strongest buckle under the threat of nothingness. But consider those brave enough to say *To hell with all that. I'm here now and won't be tomorrow.* What brighter more honest lives they live.

Michael Long, who was our neighbour, was an old man when I was born and so was always old in my memory. He laid out food for the birds and the animals. The squirrels and deer came to him. He was an eighty-year-old activist. He disrupted hunts and protested chemical plants. He wrote letters and joined sit-ins. He told people to forget Father John Berntsson and the afterlife, to think about the current life and make a difference. He didn't buckle when death came knocking. He never wilted under the threat of hell. How brave. Mother would wave to Michael Long as he passed our house. I think she liked him, but she never spoke of him or to him as far as I know. But then she spoke of few in the town, apart from Father John Berntsson. Mother had cut ties long ago on that front. Was that her bravery? I often wondered what made her who she was. She had not sat at a window all her life. A young woman has to get out there and face the world. She can't wait behind glass hoping someone will pass by and be struck with a bolt of love. She met my father on an evening's outing to a town carnival.

'I had gone with some friends. I was seventeen. A reader even then and even on nights out I would carry some book or other with me in the event I got bored. It's an emptier life without a book. Anyway, two of us girls got stuck up the Ferris wheel, and while we waited for the ride to start again, I fumbled in my bag for God knows what. But then my book fell out. As we were at the very top it seemed to float in the air before falling. It looked like a bird that had been shot. Well, the bird landed in your father's lap. He was a good bit below in one of the carriages. And what he did was climb up to me. People were shouting to him to be careful and calling him a damn fool, because it was pretty dangerous. And so he delivered the book to me. He was so lithe and strong and handsome. The whitest of teeth, and I could see the muscles move under his tee shirt. It was quite exhilarating.'

'What was the book?'

'Oh, the book? It was Sylvia Plath, *The Colossus and Other Poems*. I'd really fallen for that one. *The Beekeeper's Daughter*...Oh, my...*circle after circle...*'

I never asked mother when she took to the window. I never asked if she still got exhilarated.

I have pushed something out of my thoughts for so long that it has become a monster in my mind. It terrifies me more than death. I think my father looked after my mother. I think my mother suffered from mental illness. Sitting by a window for twenty years goes beyond *quirkiness* or *eccentricity*. She was clearly ill. My father would walk from the garage, come into the room where she sat, and say *How's it going?* I thought for years that he was asking about her artistic endeavours, but after they had both gone I began to understand that he was enquiring about her mind and mood. And knowing her state of mind then how could he leave her? He retreated to the garage to survive, the physical weights he pushed balancing out the emotional burden he carried. Was it too much for him

R D McGregor

eventually? Was that enough to make him take his own life? These are questions I ask myself, knowing that I will never find an answer. It is one thing I detest about the novel form: the practice of tying up loose ends and answering every damn question and giving order to a disordered universe. I hate the neediness of readers and their craving for resolution. That is not life as I know it.

To prove the disorder my memory returns again to the summer streets where I grew up. It wasn't just the heat, it was the smell of summer. The heat dried the air. Back then nobody had air conditioning. Just maybe a fan hanging from the ceiling or maybe one that sat on a shelf. Outside, there was no escaping it. You felt like a window was closed on the world. The heat was trapped and you were trapped in it. That was the summer, and it seemed to go on forever. No summers are like the summers of youth. Forever we yearn for their return, but there's no going back. Another loss to memory. I curse the past. I curse memory. I curse this mind that never stops.

Boulevard St. Michel, Rue Soufflot, Rue Saint-Jacques, Place de la Sorbonne, Rue de Vaugirard, Boulevard Saint Germain. I have passed this building, this statue, this fountain, these shops and cafés a hundred times. My head goes down and my chin out: onwards is all that is left. The past shall stay where it has always been: in memory and in the here and now of thought and memory. And so my mind sweeps me past the town bank coming crashing down, and a hand held, the bedspread of a hotel bedroom, a bomb exploding; all in a few steps on hot concrete. On, I say, on.

The Flaneur

18

I reach the bookshop early. The plank of wood that lay across the ground in front of the shop is still there, but the water is gone. The street is now dry. I have to sit on a bench. This heat has taken its toll. I feel tired and exhausted. All I can think of is the ache in my shoulder so deep it has drawn the pain from my cut knee, which starts to twinge now I have thought of it again. These injuries bring me closer to the city. They are more the injuries a resident may suffer, not a visitor. I am strangely at home. I am where I belong. At last.

Two doors down there is a tea room. It has not long opened, I can tell. The window is polished and adverts for various teas are on show: white tea, black tea, yellow tea, green tea, blue tea, oolong, chamomile, matcha, Earl Grey, pu-erh, jasmine, masala chai; there are fruit and flower teas and leaf teas. As I enter a bell over the door tinkles my arrival. A woman appears from a room behind the counter and smiles a welcome. She is attractive, with dark hair, and bright eyes. She is in her fifties.

'Bonsoir.'

She replies in English. 'Sit anywhere.'

I choose a small table by the lace-curtained window. She hands me a too large menu of teas on offer, much more detailed than the window display. I scan it quickly and order the English Breakfast. She looks disappointed.

'Would you like a fruit scone?'

'No, thank you.' The idea of food of any sort at this time makes me feel nauseous.

'Do you take milk?'

'No.'

'Sugar?'

'Yes, please.'

This last reply returns the smile to her face. She positively skips across the room and behind the counter. I let my gaze settle across the street on the small bookcase beside the door of the bookshop. It looks like the one that I had returned home to collect after my first year of studies. I had been putting off going back at all and had lied to both parents that I had been too busy with studies to visit even during semester breaks. I took jobs that tied me to my new life. Selling books in the university bookshop and selling Christmas trees until Christmas Eve. All these excuses not to return. But as the first year came to an end the excuses inevitably wore thin. I thought that it would be better me contacting home rather than home contacting me. And so I phoned and asked if they still had the small oak bookcase in the corner of the garage. They seemed pleased to hear from me and expressed no disappointment at my absence. Later I realised that neither parent had called me before to invite me back. We were an unusual family.

When I stepped off the bus they were waiting exactly as they had been almost a year before when they saw me off. If the world is a dream and everything needs your presence to make it continue, this made perfect sense. They had simply paused, unmoving, until reanimated by my consciousness. As my mother hugged me my father looked away and said:

'Don't have the car. It burst into flames in the driveway.'

'Was anyone hurt?' I asked through my mother's hair.

'Well, no one was in it.' He said this aggressively. There was aggression in everything he said to me, as there was in most of what he said to anyone. Some people have harsh voices, but sometimes, maybe in quiet moments, there is a sense of tenderness. My mother once told me that he was *a very tender man*. How had I not encountered this tenderness? Why wasn't I shown it? That particular night I went to sleep with a stone in my throat.

From the station we got a bus to the house. As it trundled along, I looked out on my past. *Bump's Bookshop* was having a closing down sale. It was one of mother's few ports of call when she did venture out. (In the end it didn't close. Merrie and Mackenzie kept it open, and probably bought in a couple of copies of that dreadful novel.) There was talk that the post office would close too, but no one knew how that would work. Deliveries some said would come from the city. Or from one of the satellite towns, like the one I would spend my working life in. I could see a queue at the bakery so that at least seemed to be thriving. People always need bread if not books. I had only been away a year but the whole town looked strange to me. And I realised the place hadn't changed: the change was in me. I would never be the same again. I felt that within myself I was living with a new person. It was scary but exciting. I realised that I had left my childhood behind, like a shed skin, I suppose.

I entered their house and saw it anew. Within a few moments I could see that the hall carpet was frayed at the edges and clearly hadn't been cleaned, not only in a year, but in many years; the cushions on the couch were worn and dull. The living room mantelpiece, that in most houses displays family pictures, was bare, and covered in a layer of dust. Everything smelled of them and the food I used to eat. Had I imagined my father cleaning?

Almost immediately my father brought up the bookcase.

'I cleaned it up for you,' he said, gesturing towards the garage as if continuing a conversation we had been in the middle of. 'I'd forgotten it was for books. It held my oilcans and rags for years.' He didn't mention the small mirror, open razor, and shaving cream that sat atop. I always found those items incongruous amongst the rest of the garage paraphernalia and the weight training equipment. I asked about it once and he told me that sometimes he just goes over to the hose tap, wets his face and shaves. As a child I accepted this answer, as children accept parental eccentricities. As an adult I accepted that he had forgotten the bookcase was intended for books.

I dropped my bag in the living room when he said that. I guessed it was his way of breaking the silence that had pretty much lasted the whole bus journey. He led me to the garage and showed me the bookcase. I had never seen it look like that. He had sanded it down, tightened up the joints, polished and burnished it to a shine:

'It needed some work.'

It took me a moment to speak.

'Thanks, dad. It looks great. I'll take it back. It's just what I was looking for.'

'I don't think you'll get it on a bus.'

'Sure I will,' I said in an excited voice. 'But sure I will,' and I was suddenly determined that I would.

Standing awkwardly next to him in the garage that day I wanted I suppose to hold him or have him hold me. But whatever demons were building up in him prevented any show of love and affection. I suppose he must have felt something of my thoughts because his hand touched my shoulder as he passed and kneeled down at the bookcase.

'The joint here on this side had completely come out. Wood changes with the temperature...I suppose being in the garage all these years...Down this bit was a butt joint held together with glue, but it had come apart. It's a weak kind of joint but it was easy at the time to make.'

'Did you make this?' Nothing had ever been said about it that I could remember. He made the bookcase.

'Sure. I made it for your ma not long after we got married. It worked for a while, a good few years... then it kind of broke apart.'

He lifted a shelf and pointed to the support.

'At first I was going to make a bridle joint here and have the shelves permanent and fixed, but I thought with different sizes of books she could just adjust the shelf height.'

He looked up at me and cleared his throat. He didn't know

232

that I was enjoying him talking.

'When it collapsed it just ended up in here for bits and bobs…Oil…and rags….some cans and such like…I used to keep the car in the garage but when I got training the car just sat outside…'

'Why'd you do the training? Why'd you start it, Dad?'

Standing up, he mumbled, 'Why does anyone do anything? Just to do something, I suppose…Anyway, the case is looking better than ever. You're welcome to it…'

And he walked out and just left me there with everything that could have been. I was close to tears but held them in. What good are tears? For the first time I was glad that my childhood had passed. For the first time I began to take stock of what I was and who I was. The future was what was important. I had things to do, a world to understand. In many ways I feel about my life now what I had thought of that childhood: I was glad it had passed. *Some are born to sweet delight*…Blake obviously knew.

'There you go!'

The waitress pulls me from the memory. She has arrived with a tray and a teapot, and a rather fancy china teacup on an equally fancy saucer. As she places them in front of me she boasts:

'We only use bone china. You can almost see right through it. The tea always tastes better from a china cup.'

'Indeed it does,' I lie. I rarely drink tea but when I do it's usually from a mug. I don't want to challenge her pitch.

'The weather has been pretty bad, but the sun is out now. I wonder if that will help the protests. Don't you think people protest more on the streets when the sun shines?'

'I never thought of that,' I say, although of course I have.

'I wish people would just be a little quieter and enjoy life. There's a lot to be thankful for. You see this uncertainty is hitting businesses. You're the first person I've had in this morning. After three hours. I can't run a business like that.

People are afraid to come out in case they get caught up in the marches or the...' She hesitates at saying bombings. 'People stay in and think they can have cups of tea in their flats, but it's not the same. Going out for a cuppa is an experience. It's the whole etiquette.' I realise quite quickly that the woman before me has had bad experiences she's about to inflict upon me. Her voice is slightly on edge and getting more so. 'We have bills to pay, a business to run, a small business, I have to be in profit, I can't not be in profit. How can I be in profit if I'm only selling a few cups of tea a day? How is it possible? I bake the scones myself. I get up early every morning and bake them so that they're fresh.'

I smile. I think about shooting her. Instead, I say,

'Next time I'll have a scone.' I don't know why I said that. I don't know why I lied. But we lie on a daily basis to keep the peace, to make others feel better, to keep life on an even keel. I had stopped lying back home. I'd started being honest with people and perhaps that's why they thought me odd. Or did they see my honesty as an attack on them, as an act of aggression?

'You'll come again? Are you a tourist? Are you working here?'

'I'm visiting.'

'Even with the unrest the tourists come. I left England because there was something in the air. Like what's happening here now. And around the world. There's anger whipped up by bad people. Are you political?'

'I try not to be, but it's difficult. You're pulled in.'

'I don't get pulled in. I just stay here. In my shop. I serve tea. I bake scones. Why should I get pulled into anything? I don't want a side. I want to be left alone. Why can't people be left alone?'

'Maybe it's to do with being part of society. Maybe you can't opt out.'

'My mother opted out. She was a hippy. I was born on what

they called the summer of love. There was only one summer of love. She named me Rose. Rose from the summer of love.'

She wants me to comment on this but I am silent.

'If there's anything you need I'll just be around the back.' At that she disappears behind the counter and pushes through a beaded curtain.

I pour my tea. I don't use the milk she has put out. The milk I hadn't asked for. Nor the sugar that I did ask for. That was how my mother drank tea. She said she wanted to taste the tea, not mask the taste. She sipped always at the rim of the cup, which may well have been bone china.

'The bookcase looks good.'

'It's nice to see it used properly.'

'He fixed it up.'

'He was always good with his hands. He had lovely hands. When he returned my book to me on the Ferris wheel it was something I noticed. I haven't thought of that in years.'

Then there was silence, and I could watch her revisiting old memories.

I drink the tea in one and stand. Walking to the counter I pat my pocket for money. I feel my gun.

19

The river is about twenty yards from the bookshop. I stand at the iron fence and watch the flow. The high-water mark above which the river had risen in the last few days was visible again. It has abated to a familiar level and is lapping gently against the wall. Around the city many of us must be standing looking into the river. But only I am thinking of Martha Sweet wrapped around a tree trunk. Only I. We each have our memories, individual, unshared. *The rains of summer join together, how swift it is…*

The feeling I have now is unlike any that I have had before. If I wanted to be alone then that has come to pass. I never thought it would be like this. Cold in my core. Alone. Is this what I have asked for most of my life? To be outside of community and society? I am my parents' son. Is this what brings people to bombs and mayhem? Haven't they all stood by the river and sensed this aloneness? A soft breeze brings with it the faint perfume of cherry trees. Do I imagine this? I know that smell, from our garden long ago. One grew in the front, two in the back. My father said they don't have an aroma and I told him 'But of course they do. You just have to stand close to the blossom.'

'Well, I can't smell nothing.'

'Mother, do you smell the blossom?'

'But of course I do,' she smiled.

I was breathless, giddy that time. Giddy with breathing too much in.

Only by standing by the sea or a river can we have such feelings. Something to do with the unrelenting passage of time. When we stand before moving water we see our time, stretched out before us, in constant flux. I am the river at this point. Flowing towards the mouth. And at the river's end? The filth that has been collected. I will not flow into a sea but die on a bank of mud and plastic, the garbage of my days. I lean over and see my shape. Who could have guessed such a pathetic journey's end? Who would want this shabby life?

Rivers have always had a magical pull for me. I would spend hours on a Sunday afternoon down by the river that flowed through the town, waiting on the church to release its captives. I could often be found Huckleberrying it along the riverbank. Even then I was aware that everybody is alone when all is said and done. We all know that there was always an adventure, though, to be had or made.

There is chatter behind me. I turn and see the author enter the store. There are others with him. They're all talking at the same time. And laughing. Laughter has no place here. All my life moving towards a point, and then a point. And on. Always a destination somewhere there in my future, always a road to take. Never for me the root and hearth. The constant movement. I was never still, even when I stayed in the same place. A suitcase always ready at the semester's end. Not for me the sitting at a window. But did I see less on the route I walked? There seemed only ever shadows and glimpses as I hurried on. And where did it all bring me? Here. What a disappointing journey it has been. I wanted more. I have always wanted more. I have never been satisfied. Should I have turned back at some point? All these damn ruminations taking me back to the first moment of decision.

At what point in the writing did the author realise that there was no going back? His description of the first death? The point where his protagonist's purpose becomes clear? At the crossroads, at the church, in the storm? I entered his story then, the reader-character. I stood at the top of the road in the driving rain as the weathervane spun in confusion. I became.

Jesus, I walk around the block, and I am tired of everything. When my work is done a map of my traipsing will no doubt be attempted by investigators. Some busybodies will no doubt be eager to help compile a cartographic record of my steps. I have avoided tourist spots as they are by their very nature attractive to the visitor, but no doubt they will remember me there. *He was at the top of the Arc de Triomphe. I thought he was behaving suspiciously…I saw him on the first level of the Eiffel Tower. He was limping. I said to a friend, that fellow doesn't look right…He was in the Louvre. In front of St. Francis of Assisi receiving Stigmata. Looked damn suspicious, and surly. He obviously had things on his mind other than Giotto…He sat at a table downstairs in Harry's Bar, sipping a whisky sour and listening to jazz – well, jazz was playing but his mind was obviously somewhere else. He looked troubled…*

No, I was avoiding the tourist traps. Let them track down a grieving lover, a beaten policeman, a tea house owner, a Welsh nurse, an abandoned husband, a waiter, more waiters. That is, of course, if I'm not done for immediately after the shots are fired.

When you come to mourn me I shall not be there. When you weep I shall not touch your tears. When you speak I shall not hear your voice.

A few hours after the rains and I am tired of the sun. It pulls at me, sucks from me the energy I have left. If it keeps up at this rate the ground below my feet will be dust in a hundred years. Will anyone be around to care? What with all the trouble in every nook and cranny of the world only a fool would bet on it. Although I haven't taken my medicine in a few days I'm not experiencing the tremors that the doc predicted. The old bastard. Kept me on that medication for nearly a year. What, was it going to wipe out a lifetime of memories? Something is building up in me. Thoughts are sparking in my head like a meteor shower. Mother said life without books would be an empty and unfulfilled life. And what about our head janitor, Johnny Jackson. I recall a recent conversation along these lines:

'Johnny, the reason kids aren't reading is no one on TV reads. They don't talk about reading and they aren't seen reading. The only time you see books are in the background in a lawyer's office in a courtroom drama. Books are a signifier of the elite: the ones who went to law school. We have a nation of philistines and they're making the programmes and they're running the country. In short, the stupid have won. The intellectually lazy have outsmarted the clever bastards. To hold a book or discuss books on a serious level is to be called elitist. That's where we are. A reader is viewed with suspicion. Burning books is a legitimate option for some. It's no longer damning evidence of despotism; it's an acceptable choice. Attacking the educated is a Sunday sport. The dumb oxen of society are taking over. Then, you might ask, what are we all doing here in this seat of learning? I don't know about you but I'm here to dig my own grave. Here's a piece of advice, Johnny boy: go out tomorrow and buy your own shovel because you too are *de trop*.'

Johnny looked at me for a few seconds. He seemed confused and not a little frightened. I'd been having that effect on people over the last year. But then his face lifted into a smile.

'Hey, you're putting me on, aren't you?'

Quite clearly Johnny thought well of the world and the people in it. Who the hell was I to spoil his dream?

'Sure I am, Johnny. You think I'd still be here after so long if I thought like that? Why, a man would have to be a fool. Or sick.'

'People say you have some humour.'

'That's me, Johnny. A man with some humour.'

I remember me saying *de trop*, but I would not have said that to Johnny. My memory has embedded that phrase in the conversation. But it could not have happened. Emily at college. I imagine her walking about the streets recording sounds of the people passing by. Just like she said she'd do. Was she still doing so? Was Emily still walking about the streets with her grey hair, picking up conversations for her scrapbook of sounds? Did she forget about it? Maybe her youthful exuberance and creativity eventually petered out and she looks back on her younger self as foolish. She's settled down and keeps her rebellious head beneath the parapet. But to me she is forever the young girl sitting under a tree dreaming of creating an historical social document. It's many years on now, Emily. Do you even remember me? The boy reading *The Iliad* on campus. It was a warm and sunny day and I remember you so clearly. I remember that moment and our conversation. Why does one among all the remembrances catch the light now?

My mother smiling up at me…My father talking about the bookcase…The boy standing in the rain and wind…The young couple crossing the quadrangle…Clara telling me to return home…a blue scarf removed and the tumble of mother's hair… *His hands were buried tight and deep in the pockets of a long dark coat, a hat pulled low over his eyes*…lines stuck in here somewhere for no reason…fact and fiction all one…and still they come as I see myself opening the door and entering the bookshop.

The room is warm. Too warm. But to open the windows is to let in the stink from the street. There is no blossom smell. Each time the door is opened a waft of sewer stench blows through the room like a corpse. There are only a few seats and they are taken by people half my age. A very attractive woman sits at the front. I recognise her immediately as the customer in the café who left the magazine that told me of this event. Perhaps if she had not left the guide I would not have been distracted enough to forget to pay for my coffee. Then the waitress would not have chased me across the street for payment. Then she would not have rushed back onto the road and been hit by the number 63 bus. The happenstances of life never cease to interest me.

In my right jacket pocket my hand grips the gun. The palm is clammy and gritty as it clutches the rough handle. Against my knuckles I can feel the unexpected outline of another object. There is a moment's panic as I consider that I am wearing the wrong jacket, despite the evidence of the gun I'm clutching. I release the pistol and pull out the other object. It's the salt cellar I stole some days ago. I encounter it like an artefact in a museum. I put it in the other pocket to keep the gun one free. Every bone in my body is aching, every joint, stiff. What has truly brought me here? We seem to travel so far, a lifetime with each step. We journey and reach the start at last. Where was my mind when it was convinced that to assassinate an author for a book I disagreed with was a legitimate response? At what point had I started to believe in the rightness (and righteousness?) of my diabolical plan? I cannot say, but it was a natural and obvious decision at the time. There were no deliberations or dilemmas considered. My mind moved quickly to practicalities and I booked a flight and a hotel without hesitation. If asked I would have said *I am a reasonable man, I am a decent human being.* And that is usually true. Why, of late, have I fallen into petty pilfering, the unexpected tempers. If I had to posit a theory of everything − and I believe everything is connected − I would say that I have been somehow away from the business of life for some time. I have been…untethered. I have turned to words and phrases that seem unlike me. Like just now. Untethered; does it sound like me? I have only used it recently. Simple anomalies like that make me pause and think. When I consider everything, I feel that this is really not me, not me at all.

The truth is I have no business here. I have never had business here. I have become one of those people I have scoffed at in the news, one of those sad figures in society who kill the famous to be forever linked with them. My author is not even famous. Can it even be called assassination? I have no reason. Here am I carrying the *Barthesian* notion one ludicrous step further. This cannot stand. Wrong must be wrong.

I see now what this crime is and feel deep shame as I stand before him with my hand on the gun in my pocket. But I'm on this road from which there can be no divergence. There can be no backtracking. I've come to execute and that will be done. To kill someone for a book? But people have died for less.

At what point do I take the gun from my pocket and aim it at him? Will someone say a key word, as in an act of mesmerism, to unlock this tragedy? But I am no Manchurian Candidate. There are no politics here. And there are no words, just the pounding of blood in my head.

As I pull the gun from my pocket I start to scream. What I scream I cannot tell. Is it words? The last cry of a tortured animal? The author stops and looks at me as if he understands. Other people turn towards me. All their mouths are moving but there are no sounds. And then, as silent as the sun, a white flash fills the room and light obliterates all faces. I watch as the window shatters and blasts glass, while shelves of books are ripped through the air. Time collapses and folds into a blur of quiet movement. Then sound: a dull roar and a bang, and slow screaming. There is nothing for me to do. Someone has me in a bear hug and I am being yanked upwards. My chest seems heavy, as though it is being crushed, but I feel nothing on top of it. I feel nothing anywhere.

I am not afraid but I am curious. This is familiar, what I've done all my life, the detachment from the physicality of being. Me, a youngster, being chased by some local thugs and knocked to the ground. Their fists and boots striking my body and face, switching off. I'm not there, and the attack cannot hurt me. They do their worst, but I remove myself to unconsciousness.

I am not sure if there is a weight on my chest pinning me to the floor, or something inside my chest stopping me moving. My eyes are closed, I think, or they might have been

242

blown out of my head. All is dark. The smell released from old walls. We stood near a building — it was the town's old bank — as it was being demolished. Dust, blooming up from its collapse, sweeping across the road and enveloping mother and father and me.

Breathe...

I'm crying. My parents now gone from this life. Myself at such a young age. If I could return to then I could get things right. If I could go back to the moment the town bank was torn down. It was a summer's day and my parents' hands held mine. I stood between them. Safe. Does life come down to a single moment? No, there are more. A turned back, a glance across a room, other hands held. All lost, and not through bombs or bullets. I remember...

Breathe...

What have I left behind? The past sitting in the present. The here...the now...

Breathe...

Has it been seconds? Minutes? Longer? Eventually someone will come. They will lift the weight from me. They will stroke my brow. They will offer soft words while pain finds its voice. And they will hold my hand...

Breathe...

R D McGregor

Books By This Author

A Funny Thing

Disposing of a body is a daunting task, but funny man
Freddy Foster, half of a once-loved double act, gets through
it by recalling better (and worse) times spent with his victim
and comedy partner, Norman. His recollection of their
quest for success takes us on a journey through British
slums, exclusive clubs, TV land and cruise ships from the
1960s to 2009. How, Freddy might ask, did it come to a
'mercy' murder of my old pal in a run down flat in London?

In this darkly comic 'memoir', R D McGregor gives a
moving portrayal of the complex relationship between 'a
couple of guys' and the society that shapes their lives.

Bad Things

Charismatic student, playwright and ship-in-a-bottle maker
Gladbody Holiman thinks he's pulling the strings of the
band of socialists and thespians who populate his life and
fantasies while he blags his way through uni and into the
review columns. His murderous odyssey to steal literary
stardom from a family friend takes him from Glasgow to
Orkney, and back. But there's more to his comrades and
girlfriend, Calvert Makeme, than meets his sick eye, and as

the cast of bodies and lovers pile up, Glad has to work harder than planned to stick to the plot.

The players in R D McGregor's psychopathic love story are driven by ambition and an unhealthy desire for control. This portrait of 1980s studentdom leaves us wondering if love is, in the end, a good thing?

R D McGregor
Next novel will be The Marble Index.

The Flaneur